THE ROSE
CROSSING

BY THE SAME AUTHOR

The Possession of Amber (short stories)
Rowena's Field
Feathers or Lead (short stories)
Paper Nautilus
Avenue of Eternal Peace

THE ROSE CROSSING

Nicholas Jose

THE OVERLOOK PRESS
WOODSTOCK • NEW YORK

First published in paperback 1997 by
The Overlook Press, Peter Mayer Publishers, Inc.
Lewis Hollow Road
Woodstock, New York 12498

Library of Congress Cataloging-in-Publication Data

Jose, Nicholas
The rose crossing / Nicholas Jose.
p. cm.
I. Fathers and daughters—Indian Ocean Region—Fiction.
2. Roses—Breeding—History—17th century—Fiction.
3. Rose breeders—Indian Ocean Region—Fiction.
4. Castaways—Indian Ocean Region—Fiction.
I. Title.
Originally published in Australia by Hamish Hamilton, Ltd.
PR9619.3.J73R57 1996
823'—dc20 96-3577 CIP

Manufactured in the United States of America

ISBN 0-87951-673-9 (hc)
ISBN 0-87951-797-2 (pbk)

1 3 5 7 9 8 6 4 2

for John Clive
(1924–1990)

traveller
soave sia il vento

PROLOGUE

Edward Popple saw the axe fall but not the axe-head find
its object. The block was low and the platform was hung
high with black drapes to hide the meeting of metal and
flesh from the pressing crowd. In the instant at which the
king's head was severed from his body a visceral groan
rose from the assembly, as if the people feared that their
world would end too. Despite himself, a sound gurgled in
Popple's throat. The bearded fellow in front of him, hat in
hand, bowed his head in respect, and the jolly boy on top
of the wall made a sign of the cross, not knowing how else
to proclaim that he was alive on the blackest day of the
creation since the crucifixion of Our Lord. A man and
woman fainted in each other's arms. Edward Popple gave
only a sour smile. It was sheer chance that he should be in
the street on this coldest London day of his memory.

The bearded fellow had asked his profession, and when
Popple said he was a horticulturist, the man, who was
dressed in an outlandish, old-fashioned style, asked then
what he did there. Popple explained how he had come
down from the north to deliver letters to his patron on this
day. He did not add that he had been unable to find Lord
Brougham in the chambers of Westminster Hall, or that a
messenger had come to him with a laissez-passer to the
yard outside the Banqueting House. It was a plea, Popple
understood, from his Lord for a space to deny the act of

I

blood. Lord Brougham did not want to be there, and Popple was standing in as his witness, craning to see the scaffold, obliged to his bearded companion – who confessed to being a seaman – for doffing his plumed hat in good time. Popple saw the king remove his cloak and his doublet to expose a white shirt. Then the king wrapped his cloak around himself again for a spell from the cold. As the royal face turned to the executioner, a smocked man in a grey wig and false beard, Popple was reminded of the time he had seen the king and his queen years earlier, with Viscount Falconbridge, as players in the masque of *Albion's Triumphs* inside the selfsame Banqueting House, the king as the god Apollo exposing his flesh to public gaze with a red swathe of satin across his ivory chest, and a black lady masquer as Peace. Today he saw the king lift his hands and his eyes to a white dry silent sky. The king's lips recited no more words, save for the mild order, as it was afterwards reported, for the headsman to stay for a sign. Then the king dropped down behind the black scene like a puppet.

His head alone reappeared for the spectators, dripping from the axeman's hand. The crowd was sucked helplessly towards it, even as the double ranks of mounted horse broke forward, hooves striking stone, to drive off those who were determined to dip themselves in the king's blood. In a matter of minutes the yard was cleared.

Popple found himself hurrying with the bearded seaman, whose feather waved in the air. The man gripped Popple's shoulder by virtue of the bond they had entered into that day and from his dangling coat pocket he extracted a token he was willing to part with as a memento.

'Look at it, sir. It is no ordinary stone. A fellow at the docks brought it to me from Tartary. Look carefully, sir.'

They stopped at the crossroad and his palm opened to reveal a smooth green stone with a black marking that had been picked out in relief.

Bringing the stone close to his eye, Popple made out the black shape of a rose. He looked up in wonderment at the bearded man whose eyes, hidden under the brim of the outlandish hat, seemed to gaze from the furthest reaches of the orb.

'The curio is jadestone. It grows warm to the touch.'

'What do you want for it?' asked Edward.

'On this day? A half-sovereign to see me through.'

They parted with a handshake, commending each other to fare well through the troublous times. By now the troop horses were returning calmly down the empty street. The frozen sky shone white. Heaven had no tears for Charles.

Monarchy is dead. Long live the republic!

In his pocket Popple closed his fist around the warm stone.

Popple stayed in London for some days, watching for the uncertain consequences of the execution, until he felt it safe to go. His innkeeper got him a copy of the secret book of the king's image, *Eikon Basilike*, which he would give his son Henry to remember the day. Rosamund his daughter would have the curio stone. It occurred to him that he had nothing for his wife. He would buy her some black cloth.

On his journey north he found himself spreading the news. He disliked having to report, but could not deny, if he was asked, that he had been there, and when folk found out, they flocked to him, to look and touch as much as to hear. Then as quickly they shrunk away, as if he were infected with the horror he had seen. He soon learned to avoid talk.

He travelled over miry roads that were troubled by people on the move, men on the way to be soldiers or others escaping that duty, masterless types driven by rumour and fancy, broken families, or souls just making for anywhere they might be safe and free. The citizens of broken England roamed ground that was slippery with blood and as cold as death. Muskets and hayforks were what people heeded when a shape approached through the drizzle. Passes, uniforms and credentials counted for little. He travelled in a rough woollen cloak with high collar and cap, and an unsheathed dagger on his belt. He was relieved to reach safe home.

His family was in the chapel with Lady Brougham. The news had gone before him to Brougham House and Lady Brougham already had by memory the last words of Charles, the unbreakable diamond.

'I go from a corruptible to an incorruptible crown,' she recited with tearful admiration, hopeful of doing the same herself before long.

Delia Popple embraced Edward, fixing him with her shrewd eyes to see how his presence at the event had changed him and might be turned to account. Rosamund and Henry saw their father in a new light, aware suddenly what enormities of experience his paucity of speech concealed.

Lady Brougham insisted on a grace from Popple at supper.

'We give thanks for deliverance, sustenance, and the grace of fortitude. We beseech Thy guidance in darkness and Thy helping power against destruction, that we may once again enjoy Thy love in light.'

The women sighed. Henry Popple smacked his lips.

The servant carved the cut of venison. A draught blew through the hall when the groom opened the door to bring a jug of water. On Lady Brougham's instructions they drank only water in the house. They were in mourning, and in transition to the new puritan ways.

PART ONE
England, 1651

I

Delia was a girl, when Edward married her, scarcely older than his beloved daughter Rosamund was now. The match was arranged by Delia's brother when Popple was a youth of promise at the Inns of Court, and Edward, at any rate, considered himself lucky to have a pretty, smiling bride whose fair complexion complemented her well-informed mind. Delia had been a good wife to him these near twenty years as the wheel of their fortunes turned with the times, moving on through descents as it failed to rest at the heights. Popple's talents found patronage, but some discontent in himself would bring him sooner or later up against his patron's limits. Then Delia complained in case the family's fortunes should alter irreversibly too. She had matured well, with a splendid head of hair and a delighting eye, but she knew that Popple would have the benefit of youth for only a little longer. His particular successes in the garden or at the desk scarcely justified his high aspirations. Yet she had faith in him, if only their future could be secured, if only, in these spinning times, she could hold fast to something!

Lord Brougham was a weathervane and his Lady a beacon, and distinguished people passed through their retreat at Brougham House to take guidance for the new world. In conversation with the household the visitors also discovered that Edward Popple was a delver and his wife

Delia Popple a charming optimist who sought advice in the most unaffected manner.

Once, on an excursion through Brougham Park, Delia fell behind with Lord Brougham, whose gout made him florid and as slow in setting one foot before the other as he was tentative in his political move-making.

She asked him how, when things were settled, Edward might best advance in the new order.

'A natural philosopher must serve by bringing to light things that benefit the common good. Edward has yet to understand this. He must give form to things that glorify the polity. Do you hear me?'

'I do, sir.'

'His ideas must turn to gold and in that strengthen the foundations of the state.'

She took the breathless old man's arm. Her son Henry was bowling through the meadow with two unleashed hounds. Edward had stopped ahead with Rosamund and was pointing at the sky.

'Do you have any particular advice?' Delia asked Lord Brougham.

'He must compound with the Society of Fellows. Politicians all.'

Delia cherished Lord Brougham's words after he passed from their midst. In the summer of 1651 he set off with doubtful heart to command a parliamentary force and only his corpse returned, in state.

Lady Brougham, long prepared for grief, made the house his shrine. The day came when she must ask, not Edward, but Delia Popple, what the family's plans were. To expel Popple and his brood would defile Lord Brougham's memory and she had no intention of that. She wished only to know how they proposed to honour the charity Lord Brougham had boundlessly bestowed. Lady Brougham fancied that the boy Henry might join the army, not perhaps the wrongfooting parliamentarians, but the old royalist remnant.

'A reciprocity of loyalty,' whispered the lady, making Delia's eyebrows jump.

Then Lady Brougham asked what Popple did all day in his plot, in his laboratory, living off the estate while producing nothing of visible use.

'He makes a fine lazybones, dear.'

Delia made quick reply that her husband was preparing for admission to membership of the Society of Fellows. She was never so cool. She saw that if her husband and her son could be disposed to Lady Brougham's satisfaction, then the way was open to establish herself with the lady on proper and propitious terms. Lady Brougham was frankly mad. Although she had not declared that they must depart Brougham House, she might in future provide for them less and less. But she would not lightly cast out an anxious mother and daughter.

'She doesn't notice me,' protested Edward when after another uncomfortable meal they retired to their chambers. 'She's mad,' he repeated.

Snuffing the candle, Edward came to bed. Delia waited for him with creamed face under the puffed-up feather quilt. They lay on their backs, apart in the darkness.

'My dear, you shall apply to the Society of Fellows.'

Creaks, groaning. There was no sound but for the house noises, and the elements, as she waited for his reply.

'Go into London again?' he questioned. 'No! I miss you too much.'

She was taken aback by his flattery.

'We cannot afford to miss so much.'

Popple knew his fruitless activity contributed to the

family's difficulties, and when he feared that their standing at Brougham House would be upset, he trembled to think of the haven as temporary, his garden and the avenue of trees down which Rosamund cantered towards him on her dappled horse. What if he failed to gain membership of the Society . . . ? It was, he scarcely dared acknowledge, his only recourse.

'I do not know their conditions.'

'You are too proud. Go into their service in whatever way they want you.'

'I cannot bend myself like that.'

'What holds you? It can be made right with the Fellows, but only if you comply.'

He stared at the ceiling. He was thinking of his daughter. Then he saw, behind the black curtain, as he had not seen on the day, the axe blade slice through the king's neck. A prophesying image . . .

'Be my husband.'

Her hand reached for him. Her fingers ran down his motionless and unresponsive body. She tried to arouse him. He lay as if on the dissecting table, his body lifeless, his lifelessness a form of cruelty and denial.

Her silence balanced on a knife's edge of despair and wrath.

'You are a spent man indeed,' she judged harshly, and turned away to sleep.

★ ★ ★

Edward Popple went on foot to the Society of Fellows through the obscure winter daylight. His black cloak was crumpled and soiled from travel, although he had hung it out overnight. The sun had no warmth, diffused through ice-laden cloud, save to thaw the hard mud, causing damp to seep through the leather soles of his boots, and perhaps, in a hidden way, according to his theories, encouraging the underground seeds on their journey towards germination. However harsh nature could be, her processes were impartial, unlike humanity's. If nature were to judge him, Edward Popple knew he would impress. His merits were clear. But it was a different matter with men whose perspectives were clouded by intrigue, caprice and the noxious motions of self. It was a mere interview that would decide the outcome! The chance fall of a moment.

The luck the innkeeper had wished him turned to a sense of doom as he entered the Society's stone portico and knocked. His cloak caught as the smirking servant closed the door. From inside came a strain of bass violin music, and a woman's voice holding a phrase in the modern manner . . . *a bed of down* . . . broken off. He was in a high state of anxiety. Yet confident, quite confident, that he could impress the Society of Fellows. He must show his abilities, his projections, the superlative possibilities of the results he would produce, absolute and beautiful beyond any awkwardness that might be found in him. But the more he was determined that they should see through his manner to what he might achieve, the more he would draw attention to himself as an agitated figure reaching for his last desperate chance.

The meeting-room had a frieze of mahogany panels carved by an artisan from the Low Countries in the costly heavy style of the new era. Garlands of crude rosebuds looping the chamber in chains of dark wood polished to catch blood-red lights, with tumorous cherubs lolling and strangled at intervals among the flowers. Popple was satisfied by how far the artistry fell short as, taking his seat, he raised his eyes above the level of the men who turned to consider him. The interview was called to order. Already he was hiding his rage.

Great gentlemen all, and offputting in their consistency, so Edward Popple judged his interlocutors, made of one substance, their mind one mind, their flesh and style, pedigree and standing, uniformly solid. Even their allegiances, for the storm-tossed times, considering the about-face of each, had the smooth resolution of chocolate balls.

Benign and wise in wrinkled pouches, their eyes gazed at the petitioner with equanimity. In this age of the many-headed monster, the Fellows of the Society continued to see as one. Thus was their science, thus the terms a person must accept if he were to be admitted and his work to prosper. The distinguished gathering was no committee of clerks, but the great scholars of the day. Experimenters, travellers, speculators. Names like Lord Brouncker, Dr Fry, Sir Joshua Sprigg, van Wenkenhoek. The genius Lake himself. So at home in themselves and in everything that Edward Popple felt he had a sack of potatoes interrogating him as he sat more and more uncomfortably facing them.

He knew at once that the Fellows registered something unright in him. His clothes were black, exactly like theirs. The black clothes of the men across the table were the uniform of harmonizers, betokening practicality and neutrality. Yet Popple's black clothes seemed to give offence. Black was merely the fashion, no longer a badge of the like-minded, yet might still encode warring extremes, concealing extravagant mourning behind severe austerity, or, the other way, letting the shabby dignity of the past stand in for the Puritan cut of the present. The king's head was chopped off more than two years ago now.

Or was it his provincial accent they took against, displaced as it had been during his secretary's years, in roving emissaries, when a form of Latin was the language spoken? Would the committee have liked it any better if he spoke in Latin? The more he tried to conform, the more he seemed to reveal his resistant grain. He wanted only not to draw unfavourable attention to himself.

The execution of the king had stiffened social relations once and for all. Any sort of relaxation might open up another jaw of the many-headed monster that had entered the kingdom, or commonwealth as she was proclaimed. While army men feasted round large tables, saying it was all for duty and never enjoying themselves, the royalists drowned themselves in oceans of wine at secret parties, and some drank blood from each other's veins in vows of faith. Yet it was not done for someone lodging by himself in an ordinary London inn to eat other than frugally, nor to dance, nor to accept the entertainment offered by the innkeeper. The wrong tone, like vinegar, would curdle the milk of getting-on. How could Edward Popple hope to be embraced by those whose patronage he must secure? By avoiding feasts he had become skin and bone; underfed, hungry, starving. The Fellows, solid as their science, must wonder what sort of philosophy inhabited his frame. How reliable were the lesions of mind to body in him?

Hands laid flat to the oak table, Popple breathed steadily. The chairman thanked him – Sir Astley Neville, a dabbler if ever – and Popple returned the thanks. Predictably a passage on the training of bees was singled out. Neville was little more than a gardener after all, distinguished for his grapes. Could bees be trained to pollinate grapes such that new varieties of wine would occur? The clown had, of course, missed the point. Other Fellows butted in with experiments of their own that they deemed more pertinent than the bees and the grapes. How pertinency defines itself in such a gathering!

The optics of the fly, hybrid honey-scented garlic, rare stones that behave as sponges, whales and guinea pigs, frost-hardy lettuce, fleas in amber. The Society was committed to identifying characteristics and cataloguing species. The more that could be listed, the better. It was like counting money. The scientists might seem to heed each specimen in its own right, as an example of the manifold handiwork of the Demiurge (God non-personified in the modern style). The greater purpose was to achieve an expanding aggregate in which each specimen was merely one further addition to an impressive total. Popple offered a different view.

Nevillia nevilliensis. The chairman was preoccupied with having new species named after him. He had been fit and handsome once, was tired now, and judged his life by the simplest measures of performance. His eye was sleepy, his brain shrunk, his flesh responsive only out of habit. Once more, once more, would it be possible? Would it happen again this time? When the young man said that there was a 'higher motion' to perceive, Neville was irritated. (And Popple, at forty, was scarcely young.) Nothing showed up the withering of faculties more than a new idea that did not immediately declare itself. Neville hated unthought-of ideas. He farted aloud, making Popple's mouth tighten like a fish's anus.

Popple said: 'I tell you, each delicate astonishing little study merely proves that there are laws of creativity in nature of which we have no understanding. And in ourselves, as natural phenomena. Laws, I call them, of which we have no earthly idea. I am not a philosopher. My concern is for what can be made. Each of my experiments shows that the laws of creation, of connection and union, invisible and abstract as they may be, can be drawn on in particular cases to produce things of which we cannot yet dream. I speak as no virtuoso, but the most humble beginner. Gentlemen, we can move to a further sphere of our humanity through your natural philosophy.'

'Refreshing,' murmured the brilliant Lake, stirring from intense dormancy. Others sniffed. The man's hot air was a bad joke after the chairman's flatulence. Popple knew he had gone too far, though not far enough, not far enough at all.

Neville replied that the Society was dedicated to the Light of Reason, indicating that he had missed what Popple was saying.

'Our principles are tablets of stone. Our means are few. Through not diverging from our way, we have achieved great things.'

'The reforming of the state,' observed Popple slyly. There was still some hope.

'Our work continues unabated, of course, and we hope you will join with us, sir. We are impressed. Gentlemen?'

Popple felt himself grow excited. 'I should be honoured.'

'We have our requirements, you see. I suggest you approach piecemeal. We are not in a position to accommodate all that you propose.'

'Chop your logic,' said Lake. Bulging tendons worked his cheek. 'Step by step. Block by block.'

'We should be most grateful if you would return another day. Be present at our next meeting. You'll be informed. Now, sir, I'm sure you would be pleased to join us in the dining room.'

'I am talking about life . . .' bleated Popple.

'Yes, of course.' Oaken chairlegs scraped the stones.

'. . . and what *makes* life.'

'Let's banter as we consume. You'll be intrigued by our several new wines.'

Popple was excessively angered. All they were good for was cash, which he could not do without, alas, and could think of no other way of getting. Science was for them a hobby, knowledge mere cultivation, where for him it was existence itself. In his mind he poured buckets of sour milk over them as, over dinner, they admired the tastes and colours and sensations they were stuffing into their mouths.

'To the advancement of learning,' came the toast, followed by a brazen expression of thanks to Edward Popple, Esquire.

Their wine should have been vinegar.

Popple sulked. 'I shall return,' he said, when forced to reply.

The Fellows were relieved they had kept the uncongenial petitioner at arm's length.

Then Lake threw him a lifeline.

'Have you thought of a journey, sir? Our ships are in need of observers, our oceans of observation. The Society is frequently asked to supply such competency yet for reasons of health or obligation at home most of our Fellows are unable to avail themselves of the opportunity. For you, sir, a place on ship might appeal.'

'Is it your courtesy to pack me off in a cramped, stinking, unsecure vessel?'

'You fantasize,' calmed Lake.

'You don't know how cosy, how rich in rewards, a sea life can be.' The chairman applied his persuasiveness.

'You do not dispose of me so easily, gentlemen. I have commitments too, and a skin to save.'

'They are not as proper as they seem,' said the innkeeper, who knew perfectly what men and women wanted.

'How's that?'

His legs splayed by the fire, Edward wiped the ale froth from his whiskers and raged at the treatment he had received. The Fellows were nothing better than complacent committeemen living off intellectual annuities. They had earned no power over him. Even the best of them, Lake, confined on all sides, had been moulded to their shape. Mediocrity, self-satisfaction, the stupefying forms of dullness. Why should Popple play their game, except that his own burning genius, if it were nothing more than a grass fire in his head, would be thwarted otherwise? His mind ran fast on stratagems of revenge.

'They've shuffled and trimmed too many times, especially Sir Astley Neville, a false Puritan if ever there was one,' continued the knowing innkeeper.

'You're acquainted with the man?'

'London's a village.'

The innkeeper's face was a baked apple stuffed with raisins and other such good things, a contrast to Popple's lean cheeks and hawk's nose, his fretlines and scoring.

'What's his medicine?' asked Popple, raising his brow scholastically.

'Neville? Tears and a tickle will bring Sir Nasty round. The chance to be generous to the right female person.'

'Ah, the motions of pity,' laughed Popple savagely. 'How he disgusts me.'

It was a weary journey homeward in unsuccess. When he reached Hull he cautiously sought out a friend's stable. The docks had disappeared in pale grey fog but his friend did not let him down. The black gelding waited. And easier on horseback, Edward could fly, his whiskers frozen and cape billowing, over the gloomy green moor, the ice-hard ground making for pace.

He was feeling comfortable as he reached the gentle valley, the orchards of the Brougham estate, the bosom of home. Books of calculus and speculation jolted about in the saddlebags with the documents of his vain petition to the Society. He had put it behind him when, as he trotted his horse along a lane, a voice cried out.

'Stop in King Charles's name!'

A masked man scrambled out of the hedge to block his way. He had a sword in one hand and a pistol in the other, and a black bag with two eye-holes over his head.

'Hey up!' shouted Popple. But his horse slowed to a walk.

'Who are you for?' demanded the masked figure.

Popple took out his dagger. 'I am within reach of home. Where the way divides. Let me pass.'

'And if I slit your throat?'

There were nicks and cuts over the questioner's leather jerkin.

'You have no reason to do so, sir,' insisted Popple, and with a sharp kick to his horse's flank cantered by.

'Ha, ha, ha!' he heard at his back as the bold young highwayman skipped aside into the grassy ditch. He was wondering at the peals of laughter as he rode through the gate and up the grand steps of Brougham House.

The groom came striding to take the horse, exhaling white cloudlets as he rubbed his hands against the cold. Popple dismounted and hugged the man, slapped the horse, the eyes of all three creatures rolling.

'You've made a tedious excursion,' welcomed the groom. 'Safe home!'

'Seeing great places I know that in this graceful valley of our Lord's lies humanity's only jewel. Our garden beds and our greenhouses have richness and wonderment they cannot dream of in the metropolis.'

'We may not stay protected here for ever, sir,' said the groom, examining the horse's hooves as Popple unstrapped the saddle.

'You are right, alas,' nodded Popple. 'We are given over

to rulers in whom sluggishness and fear congest. Shoppers, jobbers, accountants. To speak plainly, unless we safeguard our space for perfection we shall indeed lose it. Where's Rosamund?'

'In the park.'

'Will you call her?'

'Your wife is inside. They await you. They say your son is to follow the king's party.'

'We have no king.'

'Charles the Second.'

'Business, business,' Popple snapped at the spade-faced groom.

Inside and upstairs, along the cold passageway, in the set of rooms where his family camped by courtesy of Lady Brougham, Delia sat by the clerestory window, a wall of distorting glass that made the landscape swim as if under water. Set off exquisitely, Delia could not help a shudder of disappointment when her returning conqueror came in. She had waited too many hours by the window. Wound up as tight as her golden wiry hair, she saw at once that Edward Popple was the vanquished.

'Greetings, Father,' said broad-shouldered Henry, swaggering in with his sword sticking from his breeches.

'You're for the abattoir then,' retorted Popple.

'Is it so bad?' asked Delia musically.

'Bad. The country is turning around. All our old wisdom is out the door.'

'Then we shall go with the new,' she laughed, rising to kiss her husband. He deserved humiliating in front of his son, the manikin who would prove her real victor. 'Oh Edward, love, do they reject you? Oh what shall we do?'

When he held his wife, Popple appreciated the balance of her form, like a human set of scales. 'They ask me to come back.'

'When?'

'They don't set a time.'

The pretence of calendar months continued, even as the country was split asunder, with Time itself broken. People still remembered Time, backwards as it were, day before day in a coherent sequence, imagining that the days forward would go likewise, until eventually a pattern was formed again. It was necessary, always, simply, to look to tomorrow.

'Did you run into trouble on your journey, Father?' asked Henry, pawing the hearthstone like a prize steer.

Popple recognized something familiar in his son's shape and the scarred leather jerkin.

'No!' doubted Popple. 'It was not you who challenged me?'

'I patrol for the fugitive king.'

'Fool!'

Henry laughed raucously at his father's redness, and Delia's eyes danced in admiration of her son.

She had been attracted to her husband as a man of ideas and temperament. If he was ineffectual, therefore, unable to make a living, support the family, or even use his talents properly, she must not resent him.

'Let me go to them myself,' proposed Delia, composing herself. Her teeth were a string of tiny pearls, inadequate for the incisive determination she showed. 'I can persuade them.'

Edward sat down careworn in the chair. He could not stop his wife interceding on his behalf, nor his son following the king's cause, though there were few enough in the south, even among erstwhile loyalists, who took it seriously.

Through the high windows of the gallery he saw a dimple of rose-gold sunlight break through the roiling clouds over the moor, for a passing moment amidst the rainy storm. He could not mix with men, he could not function in the ways of men's society, nor manage their world. He feared his incapacity would destroy him entirely one day, but before that day came he must have a chance to prove himself. He *could impress*.

If only he could find an opportunity to make the one perfect and pure demonstration of the things his brain conceived.

He turned glumly to his family. 'I won't stop you, either of you.'

Henry sneered. The son should not have been stopped, even if the father objected. Might was on his side, he showed, rousingly squeezing his mother while his father curled away from him in the hard heavy chair. His father had always turned away, ashamed of Henry's robust simplicity.

'I cannot be confined here, Father, while I have strength in my arm.'

'Always a boy for a fight. Well, you have brawn enough.'

Henry moved behind the chair and clapped his father's vertebrae feelingly.

'The king's cause stays but a little time.'

'Go then. Stay out of drinking bouts,' Popple warned. 'The king's is a lofty cause after all.'

'Whom should I see?' asked Delia.

'My dear, the roads are extremely dangerous – thanks to the likes of our son.'

'Whom should I see?'

'I believe an interview with Sir Astley Neville might assist.'

'Very well. Henry shall escort me.'

'A man's wife going to those uninformed shifting bastards to beg a favour,' groaned Popple.

Delia smiled. 'We must shift with the powers that be. If we serve them, they also serve our ends. It is my duty, husband, to improve our conditions.'

Popple, unkempt and exhausted from the road, brushed his hair from his forehead in a gesture of despairing neatness and gave his wife a cold grin. 'How I admire you, woman!'

Left by his wife and son, Popple slung his legs over the chair and righted himself to go in search of Rosamund, his comfort. She was in the park, the groom said, beyond the formal garden that Popple had laid out for his Lord according to the principles of mathematics, herbal medicine and astronomy; beyond the apple orchard in the wilder space of the park where magnificent trees, standing like gods, hung with pearly drops.

She was between the trunks and boughs, in dark mist, the horse rearing in a flash of whiteness that disappeared at once behind the scene. He hurried, almost running, over the sere grass, following the rapid movement of the animal, a dapple-grey pony, and the rider, divulged and as abruptly concealed among the trees.

'Holla! Holla!'

Hooves padded on grass, ringing occasionally against stone.

'Ros!'

He ran forward into the clearing where she exercised. In the wintry gloom, under the trees, the dapple-grey pony was intensely pale. Swathed in a dirty pink brocade that draped the pony's sides as well as her own, the girl rode with her head back and thick fair curls flying out.

'Rosamund!'

The girl heard and turned her head, the horse shied. The man scampered aside as the horse curved in his direction at speed.

She brought the pony up in front of him. The animal's champing and whinnying drowning the girl's cry.

'Is something the matter, Father?'

'I'm back, dearest.'

He took the bridle and stroked the quivering veins of the neck. His daughter tossed her ginger-blonde hair. Hot rosy pulses from the riding flushed her skin. Her father stood like a scarecrow, the damp cloak hanging heavily from his rack of shoulders, his hair like a crow perched insolently on his head.

'Is it not too cold to be riding?'

Her green eyes played over him with delight.

'Nelly's joints will be stiff otherwise,' she answered. 'You are tired from your journey.'

'I have not hit my aim.' The horse was restive. 'Your mother will try again for me.'

Ros laughed. 'She would.'

Round-faced Rosamund's swelling curves caused the ample dress to model a form almost top-heavy for the slender little grey that, trusting now, nuzzled the man's armpit.

'I don't care,' he beamed. 'I prefer to be here in my own domain where I can work unhampered. But I lack the means. Who will provide for my loved ones?'

'My brother is about to remove himself from your care,' she said. 'Dashing fellow.'

'The stupid ass. My own adventures are more thrilling.'

She reined her pony away from him.

'Ros, are you lonely here?'

'When my mother sets me to needlework.'

'A girl your age should have companions.'

'I am never lonely out riding. The trees stand and whisper as I pass.'

The pony twitched.

'It grows dark. Shall we meet at the house?' His awkward smile pinned her eyes. The boughs rustled in dark knots overhead. He was so tired from his travelling that his feet almost froze to the earth.

'We'll let you up. Come on!' said Rosamund. 'Come on, I said. At once.'

She loosened her foot from the stirrup to give him a hold. He vaulted his leg over the beast's rear, squeezed in behind her on the saddle, his thighs enfolded in the rumples of her brocade.

'Are you set?'

'Let us walk, girl. Slowly.'

'No,' she shrilled, kicking Nelly's sides to make the horse gallop.

He steadied himself against his daughter's bouncing hips. She was a sure rider. She quivered with motion, making her brocade catch and rub in bolts against him.

Their eyes streamed and stung in the freezing air. The trees closed in on them; horse and rider knew the way. Slipping a little, Popple moved his hands to Rosamund's waist, holding himself with his legs against the pony's hot sides, lurching forward indelicately to clasp her bodiced breasts. He swallowed for breath. Her hot, shaking body generated its energy, spirit of fire, mysteriously from the chill and dusky air, and from the animal's flesh, and from the man's heavy thighbones and kneecaps pinning her legs. She panted and laughed with such vitality that it made Popple's blood race.

They passed through a gap in the stone wall, intruding down the gravel paths of the formal garden to the flower beds where pruned roses stuck from black compost like nail ends, bed after bed, for the horticulturist's experiments. Rosamund twisted round to whisper in her father's ear as they came to rest in the kitchen garden, 'We could go further like this. We could gallop far.'

He stared with shock and fear, unfolding swathes of sweaty brocade from his midriff, as Delia his wife appeared from the house.

'You have some energy remaining, Edward, I see.'

The horse, head bowed to chomp parsley, dropped a bright slug of manure.

'Lady Brougham awaits you for supper,' Delia called. 'She is fasting. You are to give thanks to the Almighty for the pea soup she has consented to take with us.'

'I anticipate your success,' Lady Brougham warned Popple as she left the table.

'Rest assured, your Ladyship,' obliged Delia.

The unpleasant meal was over. When they were in bed, Edward waited for his wife's breathing to steady before he rose and cloaked himself. With a candle he walked the passageway and down the stairs to his study where the candle's flickering light reflected shimmering miniatures of gold in the flasks and jars laid out on his workbench. Books were stacked, papers weighted. Pots and boxes concealed smelly organic and chemical matter, pickled, moulding, fossilized. A jewelled cross stood potently between the burners, with heathen relics in a row alongside. Popple reached for the jadestone of Tartary that rested on a stained wooden stand and let its weight sink his hand to the table. His mind glowed as the little piece warmed slowly to his touch. The piece of green jade had been chosen for a jet-black flaw, from which the artist had carved a tiny multifoliate black rose, the rose appearing to rest on the green surface to which it was inseparably joined. The jet and jade, opposed in colour and substance, grew one from the other, part of one stone, one entity.

Running his fingers over it, Popple felt the possibilities of union and division suggested in the stone, its promise of a black rose to be found in the East, of new kinds to be uncovered, and mixed kinds, once the underlying principles and polarities were understood. He was riven with longing for such intelligence, and such creation. As if they were keys to a theatre of his imagination, the tools of his science could be manipulated in his study in the darkest hour of the night, unlike people, such as the committeemen of the Society of Fellows, whom he could not manage. He squeezed the jadestone, friendliest of all. If he had been able to think about it thoroughly, Popple might have realized that only his failure to convey the superior vision he possessed prevented him from thriving in the world. It was all a question of words. Words were his failing. But he was restless too. Shivering, he cloaked himself and, taking up the candle again, roamed on, his footsteps leading back upstairs to the floor where his family lay sleeping, to the room at the end of the passageway where his daughter lay.

He snuffed the light and slipped through her half-open door.

Rosamund's body was bundled under the quilt in the black room, the white embroidered collar of her night-gown buttoned at the neck. In the rich heat of the quilt's cocoon a sleep of deep physical exhaustion replenished what the cold winter's day's riding had taken from her. Virgin, perhaps but for her Nelly, her pony. Thick breasts, swelling stomach, thick thighs, closed eyelids smoothing her eyes, profuse golden down that crept in patches down her body from haloed head to upper lip, to armpits, navel, groin and fluffed calves. Rose lips, rose cheeks, pure and true. Was she his creation? Her own life was finer than that. She was her own creative power, which he adored in her. She worked on him, and *his work* was all for her, his daughter, the one true love. Shaking still, he became hot under the heavy cloak. He imagined his feet nailed to the floorboards not permitting him to move an inch closer to her. He burned like a red-hot poker as blood ran to his head and blinded him. His passion concentrated in one point, her, Rosamund, where all his desire fused. His hands lifted, his arms reached out. Lust surged, inflamed, ached. He towered. The Destroyer. His daughter. Tears dropped down his cheeks, wetting his whiskers. He would not touch her, never. His sin was his secret that kept him from the world, the Society, the Fellows. His secret was the work and the knowledge that began and ended in Rosamund, the only one. For a moment, at the highest levels of truth, he was convinced that what he was moved to do to her was permissible. *For* her. He was about to release himself from restraint, to let himself devour her, to soothe his pain, to touch the extremist and only satisfaction.

Then she said, 'Father, is it you?'

'I came to see you sleeping. I've been working, my darling. Sleep on, sweet. Sleep on safe.'

'Have you been watching me?'

He nodded coldly.

'Don't do that.'

'Goodnight now.'

He turned like a shadow, rushed down the passageway in flight from what he might have done, and, tripping on his cloak, staggered down the stairs.

Outside, the dogs stirred. Barely draping his cloak around him, he strode to the formal garden. By the pond that was sheeted in thin black mirror ice, he fell into a posture of prayer to a God whose Sole Sovereignty he refused to acknowledge. He was on his knees against the coping of the pond's stone wall. Treetops, with tentacles, clouds like waves, silver inky moonlight, changing murkily, shuddered in the glassy sheen of the pond's surface. He smashed his head through the ice. He doused himself in the black freezing water. When he came up, he was choking with cold. His lungs heaved and the cold water's teeth snapped at his brain. He shook himself in appeal to the horrible sky. He would go away. He would put himself apart. Stop me. Help me. Save me.

Then he sneezed. Then a second time. And, comically, thrice.

Delia Popple returned from London having played her cards well. In a private audience with Sir Astley Neville she interceded as the virtuous wife who was forced beyond modesty and propriety in order that the chairman of the Society should understand her husband's case aright. Edward Popple asked only to be included, she explained, to work with and for the Society's good, sharing its ends and a portion of its means, with the simplicity of the true scholar, solely for the greater glory of the Society's name.

Sir Astley countered that the Society's requirements were of the highest. Doubts had been raised concerning Popple's competence, even his equilibrium of mind. Nor was Sir Astley empowered to decide the question by himself. Matters of membership took time. He suggested that if Popple were prepared to undertake a voyage of exploration then a form of probationary admission might be considered. He drove his bargain hard.

The nation's turmoil had unsettled the conditions of patronage, Delia Popple pointed out. Her husband had no independent means nor resources for such a venture.

'Excepting, of course, the riches of his brain,' joked Sir Astley, warming to the woman's self-exposure.

'He has not the money for a voyage. How is his family to live while he is away? He has not the wherewithal to prove himself in the manner you suggest.'

'His family should avail itself of our support in his absence.'

'I submit to your goodness.'

So she took her trick. She was stationed demurely across the desk from Sir Astley, whose eyes swam red as the interview turned. Her hands clasped, she beckoned passively until he could not resist, in all politeness, coming around the massive furniture to take and squeeze her soft joined hands. At which juncture, her tears fell.

'I can offer you nothing, sir. You must not abuse me. I request your beneficence in all humility.'

'Am I a man to impede talent's disclosure? Am I, representative of the greatest body of learned artificers since antiquity, a one to deny the material support that feeds discovery and invention? Your husband shall be our ambassador on the voyage of the *Cedar* – to sail from Hull, I believe. He shall have the post of ship's doctor. You, madam, shall be salaried on his behalf. She sails before Lent.'

Sir Astley's hand, rough from vine-grafting, was inside her gown and tweaking the moist muscatel of her tit. She tightened her lips.

'May you speak for him, madam? Is he willing to accept the commission? The journey's mission is of such weight that it may not be disclosed until we are in agreement.'

A pinch too hard.

'You are at a rush,' she said sharply, intervening to unfasten. 'Then I accept in his proxy.' Sir Astley chewed slaveringly on the offered grape.

It was a ring-a-rosy of bruises she took back to her husband with the Society's letter of commission. Edward no more noticed the pains she had suffered than queried the Society's sudden change. But she was content, having secured her own position. Once Edward Popple was away at sea she would be found to have gone up in the world. She would enjoy her independence within the terms of what horny old Neville must continue, on occasion, to desire of her.

Forgive the roundabout way she expresses herself. Delia Popple has the prospect of living nicely off the stipend of a dedicated husband at sea. She has a beefy son in the wars and a dolly of a daughter. She has made herself a true matron of the new society.

The wan grey world seemed scarcely to anticipate winter's turning. What remained green had grown dull, as if no further change were possible, and shrubs and bushes had their roots in hard ungiving earth from which Popple struggled to dig rose stock for the voyage. The Fellows had let it be known that the *Cedar*'s high and secret mission was for the king – not the martyr Charles, but the living king, Charles son of Charles, in exile in France. They were to collect rarities and find out wonders, such as would bedeck the king's claim to restoration. It was worse than any fanatic project, Popple considered. What a duplicitous lot! Under the very flag of the commonwealth! Theirs was the folly of a wholly lost cause. With partisan stupidity the hypocrite chairman Sir Astley Neville sent the genius Lake to explain to Popple that, although the Society was outwardly for the new regime, ostentatious in its Puritanism, there was a deeper, still concealed loyalty to the king. Donations to the Society were funds channelled to the king's cause, for which the Society in turn enjoyed a hidden conduit to the king's bounty. To tell all this to Edward Popple, a man they disdained, a mere probationer, was idiotic. Popple watched for the trick. But partisanship is as blind to subtlety as hypocrisy to principle. The partisan hypocrite, personified in Sir Astley Neville, was the most blundering of men.

Lake, of course, saw that the Society's complacent policy of so-called consistency was shaky physics indeed. No matter how cunningly the double practice might be carried on, there was no sense in subscribing to one form of government while counting in secret confidence on another. There were not such constants, Popple knew as well as Lake, to make such doubleness work. All was shifting.

Yet without scrupling Popple accepted the task assigned to him. He would board ship for the Eastern Indies in search of novelties, because in those novelties lay a slender hope to free himself.

A breeze ruffled the pond. If he stayed, sooner or later he would take advantage of his daughter, and destroy her, and both of them, even if with her permission. He was disabled by burning pointed desire for Rosamund, who was unrestricted, unspoilt, innocent and unconfined, the one true being in his world, the flowing and boundless source of power and life. He craved her. He needed to take her into himself so he might complete his work, even while to do so would stain it for ever. Even in his determination to reject it, the incestuous compulsion kindled. To sea. He had not the strength to leave her. Love and care, respect, protectiveness and tender joy, all the emotions of a father joined him to her. It was too harsh a discipline to separate his life from hers, unfair to impose his loss on her, turn his penance into her punishment, to abandon her to a mother and brother with whom she had no affinity. To cast himself to sea. Seas perilous, uncharted, tempestuous. Ships prey to all that vile men and unfeeling nature could hurl. She would grow up fatherless, grief and uncertainty endangering her as much as his unlawful desire.

He would learn to keep himself in check. He would not touch her. It was the one thing, in all the peculiar domains of a soul he had explored so rigorously for his forty years, visiting all its cavities and ascents, that he could not promise. There were springs in himself that were not his, but hers. There was a depth in nature he had no power to deny. But he would take on the vocation of renunciation. He would try to trick fate by putting himself apart and away, across water.

Rosamund rode up and laughed at him. 'You'll soon have a bigger pond than that to drown in. What will you bring me back?'

'The black rose.'

'I permit you to be away for a year and a day. No more.'

'I intend to be home for Christmas. The voyage is for nine months, Ros.'

'Where will be our home? Where will mother and I be then?'

'Brougham House must be your home. I go so you can stay.'

'Ha!'

'I expect you to greet me at Hull, my girl.'

Her gold lashes flashed, her green eyes fluttered like birds across the sky.

Popple took the bridle.

'Let's in.'

He led Rosamund and her horse towards the house that with sunset panes was settling into darkness. Come Ash Wednesday he would be alone, aboard the ship, committed to his work. He would be upright and noble, sorrowing, steadfast.

The household gathered in the chapel. Lady Brougham took pleasure in reading Popple the prayer of going.

'Protect him and keep him. Nourish him and cherish him. Thy servant. Protect us and keep us, nourish us and cherish us, Thy servants. Through the wide world and over the main, under the light of Thy heaven and in darkness from Thee, in the crowded ways and the soul's deepest solitudes, bring us to paths of righteousness, letting us not to lose ourselves, but to find ourselves among the orders of angels, through the power of Thy hand, that moves all things, the mercy of Thy love, and the grace of Thy breath.'

Lady Brougham's throat caught for a moment.

Then she rattled on like a shuttle on a loom. 'Prosper our sails. In grovelling gratitude. Thine, Lord.'

II

Last seabirds leave the ship. She rocks intently over the grey billows. With wind in her sails, progress seems rapid. Popple is pleased with the movement, although he has not found his sealegs. The sea is wide and directionless. Waves tug the craft forward, she surges and dips according to the set of sails. A long journey begins with suspension. The past recedes, detaches. The future is empty and unknown. Or, like the sea, hides enormity and strangeness beyond contemplating.

Captain Macqueen, a Dunbar Scot who had spent the greater part of his sixty years at sea, was glad to have on board in the doctor – as Edward is now known – one man who had no function but to observe and record, and mend where necessary. Popple could be the captain's friend because he was not immediately the captain's responsibility. The first mate and most of the crew were swarthy Cornishmen, subdued, sensitive, bitter, unclubbable except with themselves. If they were not for the king, as it appeared, they were already against a new order that had been quickly corrupted in their eyes by ambitious placemen, trimmers and timeservers.

'You must harness the winds,' quipped Solomon Truro, the coal-eyed enigmatic mate whom the men heeded. 'You needn't always blow with them.'

Of the small bag of sovereigns presented him by Lake

on departure, on behalf of the Society of Fellows, Popple gave half to his wife Delia and another quarter to Rosamund, leaving a modest amount for himself. For the rest, he entrusted his family into the Fellows' hands. His personal needs were to be provided for by the ship in exchange for service. He fully expected to return within twelve months to make a name for himself with what he found. Yet at sea it was suddenly as if one of his lives had been passed beyond and he was entered on another. A man unmade, yet to prove himself in this new air, he breathed deeply in the exhilaration of rebirth.

The old and battered *Cedar* was a mighty creature, bobbing and tilting, an ingenious buoyant device that, Popple believed, would cup and keep her crew through all perils, a veritable world, like our greater world encased within heavenly waters. He had in his purse a letter smuggled from France with the king's seal and solemnly handed into his trust. Little did they know he was no king's man. A larger history had Popple's allegiance, in which one beheaded king and his successor son counted for little. Edward Popple was his own man, and the day of sailing, he could not but acknowledge, was the moment of a personal destiny he did not wish to share.

The sun splayed its bruised broken light over the tarry waters as first dusk fell over the voyage and the rise of ocean was quelled to rest. The first scattered stars showed Popple the image of his daughter, removed from him, as far beyond his reach as those bright points in the sky, a dream to sail for, a sparkling polestar. As he struggled to fix her face in his mind, sadness seized him that she must grow and change in his absence, becoming Rosamund in ways he could not know. And his eyes blurred the image he had of her against the cloud-streaked twilight.

The captain interrupted him with an invitation to mess.

'We form our own society on board ship. It must be taut and regular, admitting none of the revolutions that take place on land. If there is due order, whatever we encounter will be as nothing.'

But Popple had no appetite.

'I hope we encounter something.'

'Rest assured of that. As surgeon, you are essential to my purpose, which is not to be delayed or disadvantaged by encounters. If we achieve that, nothing else matters.'

Macqueen had a commandeering arm on Popple's shoulder.

It made Popple argue. 'If our task in going out is merely to come back, where's the gain of it?'

'If we gain but don't come back, where's the sense of that? Come, sir, enough riddles.'

Captain Macqueen explained the charts. Beyond the Azores lay Africa, Cape Verde and the Cape of Storms, and after rounding the Cape there was choice of two routes to the Indies, the creeping route up the coast and across to Candy on the island of Ceylon, or the route that struck across open sea with the trade winds. Were there no landmarks to direct their passage across that stretch of water? Only a few islands claimed by indifferent French and negligent Dutch, two or three, how many not certain; barren uncharted places that were inimical to Macqueen's purposes and sure to be avoided. The captain favoured the creeping route up the eastern coast of Africa.

Popple asked to be instructed in navigational skills and given daily positionings. The companionable captain rallied with a first lesson of such lengthy exactitude that Popple grew dizzy. A sailor could evidently read the sea and the heavens as closely as a farmer his plot. The figures and references that the captain provided to illustrate his faith sent Popple at last spinning to his cabin, more than a little nauseous. He closed the cabin door and clung to the handle with a prayer that the ceaseless motion would stop.

Stop it would never. Only, one day, perpetual movement might become a thing to which he was accustomed, a thing imperceptible.

The cabin was fitted with bunk beds, writing bench and stool, lockers, a washstand and pitcher. From one of the two trunks labelled Ed. Popple, he took out pen and blotting paper and sat at the writing bench trying to steady himself enough to scratch the page with a commentary on his first day's voyage.

Unadjusted to ship movement, his hand jagged. He paused to take his bearings. The nib hovered in the air, not daring to fall and wound the paper.

On leaving the university, Popple had gone to the Inns of Court in London for training in law and notaryship. It was not to his taste. He had taken a young wife, Delia, who soon produced a son, Henry. To provide for the family he had attached himself to young Viscount Falconbridge, and travelled abroad with him on affairs of state, adventures from which he returned at an interval, to conceive, he supposed, his daughter, before going out again. He had seen the world, high and low, north and south, Romish and reforming, breathed the currents of the times and scribbled on the philosophical debates of the day. He had come to understand the primacy of commerce and navigation in mutating the world. The great work of his turbulent age was to forge systems of interchange, often by violence. Where he disagreed with the viscount was on the nature of the fountainhead that centred those systems. The viscount served the monarchy blindly, served power. Edward Popple saw more complex potentialities in the making. He supported neither Absolute Rule nor Anarchy. He wanted to serve the motor of change, that was creativity, and as he grew more abstract in his application of reason, he had ceased to be of use to the young viscount, whose will hardened for political action. At the time Popple was experimenting with magnification and microscopy, using perspective glasses to propose a new unity of creation, large in small, many in little. *Multum in parvo.* Falconbridge set him loose from service and he existed on his bare wits as a projector in London until the wars broke out, when it suited him to go north, to seek employment in the house of Lord Brougham, the great and wise, contemplative decider and humble warrior, the balancer. With other like-minded friends from collegiate days, haunted still by undergraduate schemes for society, platonic visions, raptures of art and nature, Edward was drawn to the estate at Brougham House. There he began his experiments to distil the fragrance of the rose. There Rosamund had grown in happiness and vigour despite the wars outside the gates. In winter she read geometry by lamplight, in spring she gathered posies and delivered lambs, in summer they played hide and seek among scratchy haystacks, and in autumn the fat perch would run on a length of fine line. Henry ignored his sister to follow the men of the town and the girl had no other companion of her own age. Without a match there, without a cousin or a classmate, Rosamund grew alone. But the place loved Rosamund, and Popple loved the place all the more for that.

In the midst of discord Brougham House was a haven of learning, plenty and peace. Lord Brougham grew more protective of his estate as his reading of the future became bleaker. He was scathing about the conduct of affairs by the king's party. What began in provoking quarrel would end in blood, he insisted. The churchmen and members were worse than the nobility, pushing argument and counterargument, claim and counterclaim. Reduced to plots and intrigues, the king had lost his vision – and would soon lose his head. Lord Brougham lived to see his predictions come true, and the fight over sequestration of property that followed. Then he lost his own life in a senseless skirmish between parliamentarian troops and a rebel rump, an obscure end for a lucid mind.

Lady Brougham lacked her husband's arts of negotiation and was thrown into demented piety by helplessness as much as grief. Staying on the estate, Popple and his family had become as birds living off carrion, an estimate of their situation that the widow evidently shared. So, with honour, Popple found himself at sea.

A first day's jottings of seabirds, flying fish, patterns of currents, and the coast of Albion slowly swallowed by a convex horizon.

Yawning, his eyes swimming, Popple laid down the pen. He felt again a quaint urge to pray, but to what? Which Godhead? At the mercy of which deity was he? Which nameless, rocking power?

Then as he leaned back on the stool, he heard a muffled knocking. Noises outside the cabin – this noise seemed to be inside, as if a mocking rat-a-tat mimicked the hollowness of his head. In triplets, the soft little noises continued.

A mouse? He stood and traced the sound to a corner of the cabin by one of the trunks. Or was it the trunk itself, rocking against wood, or an animal trapped? He unstrapped the belts, unlocked the latches and lifted the lid.

She was rigid, lying like a foetus with clothes stuffed round her. To blink was all she could manage, her wide eyes startled by the light. She did not move or speak otherwise, waiting for his response to burst.

He gasped, grabbing at her stiff limbs, causing her pain. 'Rosamund.'

'Father!' she whimpered.

He pulled the clothes away from her, took her arms and rubbed them vigorously until they started to move. The feel of her flesh made him believe in her. He rubbed her neck and, hauling her into a sitting position, rubbed her shoulders. He helped her, supporting her whole body's weight, to unbend and step out of the trunk.

'Forgive me,' she said, draping herself round his neck.

Her skin was white and creased, her hair flattened. She wore a plain shift.

'Sit. Who put you here?'

She began slowly to move her body, loosening her joints.

'I did it myself.'

She sat on the side of the bunk swinging her feet. She was panting.

'You might have suffocated in there.'

'I had a breathing hole in front of my nose. As long as the trunk was not upended I was safe.'

'My darling.'

She was dishevelled, uncomfortable, awkward, contrite. She had succeeded in her plan of joining him. She refused to stay on the estate with her mother. She would go a-voyaging too.

Edward stared at her in astonishment. So she had faked her grief at his farewell and pretended the dutiful daughter, all the while assembling the means, with the groom's help, to substitute herself for her father's clothing in the second trunk that was sent to the cabin. And the groom, who fastened the latches and buckled the straps, and knocked to wish her God's blessing when all was done, was feigning too. The groom had his own flit planned, seeing no sense in staying on the estate with Lord Brougham dead and Delia Popple in the hands of those Fellows.

'So, my girl?' asked Edward querulously.

'I would not be left behind. You must take me with you.'

'Does your mother know?'

'She should have had a letter.'

'We dock at the Azores, whence ships ply for home.'

'You'll not abandon me there, Father.'

His flesh shuddered with the thrill of her kiss on his neck. No, it was too hard. He had put himself apart from her, and here she was in his cabin, within his space, her arms around him. As he might have dreaded, the two of them alone, voyaging.

She was the only woman on board, and that was dangerous too. No one, not one member of the crew, not even the captain, must know. She was his secret trust.

'How could you do such a thing? You bold girl.'

'I dared. I could not stay. You're not angry, are you, Father? You'll allow me to come with you and care for you?'

'How will we manage?' he asked in a panic. She had boundless courage and strength, and vitality that he would be unable to resist.

'We shall live together as master and boy,' she replied, full of excitement. 'Do you have any food, sir? I'm starving.'

'Oh my darling, you have been confined in there for a day with nothing, not making a sound. I have biscuits and water.'

'Give them to me. And I shall need to use the pot.'

'Would you prefer me to step out on deck?'

She looked at her father and laughed. He had accepted her, and welcomed her, as she never doubted. It was the last trick. Whatsoever storms, hurricanes, icebergs, leviathans, pirates, treacherous golden isles their ship encountered henceforth, whatever milky blue calms when all breath died and fierce sun sucked moisture from their pores, they would traverse together.

Closing the cabin door on her, Popple boggled at the undertaking. He vowed on his life to protect and preserve her, even as he would be tested to the bottom. But she was his, a golden lamb within the crook of his arm. He must shepherd her and not violate her. He would castrate himself if necessary, in order to keep his vow, if castration could change the nature of his desire.

They slept head to toe, toe to head, back to back. Their restlessness reflected the restlessness of the ship, as they shifted and touched, half in and out of slumber all night long.

At first Rosamund knew the ship only from what the porthole revealed of swell and sky. Edward kept his cabin locked whether he was inside or out. So they managed to conceal her presence as far as the Azores. When the ship docked in the little island port of Angra, the crew scrambled ashore. The air was warm and peppery. The men were keen to eat fresh food, lettuce and pickles, to try the dry sherry wine, the southern pineapples and crystallized fruit rind – and the spicy port roses, if they risked being left with a dose. When they returned to ship to allow the second watch to go ashore, the first group of men lay about on deck, sated and sleepy, outbragging each other or dumbly satisfied with their achievements. In the cheerful confusion it was easy for Rosamund to appear as an English lad whom the doctor had taken aboard as his apprentice. Edward had cropped the girl's hair, preserving the locks, and outfitted her roughly in his own clothes. They went for a turn on shore, to feed and to acquire the rest of the costume. The raiding English were devils, tolerated in the Portuguese port for the sake of the profits they brought the ship's chandlers. The dark eyes of the local people were drawn irresistibly to Ros's paleness, suspecting danger. Pale eyes were the eyes of spies.

The fairness of the youth, presented as 'Ross', who came on board with Popple was less a question for Captain Macqueen than what the kid had been doing in the port of desperadoes in the first place. He was an English orphan, explained Popple, brought back from Virginia – 'so far and no further' – by a black woman from the plantations who hoped only that the boy could return to his kind. Popple had paid well for her charity, and his was not the best offer the woman had received for the tender creature who would not survive long in the port. All most unlikely, thought Macqueen. But the captain was not one to exert his authority in a personal matter of this kind. He allowed a gentleman his privileges. From another port trader he had himself bought on board three Angolan slaves. For reasons of prudence. The best of their kind.

Squeaky young Ross, fair as a flower, chubby and energetic to boot, became one of the ship's characters, always under the wide-brimmed Azores straw hat to keep his skin from peeling, ready to oblige with fanciful stories of an eventful life, if the men asked questions.

Down the coast of Africa they travelled, in serene waters with friendly winds. The shore hung in a band of white sand and shadowy foliage, its mysteries never clarified as they kept their distance. They could make out smoke, but no people or houses. Occasional chopped logs or broken baskets drifted by with the bearded coconuts, but no trading boats ventured out. The most communicative visitors were a calling pair of ibises way out over the water. Africa was more silent than the sea. And silence and serenity day after day began to work on those aboard the

43

Cedar, who were, after all, tough types come for adventure. Time's slow and formless passing was the last thing they wanted or were ready for. While Popple could find fascination in the changing colour of the water, the drift of seaweed, or, at night, the wide concentric rings of phosphorescence, and maintained his diary in short, dry entries, the men tended to contract their range, turning in on their little society to find fault with each other, and with themselves, making grudges of undigested memories, turning small dissatisfaction into the cause of large injustice, until friction became hatred.

The mate, Solomon Truro, began to whisper against Captain Macqueen, urging the men to reconsider their duty. While the state of England was uncertain, the prospect of disorder on their return, hardship, destitution or worse, must always be kept in mind. While the men would ever remain patriots, Truro reminded them that there were good grounds to be absent awhile. For the Captain it was different. To bring the ship back on time would make him secure. He had backers not only in England and Scotland, but in France, for Macqueen was known to be a king's man and the hidden purpose of his voyage, Truro surely guessed, was to aid the king's cause. What punishment then would the victorious and vindictive republicans mete out should the intrigue miscarry? For the mere men, whose sea decision had been an impulse of venture and escape, no sinecure awaited their return. Was it not better to sojourn abroad until the way was clear and safe, enjoying meanwhile the freedom of the seas and gathering riches from the eastern world?

The mate argued plausibly to men who may not have granted all his logic, but whose imaginations, already fired with the thrill of masterlessness in the upheavals of the civil wars at home, were easily caught by the lure of extended freedom and easy wealth. Throw off chains and manacles! The visionaries and levellers among the crew looked askance at the captain's hard hierarchy. What did they gain from preserving order, by a neat completion to their voyage, and their booty laid at the feet of an exiled king for a cause already lost?

Glittering and tranquil the days, the sails full and steady in the sequent breezes. Discontent wove the men's minds invisibly, as they performed their tasks, yarned against the rail, or dozed in their bunks in the pleasant warmth of late afternoon.

Hanging about the deck under a straw hat for the periods of each day that Popple permitted, Ros picked up the intensifying whispers. The disguise would not forever fool men who, Edward knew, were stirring to strip away appearances. He was nervy. The fresh lithe form, a boy's loose clothing concealing curves of flesh, would arouse the fantasies of the crew, if not their suspicions, no matter the ostensible sex. The image of Ros would taunt them in the hot empty stretches of the night, when mosquitoes, breeding from nowhere, drilled at their peace. So the doctor accompanied Ros at all times, unless duty prevented him. Intensity of light and space gave some men a fever. One or two had scurvy from the mean diet. A swinging boom knocked one old man unconscious, and Popple had to cut another open to remove an inflamed cyst. It was the doctor's first surgery, and how his victim howled.

Ros, pining for her horse Nelly, fancied horses' manes in the frisking waves, certain that Nelly would be missing her, and as the ship rode the whitecaps, she elaborated her own solitary pleasures, spurring Nelly over the green pastures of the sea. She was locked in the casing of her father's protection.

Shy and shielded under the hat, the curious figure of

45

orphan Ross was a good omen to the men, never mind Ross's relationship with the lousy ship's doctor. Yet Ros was unaware of herself as an object of their attention. The men liked to have her in sight, and they talked freely in front of her, careless of what was overheard.

So it was that she came to ask her father whether their ship was *for* or *against* the king, and he replied that they were sent by the Society of Fellows of the new commonwealth.

'They say the captain supports a restoration,' she insisted.

'They? Oh, the men. I believe Macqueen may, but he is bound in sovereign duty to the new state, to deny which is to deny the very authority by which he has command over the ship.'

'Is it a paradox then?' she pursued. 'If he denies his bond to the commonwealth, the men are within their rights to deny *him*, and he is nothing.'

'Where do you hear these ideas?'

'The men talk of putting the captain ashore.'

'Are you certain? Then they're traitors.'

'They talk of either leaving the ship or sacking the captain.'

'Who is behind this mutiny?'

'The mate.'

'Who would be captain himself.'

'They proclaim themselves men without chains, masterless men, souls of liberty. Where do *we* stand, Father?'

'We must warn Macqueen.'

'Is that not betrayal too?'

Popple looked thoughtfully at his daughter. 'Are your sympathies with the crew?'

'I think of your mission. You must have means of voyaging. You must at least stay with the vessel.'

'Oppose their plan . . .'

46

'The men are the ship.'

'The captain is the ship.'

'We best stay with the sails.'

'If they give us the tacking.'

Captain Macqueen congratulated himself on his foresight in taking the three black slaves on board. Simeon, Timothy and Jonah were at least reliable, and Christians to boot, with wooden crosses chained to their necks. The captain had guessed what was afoot long before he came to Popple, feeling him out with a stern lecture about rebellion's poison working in the veins of men who failed to see how self-contempt and destructiveness drove on such acts of defiance. The captain proposed to buy the mate away from the men by divesting part of his command on to Truro's shoulders. Truro would execute decisions, but power would stay vested in the captain.

Popple diagnosed the plots and counterplots as a kind of seasickness. He wondered if they went ashore among strangers whether they would all not quickly come to love the ship again and love each other, high and low.

But if they went ashore, Macqueen pointed out, the mate would be able to rally riffraff in support of a mutiny. The struggle must be played out at sea. In their confinement lay hope. Childish disobedience needed a firm hand, until the seasickness passed.

Captain Macqueen was reluctant to negotiate with a mate whose rough heroics were his strength. He put off taking action and the kindled whispers soon burst into open flame. With three strong sailors, Solomon Truro fronted the captain, declared him an enemy of the commonwealth, seized him and trussed him in the hold.

'But you are king's men yourselves,' laughed Macqueen helplessly.

'We are no man's men,' retorted Truro.

The change of helmsman was as simple as that. The ship's sails noticed no difference.

For the time being, however, the mate ordered the doctor and his boy locked in their cabin, in case they should prove to be the captain's sympathizers. As the wind changes, so a few crewmen turned pessimistic, predicting no good outcome. Equally, they were too gloomy to protest or resist. The rest were jubilant at their new beginning.

Then from a gentle sea they saw green mountains grow on the horizon, massive inky blots that crackled with lightning and, as the ship sailed unavoidably closer, rose to block the sun. They had reached the zone of the monster of ocean whose throat was the tunnel of wind and water down which ships vanished. They could not tell day from night, hearing only the giant's roar and Macqueen's howling from the hold, until Truro had a gag stuffed in his mouth. The rudder was useless, the keel itself lifting from the sea, and all directions black. It was Solomon Truro's turn to prove his captaincy.

Simeon, Timothy and Jonah clung to the deckrail on their knees, spewing in prayer. At last Leary, the swabber with the flaxen hair, demanded that Ross, the sailors' omen, be allowed up on deck. It was not kindness, but Leary's fey knowing that Ross was one who would survive. The Angolans, when they saw, encircled the fair figure, kneeling with their cotton robes billowing. And Truro, wrestling at the helm, saw light glow from the dark glassy sphere. The waves lay down and whiteness descended. They were through the storm, but enveloped in shining mist that allowed them to see less than in the darkness. To see nothing. They were becalmed.

The patient whose cyst Popple had cut out started to moan. His wound was inflamed. The fellow's agony

became so intense that Solomon Truro, to show compassion in his new leadership, was obliged to let the doctor out – a novice quack, after all.

While Popple drained the wound and bathed it thoroughly, doing his best to ease the sailor's pain, the black men continued to pray to Ross. They sung a round-song in their own language, bulky Simeon leading handsome Jonah and lean Timothy.

'We shall sicken ourselves if you keep us locked up down there,' protested Ros to Solomon Truro.

Leary tossed his salty flaxen hair, arching his neck as if he were a mermaid. He was the actor on board, jealous to act whatever part the other men desired of him, and in the doctor's boy he scented an affinity that made them rivals.

'I'm sure your master finds it cosy enough,' he jeered in a high-pitched lilt.

'Shut up, Leary,' said Vost, Truro's deputy, gruffly, making the actor pout.

Misty air muffled the ship, her canvas wings dead. The three black men stood swaying to their charming song. Their long striped robes drifted from side to side and slowly, as if by contagion, the breeze they conjured from their skirts spread to the sails. Whiteness thinned to blue. The ship moved in response. They were delivered again. And for Simeon, Timothy and Jonah, Ross had brought about a miracle.

It was understood by Solomon Truro that the doctor and his apprentice submitted to the ship's new regime. They were restored their freedom.

The men debated the allegiance of the ship herself. There was a question of which arms she should sail under, the king's, the republican government's, or the people's. Some favoured keeping the palm and laurel flag of England, but to do so meant acknowledging the captain's original authority and made the crew mutineers and criminals in deposing Macqueen. Most were for sailing under a new sign of liberty. They would hoist a flag of their own devising, and it must be decided quickly, as they were nearing the new Dutch settlement at Cape Town where there must be no misunderstanding. So it was that Ros embroidered a black rose on a green ground made from Captain Macqueen's undershirt to provide the *Cedar* with an ensign. It fluttered as the ship entered Cape Town waters, a craft of independent designation, a free pirate ship.

The Dutch, determined to turn their new trading post to a profit, replenished the *Cedar*'s supplies of water, vegetables and fruit at exorbitant cost. Solomon Truro told Edward Popple that in the interests of everyone's health and safety Captain Macqueen was to be taken ashore. It was not wise for the old man to attempt to continue the voyage. Vost assured the doctor that the crew had voted to stay with the ship under her new command on condition that decent measures were taken to provide for poor crazy incapacitated Macqueen. Popple was expected to certify that the captain was unfit for his position, thus making good the mutiny.

'What choice do I have?' Popple asked.

'You are free to go ashore with the captain,' grinned Truro commodiously, 'but not, I think, your boy. No, not Ross, who has been a charm to us. We should not like to lose the kid.'

Three speakers of one tongue in the small settlement who concurred in their telling of what had happened aboard the *Cedar* might lead to the story's being given credence. Truro was careful to guard against such tales.

Macqueen's slaves were to be given liberty too, to find their own grassy kingdom beyond the warehouses on the shore. Simeon, Timothy and Jonah hung about the enclosure, praying forlornly. The local tribe was as foreign to them as the English and more hostile to their creed. Eventually the Dutch guards shooed them away; to be garotted by the chains from which the crosses hung round their necks; for further flight towards their heavenly homeland over the dry hills and golden plain.

Captain Macqueen was committed to a hospice for the insane in the stone fort of Cape Town. A portion of the allocation of gold sovereigns seized from his cabin was pressed on the sisters for his care. The mate feasted and paraded himself with the settlement's governor, a lardy, useless Dutch loner, and was soon bored. The *Cedar* must sail, east to uncharted waters and an uncertain goal. Solomon Truro promised his men gold when their mystic destination was reached. They were on Drake's route to the Hesperian Isles, he boasted. Only one of the sailors, Cramphorn, who had a better sense of geography, dared scoff.

Had the governor not been such a vain, narrow, hubristic dullard, and the place called Cape Town so ungentle, Popple might well have opted to stay on shore there himself – if he could have been sure that Ros would be with him. He could have worked in the hospice. But he didn't trust Solomon Truro, who kept Ros on board as a hostage throughout the time in port. The man was a dangerous self-convinced Celt willing to commit the ship to crazy venturing merely to prove a point. And Popple hated the mate's sneering interest in Ros, the oily insinuations, the dark eyes on the figure beneath the clothes. For his daughter's sake, Popple should have abandoned the voyage of the *Cedar* at Cape Town. But he was possessed of his own higher purpose too, for which the ship was needed and his countrymen to sail her. He dared not risk antagonizing the crew with talk of leaving them. For the sailors needed Popple too, however inadequate his skills. A ship needs a doctor for her good health.

★   ★   ★

With Ros proclaimed her mascot, the *Cedar* sailed from port under a blue sky. But Cape Town had bequeathed a fever that did its work with terrifying speed. The first case broke the next day and the doctor's spirits and methods were little use against its immediate effects. The fellow died on the third day, by which time there were half a dozen cases more. The spread could not be stopped, no matter what Popple, who fully expected to die himself, did. It was Vost who railed against a God he had always considered malign for the vengeful doom on their rebellious ship. Vost stood and lived, cursing, while around him on the deck, in heat and cool, in palsies of bodily evacuation, flesh was stripped from bones, brains turned to mush and organs failed. Within the month three-quarters of the crew had gone, as each afternoon at sunfall their bodies were consigned to the deep.

Cramphorn, however, scoffed at Death, who refused to take him. If one of the dead men's parts should chance to touch him, he would dance a frantic jig on the bow to throw off the evil influence. And Solomon Truro survived too, of course, unrepentant skipper of the death ship to which every day he promised landfall. He swore there were islands imminent where they would find haven and recovery. On secret Arab and Portuguese charts he had seen the hidden landmasses of the region. Cambalu, Mascareigne, Dina Arobi. But in his preoccupation with the condition that had befallen his command, in an excess of determination to ignore its ill effects, Truro had steered off course. No land appeared, because they had lost their way.

'Oh-ooh!' lamented Leary, urging the stars to play on him the trick that in their tilted angles they had played on Solomon Truro. The trick of extinction. He prayed incessantly.

Edward sat with Ros in their cabin preparing for death. He mantled himself with sorrow at the apparent wreck of his undertaking, his eyes glittering at the strange sense of their evident end. He was satisfied that he had not hurt his daughter. He had done his part.

'No hurt, Father,' she smirked, fixing him with her clear green gaze. Her condition was still strong and fair.

'Let our blood and guts desiccate to mere bones. Meal for fishes,' he sighed. 'Our souls will continue voyaging.'

But Ros was still a lucky charm. The doctor, his skills inept against the ravaging disease, managed to survive. Sweat drenched the rat's tails of hair down Solomon Truro's neck, and he was alive too. Among the remaining crew they saw furies pick away souls at night, while the mortal body sought its last renewal in sleep. At last only three men remained, Leary, Vost and Cramphorn, and their mate-captain, and the doctor with his apprentice. With so scant a complement they could barely handle the ship. They sailed with the wind, and the winds treated them profligately, driving them many leagues a day. In their ailing state they would be lost if serious weather came. Watery graves would gulp the morsels that pestilence had not bothered to chew. But every day continued their progress until, at last, a graph of porphyry crests rose unexpectedly like a whale from the sea.

Land beckoned, an island seemingly, or the end of a peninsula, their last hope, a pale turquoise lagoon stretching from the land, and between their ship and the lagoon a crashing line of breakers, a reef, towards which they were driving with wind full in their sails. The small weak band turned from scrutinizing each other for who would next be food for fish and heaved the set of the sails around for what appeared to be a break in the reef. Vost managed to shin up the cordage to the crow's nest to sight a narrow channel through the ceaselessly pounding waves that formed a natural rampart to the shore. Their steering helped, but it was the friendly wind that took them in. They heard the keel scrape. Without an order being given the longboat was lowered and, as if in desperate flight, all clambered down the ropes to abandon their vessel to its emptiness, in favour of the smaller boat, to row resolutely for the white sand and the green hills beyond. At the last moment Solomon Truro reclaimed his leadership, with a firm order for Leary, Vost and Cramphorn to stay watch.

'Drown any rats,' he cried, brooking no objection. 'No more pests! Let no rat leave the ship!'

PART TWO
Southern China,
Yong-ch'ing year one . . .

. . . or February 1652. We begin again, from a different starting point, on the other side of the world. In 1644 the last Ming emperor to rule China was found dead in Peking. The Manchu invaders became the new rulers, inaugurating the Ch'ing dynasty, while in the south a rump of Ming resistance remained.

III

Eunuchs are either indolent or overactive. Old Lou Lu, eunuch commissioner of the Ming, rose before dawn for his meeting at the quay. The arrangements were of the utmost complexity. Only with a lifetime's experience of intrigue, in the most taxing circumstances of history, the fall of a dynasty, could one hope to succeed. So Lou Lu, after fourscore years and three, did not rest. He slept for a few hours, rose, performed his peculiar ablutions in darkness and privacy, hurrying always, with scant thought for himself. All was for his master, young Taizao, Prince of Yong, Ming heir, and the futurity Lou Lu expected to see. Being sexless, he had been spared the burning-up of his life. He had watched while generations wasted themselves and he, like the old tortoise, seemed assured of longevity. Placing his long bony hands in the padded sleeves of his gown, he observed the fishermen unloading their catch. There was always a profit to be taken. It was chilly waiting at the docks in the last hours of night. The old eunuch commissioner stood in the darkness resisting the temptation to drink tea or eat hot porridge at one of the warm lamplit stalls. He was prepared to wait until the messenger arrived.

Lou Lu recognized his man at once, shambling down the gangplank with a pack on his shoulders, his patched and tattered clothes indistinguishable from those of the fisherfolk. He came off one of the fishing boats from

Ningpo, having hopped from wharf to wharf in a journey through the riverine lands of several days from his home town of Hangchow – a middle-aged man with lined face and a gammy leg. From the shadows the old man extended a hand to help with the pack and hurried the traveller down several lanes to an inconspicuous waterside inn. Only when the traveller opened his mouth to comment on the lavish welcome that the eunuch commissioner offered him was his scholarly irony apparent. Both men had the awkwardness of those whose certain standing in the world had been displaced by events. The traveller, once a frequenter of courts and academies, followed ingrained rules of etiquette in sipping his tea. He was tough and had suffered unspeakably, seeing his family put to death for his loyalty to the collapsed dynasty. Barely escaping with his own life, he vowed to work relentlessly for the re-enthronement of the Ming, and already eight years had passed.

Facing the messenger in the stinking eating house, the ancient eunuch was reminded for a dreamy moment of the vanished exaltation of his youth. The other man's circumstances were far more wretched than his own. In Zayton, through Lou Lu's tireless efforts, the claimant prince of the Ming, the Prince of Yong, Zhu Taizao, had garnered powerful local support, establishing a most useful allegiance with traders who had grown large enough to chafe for immunity from the interference of a capital more than three thousand *li* to the north, in Peking. By mixing with the merchants of southern ports, who had commercial reasons for rejecting the Manchus, Lou Lu had built the plausibility of a Ming recovery. But there was no question of a court in exile, not yet. Lou Lu recognized all too well the lamentable falling-off from the splendid sovereign supremacy of the Ming courts of earlier times. The traveller was a relic of that glory, his zeal derived from the true source; however much he had suffered, he had not compromised, and had engendered great virtue. Lou Lu thrilled inwardly to their oblique courtly chat, and might have felt ashamed at their present circumstances if it were not for his long vision.

To make certain that they were unfollowed and unobserved they moved from one shop to another, until the traveller felt it safe to disclose the letters and assurances he had brought. It was in a pavilion of the great Kaiyuan temple that the traveller at last let Lou Lu see the treaty that had been negotiated with the foreign priest, long-trusted servant of the empress, a Neapolitan father who had since been recalled to Macao to discuss strategy. The Macao Dominicans were convinced that the pope would see the wisdom, at the cost of a few muskets and men, of restoring the sincerely Christianized Ming to lawful control. The Manchu ascendancy had been disastrous for their mission in China. The Jesuits had succeeded in gaining the ear of the new rulers in Peking, offering their usual shameless promises and duplicitous bargains. Accordingly the Dominicans undertook, on behalf of the Vatican, to provide military support for the Ming to reclaim the throne.

The traveller confirmed intelligence of the death of the empress. With the last rival gone, Taizao would be recognized as the leading claimant if his existence were known. Lou Lu's silence encouraged the traveller to jump ahead and summarize the situation. Whoever had the support of the Christian pope would be emperor, and whoever would have the pope's support must go to Rome.

Lou Lu peeled back the difficulties as if they were the skins of an onion. Was the messenger to be trusted? The man, hardened against all risk and danger, wanted to see the dynasty restored. The eunuch commissioner wished his prince to be emperor. There was no reason that they should not join purpose in a time of desperation. There was room for divergence of aim. But was the man to be trusted? That prior question he left in suspension. And was the Neapolitan to be trusted, a Dominican priest? For their order too it was a time of extreme measures. The extinction of the old dynasty had seen Dominican influence bow to anti-foreign edicts and Jesuit supremacy. If the Dominican mission at Macao, a cover for territorial and mercantile interventions after all, was to be challenged by Manchu force, why not augment the counterforce with the discontent of Ming loyalists throughout the empire? Were victory achieved, the gains would be considerable. If failure, then no worse, although more costly, than the present. Could foreign armies achieve victory for the prince of Ming? Their boasts were easy. Could they? Would they? What would they want in return? Could the Dominicans persuade their Roman father, this pope, to give support? Was the prince needed in Rome or would a deputy suffice? These questions were difficult to weigh. How far was Rome?

The port of Zayton was sluggish, its greatness silted up by centuries. Fishing boats, coastal transports, traders to Manila and Formosa, occasional privateers were its regulars, and the craft of the unofficial navy of Koxinga, moving in glimpses up and down the coast. Long oceangoing voyages to east and south had ceased by imperial command, and the mighty vessels were no longer built in the shipyards. Would it be possible to find a ship worthy of bearing Taizao, Prince of Yong, as far as Macao, let alone to the western hemisphere?

Nodding and frowning, Lou Lu rubbed his smooth chin.

And if the prince declined to act according to the treaty, would the traveller be within his rights to negotiate a deal with another of the contending claimants, although few remained and none had a claim to match Taizao's?

And if the prince left Zayton on a journey of twelve months or more, would the swollen local traders continue to acknowledge his legitimacy? Would the comfort and standing that Taizao and his train enjoyed in the region survive? As things stood, and it was preciously achieved, the cherished prince expressed the people's confident indifference to the tax-leeching regime in Peking. He was the darling of new-won local prosperity and independence. They had bought him at that rate. Would they want to push his challenge further, to risk confrontation? Only if to do so was clearly in their interest, with feasible outcome. Or would the prince's absence provide them with an excuse to renege on their support?

Lou Lu, antique, could not be content with waiting. Persuasion, expense, effort and danger lay ahead. The process was arduous. If the plan failed, he would have failed his prince. Lou Lu found himself hurrying the messenger along almost impolitely. There was not much time, if courage and righteousness were to prevail. Down an alley so narrow that the black-tiled roofs of the houses on either side overlapped in the middle, giving it the name Never-See-the-Sky Lane, they went, the fragrance of narcissi growing in straight thick clumps from earthenware pots on balconies falling to their noses while Lou Lu explained to the messenger that he would accept the offer of help from the foreign fathers *only* once he was sure that the bosses of Zayton would permit and pay for a voyage to the western hemisphere to enlist support. He reiterated that Zhu Taizao, Prince of Yong, was now ranked prime among rightful claimants to the throne. The messenger must spread the word that there was no other. Thereafter communication must be kept to a minimum.

Lou Lu left the man by the harbour wall. The water was grey and tranquil, the coastline changing in definition as the light came up. Having no purpose in the town but to elicit Lou Lu's involvement, the traveller at once sought passage back on the fishing boat on which he had come. Lou Lu was apologetic for the lack of proper hospitality Zayton had offered. As the sun rose over the wide horizon beyond the crumbling breakwater, the two men bowed, collaborators in the cause, in final bond of trust, and Lou Lu left the traveller to fend for himself in the strange town until a boat would take him through the waterways away into the hinterland.

Lou Lu, who had seen a great many changes in his lifetime, continued almost despite himself to have a keen interest in the emergence of new possibilities. It was perhaps more a matter of curiosity than hope. He was no visionary but a practical, open-minded man who looked to solutions. As he walked he found himself, to his surprise, intrigued by the idea of a voyage. He was curious about boats, the science of the seas, navigation. The thought of the world out there aroused him. It surely would contain a great many novelties, offer unforeseeable advantages. Curiosity nibbled at him, tickled him, and in vain he pressed his thick jacket flat against his body to crush the itch.

He must be careful not to forget that the traveller was a scholar first and last, a dreamer who could not distinguish between elaborate speculation and the analysis of facts.

The doctor was waiting when Lou Lu returned and Taizao had not emerged from his apartment. The doctor preferred to present his report on the prince in private to Lord Lou.

'What's the news this morning?'

'The patient submitted successfully to the medical treatment prescribed.'

'Was the medical treatment successful then?'

'No results are visible at this stage.'

It was, predictably, another failure.

'I see.'

'We continue the treatment tomorrow,' said the doctor with restrained glee – a disgusting quack who had ingratiated himself with the town's leading figures and stuck like a leech, scheming the while to deny access to the queue of midwives, shamans and travelling salesmen who professed to have miracle cures for the prince's condition. But there was no point in resisting. The doctor knew how to protect his inexpertise. He wrung his hands at the sensitivity of his task, lamented the setbacks and delays, and grudgingly, miserably, measured out the all but imperceptible progress, while all the time money was spent on the most expensive, most preposterous medicines, none of which did the trick, and all the time the doctor's purse swelled. It was possible, perhaps, by adjusting doses, to achieve the degree of recovery or decline that was expedient. The doctor was not above poisoning the prince, Lou Lu conjectured, to prevent anyone else from coming up with a cure.

Dismissed, the doctor backed from Lord Lou's presence. The eunuch's eyes were sunken and rheumy, heavy lids closing over his unfocused gaze. He thought merely of his charge, Taizao, Prince of Yong.

Seeking relief from the weight the day, Lou Lu stepped out into the garden and found no change. The air was humid and heavy, the sky blanketed with thick grey cloud. Leaves of bamboo and cumquat sat dully, beneath which the goldfish, compliant club-shaped creatures, hid in the unreflecting water of the ponds. By the stone path in the plantation of lilies Lou Lu found a tight apricot-coloured bud rising on a stalk amid the thick leaves. He looked at it with satisfaction before walking on. In the darkest corner of the garden a large evergreen magnolia tree with damp emerald moss over its skin offered cool shadow, its great white flowers like seabirds drowned in its boughs, dripping perfume. Lou Lu stood there breathing, pressing together his blue-grey fingers, their pale aged elongation an amusing contradiction to the creamy cups overhead.

Refreshed a little then, the old man followed the path back through the zigzagging corridor to the front hall, where his servant, emboldened at last, wasted no time in fetching the mountain woman.

She had waited several hours for her audience with the eunuch commissioner. She sought entry through a village connection, a household manservant who had attended solicitously on Lou Lu for days before daring to ask if the woman might be admitted to his lordship's presence. She was a peasant housewife who wore an embroidered smock over blue cotton trousers and had her hair pulled back in a knot from her creased face. At once brazen and shy, mixing suspicion with simple country opportunism, she stood and waited for Lou Lu to question her.

'Speak,' he snapped.

He knew her purpose, even as he felt contempt for her motherly ambitions. A hundred virgins had been paraded past the sexless old man, and with a diligent sense of irony he had carried out his duty, ensuring each her chance, and still the peasants came meekly forward until he despaired of finding the solution.

'It is said that our most lofty prince seeks his rightful companion. I bring my daughter to beg an interview with him. She is known in our parts as the Fire Fox.'

'Then she may burn the prince's spirit. What you suggest is dangerous.'

'She would serve only to give him pleasure.'

'Do you trust your daughter with a stranger like this? Do you not fear for her?'

'He is our prince. What harm can come to her with him? All is advantage.'

'Except failure.'

The woman bowed her head blankly, acknowledging the risk she dared to take.

'She has entranced the men in our village, including my own husband. Our prince would regret not having the opportunity to enjoy her company.'

'Is she here?' he asked unnecessarily. The candidates were always at the ready. Hearing Lord Lou's interest, the servant bundled the girl in.

Running to her mother, she breathlessly covered her face in her sleeve, a vulgar little thing, sinuous, charming, with lovely painted eyes, a ruby mouth and white skin, and a tight gown of red satin picked out with silvery-white chrysanthemums. Big feet. Heat brought moisture to her forehead, her mouth, her thighs. Curling against her staunch mother, she was hot with senseless longing, irrational desire, animal appetite.

'She dances,' said her mother, pushing the girl forward so she might divert the lord. But Lou Lu scoffed at her. Fire Fox left the eunuch cold. 'Will you receive her?' asked the mother bluntly.

'Of course. With gratitude.'

'May I also be permitted to cook some dishes for the young pair?'

Nothing was left to chance by these mothers. Lou Lu stifled a yawn as mother and daughter prostrated themselves. This one wouldn't work. He knew that as he signalled for the servant to lead them to the apartment where they could prepare.

He turned to his writing table and dipped his brush. The

ink, prepared too early, was already drying. Long decades of administration, petitioning, ordering, manipulating, had enured Lou Lu to correspondence. He was no scholar. His brush hesitated before sweeping across the paper. He was writing, after all, to one who was less of a scholar than he. The merchant chief, Cheng, knew only triumph, Lou Lu reminded himself with a smile.

The vigorous sea commerce carried on by the traders of Zayton, despite official interdiction, and not to judge by their port's forlorn appearance, had made Cheng and his kind as practical and proud as they were powerful. For decades they had ignored Peking's demands for taxes, establishing independent alliances with Malaccans, Arabs, Indians, making friends of strangers. No wonder the new conquerors of the north had grown wary of the region. The eunuch commissioner knew how to flatter the Zayton chiefs, turning the evidence of Manchu mistrust into a tribute to their strength. It was a comedy that bound them to the Ming cause, a sense of their own unassailability, so far from Peking's reach, that made them, with Lou Lu's invisible prompting, unite their commercial might with diverse and more vulnerable elements: the loyal dedication of the peasantry, the intelligent grievances of scholar-officials, the discontents of the numberless itinerants whose condition of life had been lost in the upheavals.

It was self-confidence, Lou Lu knew, that made Zayton adhere to the prince, the true hidden remnant of the Great Ming. In time Lou Lu had established the relationship of trust and identity.

Taizao lived in seclusion in a house on the hillslopes above the town. His involvements with the world outside were handled by the eunuch commissioner alone, who talked carefully to people of all levels, neither a remark too few nor too many, attracting by reticence, until the walled

66

mansion came to be considered the town's silent and secret treasure, containing a promise of supreme ascendancy. By subtle yielding and scrupulous insistence, Lou Lu let it be understood that the prince's power was conferred by the merchant chiefs solely and held in their hands. Ming power was their power. Their ambitions, their loftiness, were inseparable from the symbol of the prince.

Unlike Master Cheng, the eunuch was accustomed to defeat. He knew when he took Taizao south in his custody that it was the final parting from Chongzhen, emperor of the Ming, Taizao's cousin. When news of the emperor's suicide reached him three years later, Lou Lu screwed up his eyes and wept. The emperor had hanged himself on a hill behind the Forbidden City as Manchu rebels threatened to invade the palace. As news followed of old emperor Wan Li's ranking grandsons, collaterals of Chongzhen, claiming the mandate to rule, with support of valiant generals and loyal scholars, enthroned one by one and exterminated one after another by the invaders, Lou Lu grieved. The Prince of Fu was executed, the Prince of Gui sent on the road. Yet Lou Lu kept his counsel. He hid and protected the orphan prince, concealing his ambitions for the youth. And now, with confirmation of the empress's death, the last vestige of the Prince of Gui's claim was gone. There would be no more pretenders. The woman who had argued that her son was unfit for the throne, driving him into exile for the sake of her own claim, was now gone herself, like her son, beyond hope of return. Only Taizao remained, unknown, his survival barely a rumour, suspected by no more than a few.

He was unformed. Yet Lou Lu knew that the prince's reclusiveness and obscurity were requisites for the role. His destiny was latent and must remain so. His tenderness it was, his lack of hard driving purpose, that made him the chosen one. In a secret ritual the eunuch named the new reign: Yong-ch'ing, year one of Rejoicing Forever. And here Lou Lu must be more careful than ever. Whispers, distortion, a few stray threads of gossip unluckily caught and worked to inflate a spy's importance in the demanding new court of the Manchus could bring attention to the youth. Which of the many rejected companions, those writhing girls whose flesh proved worthless, or the musical boys, or those sullen muscular beasts who had been given their turn with Taizao and lost face, which among them had turned informer? It was dangerous to continue much longer, until the will arose for another claimant. And once a threat materialized, it would be too late to dart out of sight.

He wrote to Cheng, recognized leader of the Zayton chiefs:

Respected Sir:

It is your servant's honour to carry out his duty towards his distinguished superior through whose tender concern for the welfare and livelihood of the citizens of the region the prosperity and standing of Zayton have risen to heights unparalleled; and whose selfless efforts and wise understanding have pursued with success the glory of our people and empire. The defection of the rebel Prince of Gui and the decease of his empress mother are reported. The honourable sir would be advised to ensure the future stability and welfare of his territory by removing from within his boundaries any further threat of danger, thus clearing the way for the eventual restoration of harmony to all under rule.

May all things run with your honour's will.

Greetings from Lord Commissioner Lou Lu.

It was oblique enough, the required reverse-talk that

must characterize all their correspondence and discussions. The servant, who might be trustworthy for a day, since the old man had agreed to admit the women from his village, delivered the letter immediately.

It was close to midday. Lou Lu ate the exquisite meal prepared for him alone in his chamber. Cockles, fresh-water crabs, pickled radish, pea sprouts, pearly rice and osmanthus wine. Draining the lotus-seed soup, he belched resonantly and stretched out on the satin-covered mattress to digest.

In the afternoon he went on foot, with his splayed gait, to the many-storeyed house that Cheng had built himself beside the canal, on the exact spot where he had started building his fortune by hawking fishing supplies as a lad. Now it was as a grandee surrounded by private troops that Cheng greeted the lanky, bent eunuch – from Peking, Cheng had to remind himself, as he prepared to listen to Lou Lu's calculating eloquence.

'Large carp and small fry do not happily co-exist. Sooner or later the larger eats the smaller, striking before the smaller grows large enough to threaten. With the consolidation at the centre and the sharply rising strength of our independence, is it not inevitable that power will seek to strike the root of our provincial prosperity, imposing taxes which no negotiations can stave off, taxes without end? Our prince will grow to mightiness, given time. He must be safeguarded until his rightful place is secured. With our efforts he can gain the support of prepotent foreigners who have means more forceful, more dynamic than ours, to ensure the success of his campaign. Think what greatness will descend upon his patrons then, the honourable merchants of Zayton! Think what boundless future lies in prospect! Think of a power acknowledged to the bounds of the world!'

Cheng's forthright gaze assessed the eunuch for the

hundredth time. His mind scrutinized the arguments set out and conclusions drawn.

'There are risks,' he said.

'Of course. Risks innumerable. We take them on ourselves in order to relieve you of the worry.'

'How so?'

'It is imperative that the prince leave Zayton before knowledge of his whereabouts becomes a danger. The cause must be kept secret. Through absence, loyalty can be maintained in silence.'

Cheng nodded. Lou Lu pressed forward.

'He must go on a mission. He must be fitted out for a voyage – to barbarian lands.'

'Will you go?'

'I am his pilot.'

Master Cheng disliked the rarefaction of court culture. He did not understand the abstract devotion that could take the place of love. 'You ask me to equip the voyage. Am I not then implicated?'

'You may disown us if you need, or if we fail.'

'And lose my investment?'

'A trivial outlay for what you would reap as kingmaker. A gambling misadventure of no significance to one of your oceanic prosperity.'

Cheng saw the proposition clearly. To get rid of the prince and his counsellor, whose stature events would only augment, was an advantage in itself. To offer assistance would keep the prince in Zayton's debt, if he one day became Emperor of the Four Seas. But it must be Zayton that decided. He would talk to his associates, those he had brought on and those who were jealous of him. And if the prince never came back, that too would be a gain.

'I shall speak to the merchants. The proposal has merit,' he said to end the interview.

'Your generosity is noble,' responded the eunuch without irony. Nobility was the one quality Cheng's money could never achieve without the help of courtiers like commissioner Lou Lu, who chuckled with excitement as he lowered his back into a crooked bow.

It was less the contest of the fishes that concerned him than the fisherman's profit when large and small contend. When the snipe and the clam grapple, the fisherman nets both.

The prince would not paint the rose from life. No point in such forgery of the external world. He would rather recapture its spirit in a few inspired strokes of the brush. A more profound analysis of the rose's elements was required to achieve the less superficial representation. But the prince shied from his purpose, fitfully daydreaming, as if among clouds in the sky, before he eventually returned to the rose. Rose, symbol of youth, of unfulfilment, of immaturity.

He sat on a stool by the pond where the bored attendants had left him and where Old Lou found him, passively absorbing the essence of the rose that he proposed to paint.

'Taizao,' greeted Lou Lu, pleased to find the boy alone. Taizao looked up, startled, from a deep daze. He had no words for the old man, no smile.

But Lou Lu grinned to see the prince whose flawless face was proof of his breeding, his narrow black eyes shining below smooth lids, his nose small and fine, his mouth small and regular, his long shining hair pulled back against little ears and white skin, like raven's wings opening over snow. As his consciousness returned lazily from a remote dream, Taizao's eyebrows quivered to salute the funny old man who adored him. His teeth flashed in mockery. He did not bother to stand in respectful greeting. His skirt was pulled into his lap, exposing hairless muscular calves and bare toes in straw sandals. His shirt, loose on broad shoulders, had fallen open to reveal the well-defined chest of a man who was compact and shapely as a pomegranate.

'You study the rose,' began Old Lou, 'a flower like a youthful gift, cheap, blooming all year long, shallow and flavourless.'

'It's pretty and commonplace, and that challenges me to catch its quality.'

'The idleness of youth. I have been working for our cause since before first light. Have you done your texts?'

'The study of the rose is an exercise too.'

'A lonely one.' Lou Lu turned to the matter at hand.

'They come every day to entertain me.'

'There's another girl for you, recommended by my scouts. Her reputation as a miracle worker goes before her.'

'I'm not interested, old man.'

'Let your desires float. See what enticements pry into your heart. You must try.'

'The little rose entices me.'

'Are you so unsensual? There is no excuse.'

'I'm bored, that's all. I don't know what is wanted of me.'

'In boredom lies the beginning of unrightness. You must be strong, clean and virile to rule the kingdom.'

Taizao flashed his teeth again. 'I must also have a cultivated mind. These people sent to entertain me do nothing for that.'

'It's more pressing than ever that an heir be conceived.'

'Let someone else do it for me.'

Lou Lu sighed and squatted down beside Taizao, settling his buttocks on his heels, harder than the rock.

He explained then that they were to go on a sea journey beyond the known world, to a world known only by strangers, to gather support for their mission from the Christian pope. They would sail with the covert backing of the people of Zayton, as their champion and hope. At each port on the route, Canton and Macao, Champa, Annam, through the trade islands to Malacca, they would be warmly welcomed by loyal communities of sojourning Chinese. They would rally allies and solicit funds, continuing in triumphal progress across the western oceans to Rome, the capital of the outsiders' empire. Suffering foreign seas, neither defeated nor exiled, in voluntary absence from China, Taizao would draw the love of all true patriots, until at last, godlike, allied with alien might, he would drive the Manchu invaders from his ancestors' throne. Lou Lu's eyes sparkled at the vision.

The young man's gaze shifted and wandered. What Lou Lu spoke of was far beyond his ken and he was not interested. His emptiness allowed him to survive, like a floating boat, calmly accepting the direction of the winds and currents. Like a dancer, he had only to follow their music. Graciously, he allowed Lou Lu to lead him.

'I long to see the world,' he said. 'New scenes and exotic places. I want to know all the different and fascinating things.'

'Consider that you have no choice. If you stay here you will be discovered. Surrounded, ensnared, destroyed. You must welcome the voyage.'

'When?'

'A ship must be found to weather the great oceans. Preparations will take some time. Letters must be composed in utmost secrecy for those in foreign ports into whose care we shall entrust ourselves. Loyal crewmembers must be chosen, provisions for our survival laid in, gifts made ready and collections of marvels and rarities to impress our barbarian hosts gathered. The finest examples of our arts and sciences, our medicine and our horticulture, our clothing and our cuisine, must be selected. Our ship must bear the civilization of the Great Ming, your highness, its chief cargo, a jewel in the lotus.'

'It is a journey without end, old friend. Aren't you frightened?'

'The end of our journey is the continuation of the Ming line. But you must ensure your posterity before we leave. Father a child.'

'How?'

'The doctors have instructed you.'

'I am incapable.'

'You resist.'

Looking at the handsome prince, whose beauty and purity caused more unbearable pangs than those of denied physical consummation, the eunuch could not understand how natural fertility failed to gush from the youthful body. The grafter's art that had produced such exquisite roses for the garden could surely graft some offspring on the prince. Bull's penis, rhinoceros horn, bee's jelly, turtle flesh, asparagus, oysters and musk, tiger paw and gold dust, excess and denial, manipulation, hypnosis and drugs. Every method had failed. The peasants with their fecund girls, the performers from the opera troupe, child duchesses and boy soldiers. Taizao, Prince of Yong, proved resolutely impotent. At times blood flowed into his soft member, causing tumescence to begin, which once beginning immediately subsided, until decline was complete. No climax was possible.

Taizao put up with the therapists and fortune-seekers Lou Lu sent, but after so many attempts he was thoroughly fed up. Obliging out of obedience, he became more resistant with each new experiment. He preferred to contemplate a rose in peace, and as he learned the technique of unwilled resistance he grew contained and strong.

'I don't want another one,' Taizao told the eunuch.

'They say the mother is something of a witch, and a powerful cook. Have the dishes tasted first, won't you, my dear boy.'

'The spicier they are the colder I get.'

Lou Lu squeezed Taizao's knee with urgent affection. The boy could not be emperor until he proved his potency. Take him away and send back reports, lies, inventions, to enhance the standing of the all-subduing god-prince of the Ming.

Taizao yawned. 'We shall go then.' He looked fondly at the old man. 'When's the next session?'

'They are ready for your summoning.'

'Then they can wait. First walk with me in the garden, old man.'

They favoured the wilder paths for their walks together, and climbed from the lower courtyard, with the large pond fed by a watercourse cut from the steep bank on which the house was built, through the sunny courtyard of rocks and roses adjacent to the apartment where Taizao spent his time, to the territory, still inside the walled compound, of ancient bamboo and citrus arbours, shining pipes, twisted cypress, bauhinia and golden shower trees, and myrtle groves hung with flowering vines abuzz with dragonflies and butterflies. The path snaked in and out. Following the old man, his guardian and guide, as on so many earlier occasions, Taizao submitted with pleasure. Life was easier when one was told what to do.

'A prince needs uprightness,' Lou Lu began, his statecraft informed by an almost superstitious morality. The dynasty had collapsed because the rulers had not behaved rightly. 'A prince must set an example, link heaven and earth, balance opposing elements. He must respect the rites and take new measures with decision. He must be open to the desires of his people while remaining far-sighted and superior to their desires. He must be nothing but a prince.'

Taizao liked the idea. Picking his way along the grassy stones of the path, his sandals brushed with warm dust, he wondered if Lou Lu could be talking about him.

'Is it right for a prince to leave his land and go to sea?'

'Whatever stratagem is advised is right.'

'Will I still be the prince in foreign lands?'

'If you are not greeted properly, you will not meet with the foreigners.'

'Can you sail?'

'I intend to make a study of navigation. I am interested in the mechanisms of shipping.'

'There is no end to your interests,' Taizao laughed. 'We must bring back lots of new things.'

'We shall travel as traders, our professed aim to open new markets. For your safety your identity will not be known.'

The old man stooped to examine a small golden-yellow eglantine rose growing by the pathside. 'What is its name?'

It was a wild rose. Taizao smiled keenly to be able to answer his teacher. 'Seasons of the Moon,' he said.

'You're right, you're right,' Lou Lu nodded. 'Good. Good.'

The mountain girl tried everything she knew, pressing her hot and moist parts against the prince's cold and dry being. The girl and the prince worked their eyes at each other across a gulf, where all else failed to react. The mother gave a helping hand too, the prince surrendering to their efforts. It was like trying to force a newborn baby to suckle. Charm disguised their frustrated fury, until time was up.

'Thank you. We need not go on,' Taizao said at last, and they left in a huff, muttering that the prince was certainly ill, certainly abnormal, certainly of no use to anyone.

IV

Lou Lu was interrupted in his study by the servant, who had been roused from sleep with an urgent message for the eunuch. The son of a fishwife was waiting outside, a brawny fellow who shifted his weight from side to side, cupping the hot tea with both hands, but refusing to sit down. His message was that fresh loaches had arrived, a seasonal delicacy from the mud of the Yangtze delta, and his mother, who had a stall in the market, was ready to sell them to Lou Lu. Her son would willingly have carried them up to the house on his shoulder-pole and felt disrespectful in asking Lou Lu to come with him. He did not know how to talk to the commissioner; he preferred to serve with his strength. But his mother had sent a sign of her good faith, passing on the token she had received, which Lou Lu acknowledged as he unwrapped the cloth parcel the servant gave him. It was an octavo size sheet of paper, printed in a language that the eunuch could recognize as Latin, a page torn from a foreign holy book, a sentence marked with a tiny circle that looked like a fish's eye. *The way of the righteous is made plain*, Proverbs 15: 19. A dry gurgle came into Lou Lu's throat at the scholarship of their cause, as finely spun as silk gauze. Heaving himself from the bed, he once again reached for his padded coat. The long day was not yet over. Lou Lu had no words for the fishwife's son, and demanded none in exchange. He was content to follow down the hill into the shady streets of the town, scarcely keeping up with the pace the boy set, who made up for being sullen with his shy agility. It was after midday, and the overlapping roofs cast deep shadows over the open doors and windows of untroubled sleepers. The boy led the old man directly to the market place where the storeholders, packed up after a morning's trading, had gone or were sleeping too. The fishwife had a shelter of hessian strung over bamboo poles at the back of her stall. With a brusque apology for the rough conditions, she pulled Lou Lu inside, sat him on a stool and poured out strong brown tea to revive him.

Without small talk, clearly and concisely as she lit a pipe, although in the heaviest accent of the region, she praised Lou Lu's devotion to the Ming empire and its young scion. The old man, knowing her attachment to the old order of things, was gratified to have her loyalty formally reaffirmed. He did not know that the traveller who arrived in Zayton in the morning, and who was already on his way, had also made a call on her commitment, indirectly, through her connections among the fishing people. He had been forced to switch plans. Boarding the boat at the wharf in Zayton for the first leg of his continuing journey, the traveller was aware of being observed. He suspected he had been followed in Zayton. Or perhaps the eunuch was being watched. Reaching Amoy, he decided to abandon the vessel and change course to travel overland. It was through a net of contacts which stretched to the fishwife that he had sought the assistance he needed for the tricky mountain country: reliable guides, safe accommodation, a through route. If he had been watched, it was because some particular of their plans was known by those who opposed. The danger that faced him faced their whole enterprise. It was an obligatory caution to inform Lou Lu. The message came to the fishwife with the tubs of loaches that were brought in from the estuary too late for the morning market. It came as an order to action. If they were already under suspicion and the closest observation, there was no time to seek further assurances. The voyage should commence as soon as possible. The traveller could ensure their welcome with the Neapolitan in Macao. That was all. *Proverbia 15: 19. Via iustorum absque offendiculo . . .*

The way of the righteous is made plain . . . Where was the proof? A scrap of foreign printing? Lou Lu was bound to inspect things from the perspective of doubt. The crudest plotter could think of such a device. But he knew the fishwife would be even warier than he was in the matter. She had sent her own clumsy son to command the high-ranking commissioner to her. She evidently judged that it was time. There could be no stronger guarantee than the woman's act. The time had come.

The fishwife lifted the lid from the large wooden tub to show Lou Lu the loaches that moved incessantly, squirming and arching. One, flopping from the water in a frenzy, managed an escape. But some were already torpid, slimy brown with black and russet markings, crudely shaped things, between eel and fish with the grace of neither, like stunted, unsinuous eels or fish with no fins, with only a tiny eye and a stroke of a mouth to distinguish head from tail. The loaches looked like mud and smelled of the silt where they bred, neither fresh nor salt. They were best thrown live into a boiling hotpot, their blood mixing with red chilli stock, thought the old man, peering at those that wriggled in the tub in agitated life. He furrowed his brow, excited by their vitality so close to the moment when they would be doused in soup, sucked and chewed, bones and all, as someone's nourishment. His, he hoped.

Laughing, the fishwife seized a fat one that had fallen over the side. It escaped her fingers, making her laugh even louder.

'What do you need?' she asked. 'What are you after? What must I do next?' It was her honour to serve Lou Lu.

'Who is the best of the boat captains? I will need a vessel fit to travel to the western ocean, and a skilled navigator to guide us.'

'Zayton has the best navigators in the world,' replied the fishwife, rubbing her hands as she refused over and over again the cash he offered her.

'I would need a ship.'

In a corner of her shelter, on the floor, a bundle of incense sticks sent smoke to the god of seafarers, an apple and a tangerine glowing in offering.

'Zayton has the most seaworthy vessels.' She tugged his sleeve with her fishy hand. 'Come with me.'

He clasped his hands in thanks as her son, ready to be escort again, silently took up the bucket of loaches as if in response to an unspoken order. Between the three of them was the bond of constancy to the cause they served. With shaky dignity Lou Lu, eunuch commissioner, went ahead of the fishwife up the hill. The son, tagging behind, splashed water from the bucket on his shoulder-pole. The way turned through the angled lanes of whitewashed houses with their tiled friezes and cumquats flourishing in pots to signify *ji* and *li*, happiness and profit. And still the idea of a voyage itched at Lou Lu like a crab-louse, as he pulled his padded robe around him and told himself again that the traveller was a dreamer who could not distinguish speculation from facts.

The Mosque, of austere white marble, had stood there for five hundred years. Beside it on the canal was the grand housefront where Captain Jin lived with his women behind a red-brick façade inlaid with black-and-white stone and tiles, red parquet and carved timber inscribed with running Arab script. The captain's landstays must compensate for the deprivation of his voyages. Captain Jin had chubby cheeks and a barbered black beard. Under lush lashes his hooded eyes looked out, and his teeth, revealed in a welcoming grin, were astonishingly white. His sinewy hands had iron strength. His ancestors had been in Zayton for many generations, for centuries, from the time when the place was the major port of the eastern world. Yet his people continued to preserve a degree of resistance to the enclosure of Chinese culture. As Muslims they kept to themselves at the fringes of the clannish merchant society.

The fishwife and her son waited outside while Lou Lu entered the courtyard where painted lanterns bobbed in the wind. The visitor accepted the oranges and raisins he was offered. Jin's independence recommended him. He owned his own boat and was for hire. There was little risk that he would secretly follow the orders of another. The best navigator on the coast, he was able to strike a deal. For a sum, a not inconsiderable amount, Captain Jin, ship and crew would be hired for a journey of twelve months to Macao, along the coasts of Annam and Champa, through the islands to Malacca, and across the western ocean to Europe. The fee was to be paid by the Zayton merchants, who would reap the benefits, commercial – and, it need not be said, political – while safely keeping their distance. The less the eunuch was prepared to disclose about the mission, as the discussions went on, the more Captain Jin was able to harden his bargain, always bearing in mind that the bill was to be paid in the end by Master Cheng, whom the Arab had no wish to antagonize. When Lou Lu was vague about purposes, and insistent about standards for staterooms on the trading vessel, the captain saw that he should ask no more questions and stick to sums. The agreement was made. In a spirit of honourable calling, however provisional, Captain Jin accepted the gratifying terms. The rate was set by the secret passenger, whom he might have guessed was Zhu Taizao, Prince of Yong, unthroned emperor of China.

★   ★   ★

In the guise of a young man of business, his hair cropped, and in high spirits, the prince boarded the boat before dawn. The others had been on board since the previous evening, stacking supplies and preparing the cabins. For the merchants of Zayton the voyage was an emissary of friendship to neighbouring lands, a journey to explore new markets and make new finds. To have the refurbished vessel sit impressively along the harbourfront, her dragon prow flaring skywards, the great black eyes inspiring boldness in the onlookers, and lacquered timbers glinting red-gold, was truly an auspicious sight. New ropes were coiled on deck as bright as spun silk and all the metal fittings polished. Embroidered banners fluttered symbols of good fortune into the friendly spring weather. Images of peaches and peonies echoed the hothouse peaches and melons, and the rows of potted flowers and shrubs, piled in the hold. Overhead hung the painted phoenix, below on deck finches and doves chirped in their hanging cages, chickens, roosters and ducks babbled in their baskets.

After sunrise the abbot, in a robe of brocade, came on board with a train of young monks and quivering girl dancers to drive ghosts and demons from the craft. Banners and poles topped by carved wooden hands and wooden orbs were paraded round the deck to prepare the way for Matzu the seafaring god and the lesser gods of the Far-seeing Eye and the All-hearing Ear who keep voyagers in mind of home. Horns blared, cymbals clapped, drums rumbled, and a cloud of incense blew away over the sea as the moment came when Captain Jin proudly received the abbot's blessing. The crew gathered around the captain in a tight knot, keen to share whatever good fortune the spirits might bestow. Then Master Cheng, providing further comfort, presented gifts and letters on behalf of Zayton. These were more than the usual ceremonies of departure and, while unaware of the reason, the crowd on the wharf entered into the gay, brave occasion with shouts and toasts.

Among the throng stood the fishwife, watching through narrow eyes as she smoked her pipe. She refused to let her son join the expedition. The great ocean was even more dangerous, more unknown, more treacherous than the hinterland.

Fireworks hung from the mast and along the rigging like bunches of brilliant red bananas, and when the last of the dignitaries had returned to shore, a monk lit the fuse. The rat-a-tat explosions mounted as the sparks ran, smoke puffing along the rail and the sailors laughing. On Captain Jin's order the sail of woven bamboo panels unfurled at last and caught the breeze. The crowd cheered. She was a fine vessel, of large junk design refined with elements of the Arab dhow, different from other boats in the port of Zayton. Her structure was a tribute to Jin's seafaring years, well-proven and a touch exotic. He loved her. And in the excitement the familiar figure of Lord Lou Lu, eunuch commissioner, separated from the official group and slipped below deck unnoticed. It was as if the instant he set foot on board a command was given. The sail filled, stiff and lofty in its flexing against the force of air, and the ship slid effortlessly from the dock, banners rippling, fireworks spluttering, to glide across the harbour like a swan into the open sea.

Lou Lu recited a prayer of sacrifice in his cabin to propitiate the alien gods of the elements and bring the ship home with his purpose fulfilled.

Gripped with the seriousness of the moment, Taizao appeared to shine with excitement. He made a vow to bring back the riches of the fabled four seas and reclaim the throne of his ancestors. It was a spontaneous, unformed gesture that made the old man happy.

At the helm Captain Jin chuckled ebulliently to be away, to be unconfined. He flashed his teeth to the sky, his weather eye on Malacca, the halfway destination, the free-wheeling port city where he knew well the variety of sought-after products he could acquire in exchange for his cargo of Fukien tealeaves. Arabs were there in large numbers, Chinese mixed with Arabs, and Malays mixed with Arabs. It was trade, going among the mix of people and working their desires, that formed the basis of Jin's fortune. He intended to advance himself a stage on this trip. Malacca, the acme of purpose for a captain with ambitions. The most advanced shipping of the day was there. Malacca – Jin didn't care if the voyage went no further. Time to expand his fleet, to improve his old craft, to make gold from opportunity. He began to sing praises to the Unnameable in a muezzin's guttural chant.

As dusk fell, Lou Lu came up to sit beside Captain Jin and note the skills of navigation, checking bearings and currents as the stars came out. While Jin was responsible for the boat, Lou Lu made it clear that the progress of the voyage was answerable to a higher authority, vested in himself. Jin's eyelashes lowered. He didn't care what people believed. He knew whose hands were on the wheel.

On shore the celebrations continued after dark. The prolonged crackling of fireworks eddied around the harbour and, from small fishing boats, stars shot into the sky and squirted into the water, sputtering out in their own reflection. From far away in the darkness the well-blessed vessel sent out a last flare of goodbye before she sailed from view, from Zayton for the western ocean.

Drunk on the dockside, a few boys aimed their rockets at a figure dressed in a straw smock. The creature danced and whooped in high-pitched shrieks that could have come from a man or a woman. Male or female, the creature lunged at the drunken boys, flirting with them and calling out obscenities in a mountain accent. The boys, goaded into excitement, threw firecrackers under the fringes of the straw smock. Bang-bang-bang they exploded until the straw caught alight, and the poor mad creature's cries turned to yelps of pain and terror. The straw blazed. Teased beyond endurance, in a fire of ecstatic torture that transfigured the scene and made the boys gape at the humour that had vanished from their prank, the smocked creature ran at the wooden bulwark of the dock and jumped off the edge into the harbour. In clumps the singed straw was floating to the surface of the water. None of the boys dived in to save her.

★   ★   ★

The first stop, after two days and nights, was Macao, one of the ports where the foreigners had been authorized to establish themselves. On entering the harbour Lou Lu was discomfited by the flagrant strangeness of the architecture and, noting the flourishing trade in the settlement, wondered whether the governors there would have any reason to risk becoming involved with the ship's mission. Would the letters and covert agreements be of any use? Lou Lu was quickly answered, when the foreign fathers proved uncooperative and even, within the bounds of their code,

86

inhospitable. The particular Dominican, the Neapolitan, who was said to be active on their behalf, proved not to be there. The head of the order claimed not to have heard of their enterprise and would take nothing on trust, nor on the evidence of the documents and gifts presented. Lou Lu might almost have suspected the messenger in Zayton of sending them on a wild goose chase, if the likelier explanation were not that the poor traveller had himself been betrayed, no doubt fatally.

The Dominicans would grant only that the visitors might stay, under conditions of limited comfort, while the matter underwent further consideration. The issue had changed, however, into a question of whether the ship from Zayton would be able to carry a letter from the fathers to Rome endorsing the Ming cause, a letter of introduction, no more, or, if that were too open an expression of support, whether the Dominicans would not send to Rome by their own separate channels, in their encrypted style, a plea for commitment to the Ming loyalists' strategy. To this end Lou Lu spent many hours of tortuous dialogue with the Dominican superior, while Captain Jin spluttered and sniped about the time they were wasting. The Latin negotiations were tedious and inconclusive, bar the face-saving conclusion, reached without much choice, that the ship were better to reach Rome expeditiously herself than to wait for the foreign fathers to make up their minds whether she might have the honour of bearing their letter. The Dominicans were in truth unable to convince themselves of the value of engaging with Chinese politics. That was more the Jesuits' style. The Dominican rector, to the almighty cost of the order, did not look to larger patterns. He would end his days unmartyred in an Italian abbey, regaling dinner guests with alarming tales of his ministry to the East, a place without grape wine. But for eunuch commissioner Lou Lu there was no turning back. He maintained his faith in the one foreign father who was not there, the one who had understood, and he determined to sail on.

The water turned purple as the ship pursued her way down the tropical southern coast. Captain Jin was cheerful as long as he sailed on course and his mood was reflected in those crew members, lackadaisical worshippers of Allah, who were his men. The rest of the crew comprised proper Chinese, men who respected their ancestors and whose fealty to the Ming, subversion of the usurping empire in the north, could be relied on if called for. The natural leader among them, a rough weathered seafarer called Huang, showed Taizao, whenever he appeared, a matey, intimate respect that suggested intuition of the fey young man's importance; but Lou Lu took no one into his confidence. Taizao's presence on board was unexplained, his standing unspoken. And to Captain Jin and his men, Taizao was invisible. Rather than jeer at him or break his composure when he stood languidly at the rail gazing at rainbow sunset over the sea, or when he fussily moved potplants from hold to deck, from sunlight to shade and back again, decanting his own urine from a glazed pitcher on to selected plants, Jin gave the signal in his own behaviour that the passenger should be ignored. It was through Lou Lu that the captain passed information for the princeling. But Huang could see in Taizao's invisible standing a shadow of the hierarchy which gave him his own measure of rank. Huang had skippered enough ships in his lifetime to be styled captain as well as Jin. The camaraderie and deference Huang showed Taizao, in a wink or half a grin as the boy passed, was in subtle defiance of the Arab captain. Lou Lu knew all this, reserving Huang's loyalty for later, when it might be needed. Taizao was oblivious. He communicated only with the old man, sparingly.

After the joy of sailing wore off, Taizao sulked in his cabin, lolling to and fro in a hammock. The small cabin (second only to Captain Jin's) was a confined cubicle with a kelpy odour, yet light and buoyant from the panelling of bamboo and a narrow latticed porthole. Taizao liked to daydream there.

He also took charge of the botanical specimens in the cargo; potted fruit trees, potted vines, medicinal herbs, sprouting vegetables, miniature trees, and select flowers and shrubs, plum, chrysanthemum, peony, iris and rose. His concern was to make his shipboard garden flourish. Not all the specimens relished the salt air, the motion of the ship and the divorce from earth. Some perished, while others were best helped by slowing their growth into a state of dormancy, still others could be kept healthy with sensitive attention. The plants were Taizao's work and his precious companions. Captain Jin had to warn Lou Lu about the amount of drinking water the boy wasted on them. Then when it rained at sea Taizao rolled the awning back to expose all his plants to cool freshening moisture.

A puppet theatre had been presented to Taizao for the voyage by Master Cheng's clan in Zayton: an elaborately carved wooden stage, red-lacquered and gilded, with a set of glove puppets, as long as an arm, their finely carved heads painted with opera masks. A Fukien native, Huang knew the roles in the local form of the art and showed Taizao how the puppets could be worked to perform opera in miniature. He taught Taizao the voices. Taizao kept the stage in his cabin, and when he was alone, placing a lamp behind a woven rattan shield to cast moving fronds of shadow over the boards, he was able to enact his favourite stories.

The beautiful maiden sits sewing with her nurse, forbidden by her mother to sleep during the daylight hours. She wanders without an escort into the flower garden and sees the young man. Showered with peach blossom as his arms reach around her, she wakes to find that she has been dozing and the young man has vanished with her dream, never to return again. The girl puppet, with a band of pearls and kingfisher feathers in her raven hair, lies down and dies . . .

Taizao's hand withdrew to leave the limp bundle of puppet's clothes and the downturned puppet's head staring from the stage.

The dream lover is a young gentleman who comes into the flower garden on his return from school, drawn by a wafting whim to seek the beautiful girl he has seen in his dream, nodding at his books in the afternoon heat. He sees the dead girl surrounded by her grieving family. What can he do but fall on her in protest, expiring from grief?

In tears of imitated passion Taizao withdrew his arm from the boy puppet whose sock robe emptied over the girl. The incense sticks he was burning filled the cabin with smoke that seeped through to Captain Jin on the deck above. Jin raised his eyebrows and bellowed.

'Smoke!'

What Jin most feared at sea was fire. But no one would pass the message to Taizao, not even Lou Lu. The young man heard the captain's shout of alarm and sat watching, smiling calmly, as each stick of incense slowly smouldered down its length to grey-white ash.

*   *   *

One day as the ship was passing through the islands of the

South China Sea, they were ambushed by two Malay pirate boats. The pirates gave chase, attempting to drive the Chinese on to the concealed reef. Captain Jin proved his mettle in outmanoeuvring them. He knew the currents beneath the sea's purple surface and by sailing in close to the reef, rather than sailing out wide, lured the pirates after him. The Malay crew were waving their curved knives, yelling and threatening, while Jin manipulated his own men as if they were a troupe of acrobats, until the pirates were drawn so close to the reef that they were forced to give up the chase, dropping sail to avoid having their hulls ripped open. Their stagey threats dropped like masks to reveal the snarling pout of lost dignity, and Jin laughed. His men had answered their captain's will and the ship had proved beautifully responsive until they were out of danger.

Standing by the helm, Lou Lu congratulated Jin on his nerve and talent.

Then Taizao came wandering wanly over the deck to sprinkle the line-up of rose bushes he had put out in the air.

'*Dew on roses, rain on lotus, don't disturb my sleep,*' he sang in the girl puppet's voice.

Jin shook his head. He could find no heroic qualities whatsoever in the young man. Yet as an enemy of the new Manchu regime, he was pleased to have preserved from butchery a person on whom so much seemed to depend. He flashed his white teeth. He was pleased, before the lofty old commissioner, to have fully justified his high price.

★   ★   ★

Lou Lu's time was precious. He never needed sleep. In the small hours of the night, under starry darkness, he minded the progress of the boat, checking stars, winds and currents.

While Captain Jin slept, Lou Lu watched, and by the time they reached Malacca it had been established that the nightwatch could be entrusted to Lord Lou.

Malacca – the rich, rotting stink of human transactions. Garbage banking in thick putrid rafts against the dockside, a tribute to the city's prosperity. Ships reached port and ditched the last of their unwanted provisions, knowing better stuff was to be had. Sacking and baskets, spoiled cargo, corks and the carcases of cats and rats, peanut shells, pepper husks and papers, clothes that had lost their fashion, barber's trimmings, feathers, wooden dolls and pineapple tops floated together around the piles of the wharf. They jostled to a mooring among the other boats, and a sampan took them ashore. There was no room to come alongside the pier. Since Captain Jin's last visit the dry dock had been pushed out and enlarged, and the first strange sight was the frames of the ships under construction or repair out of water on the dry side of the landing stage, a warning reflection of the fantastic array of boats at their moorings on the ocean side.

News of Jin's exploit with the pirates had run through the coastal villages to reach Malacca ahead of him. A group of turbaned Malay sailors hailed him before he was ashore. Those who offered congratulations were pirates themselves, policing the waters in the interests of the Malay sultan. Malacca prospered because of the sultan's flexible management of foreign traders. Each group of people were given their own zone, as they wanted, yet remained subject to the well-judged laws and limited desires of the Malays. Jin was happy to be remembered.

Lou Lu was less comfortable. He would have preferred to stay on the ship had not Huang and the Chinese crew insisted on finding somewhere to stay in the Chinese quarter. Lou Lu wanted no one to be aware of Taizao's presence, even as an unidentified young man. But Taizao yearned to come ashore too. The water was oily blue, the metal burning. The lilac-to-black sky pressed down like a furry blanket studded with shining heat. Tall straight palm trees tossed their heads in an affectation of arrogance and in every corner of dirt hibiscus and passionfruit flowers opened and flounced. Through the Malay centre of the town, where barefoot, barechested men and women, in bright skirts, fried spices and ate their snacks standing in the street, and the prosperous Arab quarter that smelt of seared mutton and cumin, Lou Lu, shepherding Taizao, followed Huang. Skirting the barbarian compound, they glimpsed some Portuguese Christians in baggy pantaloons. Lou Lu bristled to remember the ill treatment he had received in Macao. In the more enclosed Chinese corner, with its dried fish odour, they found the back room of a well-fortified house where they could be put up in safety. But knowing that sympathizers could not be trusted either, and having been told nothing himself, Huang told their hosts no more than could be implied by evasion. He had first to extract a promise from them. He knew that sympathizers who had not given their word could not be trusted at all.

Lou Lu waited with Taizao impatiently, and when no word came from Jin, he sent a messenger.

Jin's friends entertained him in every conceivable and entrancing way, laying a succession of business prospects before him. Despite his solemn agreement with the merchants of Zayton to escort his precious cargo to Rome over a twelvemonth, he was in no hurry to leave behind the opportunities that presented themselves. He cocked his head from the divan of satin cushions where he sprawled, and snarled a reminder that he was not in the eunuch's pay but in the pay of the merchants of Zayton. Lou Lu, in sending a messenger to summon him to leave, was treating him like a hireling. He despised the superiority of the Chinese. He was a man who kept his word. He was the captain and it was up to him when, within the twelve-month span, they chose to leave Malacca. They were ahead of the schedule already thanks to him.

A bitter argument ensued, driven not by malice but by the unbending focus of Lou Lu and Captain Jin. For Captain Jin shared nothing of the Ming mission, and the eunuch commissioner felt no excitement at Jin's personal gains.

The old man's time was running out.

There was a splendid new ship in the harbour, of Arab making and of a size and sophistication well beyond Jin's present vessel. Jin's covetous heart was set on returning to Zayton with the craft in his possession. What was the use of high esteem if his means could not expand to meet his station? The negotiations between Jin and the Malaccan ship dealers, and between Jin and Lou Lu, were tough and unfriendly. Wily Captain Jin was, as it suited him, betray-ing those for whom he was responsible, an opportunistic act almost beyond Lou Lu's ken except that he knew the nature of men. Lou Lu could never permit Jin to continue to skipper their voyage. It was decided that Jin would be released from his agreement if he gave his original vessel to Lou Lu for a lofty hire fee, allowing Lou Lu to captain her to Rome before bringing her back to Zayton. With the funds received, Jin could purchase his new ship and go home. With a turning on the heels rather than a handshake, the deal was done. Jin took his Allah-reverencing men with him to the new ship. The Chinese crew stayed with the old.

It was a depleted expedition that Lou Lu led out of Malacca towards the western ocean. Once they were at sea the command of the ship was delegated to Huang, who became captain for practical purposes. Delighted to be rid of Jin, Taizao moved his hammock into the captain's cabin, where he could enjoy an unhindered view of the water ahead.

Lou Lu was the navigator. He squinted into the astrolabe. The sun and the stars were in different places. The compass no longer read in the familiar way as the ship followed a bearing south. They travelled further on the reach, and the sky revealed stars that had never been seen before, until Lou Lu, setting course in deepest night, was no longer certain of their direction.

★   ★   ★

Taizao, Prince of Yong, rocked the hammock slung across his cabin as he idly read what his brush pen had written to fill every corner of a length of paper:

Immense ocean, a soup of creatures, water and elements, an infinity of waves repeating, and beyond, what is there? No moment remains, or can be grasped in itself, all is moving, always changing to something else even as I try to see what it is. Yet always the same, day after day, day after night. How many nights is it now? Countable, but beyond remembering. How many seas? Always the same sea, the one water, the one sky, the one scene of sea and sky divided by the line in the distance at which they appear to meet, regardless of light or darkness, stars exposed or hidden, the sun rising and setting, the moon in one or other of its phases, always the same. To live surrounded by evanescence, on every side, nothing that is not passing in the same instant that it comes into being, such pure, philosophical transience, permitting the perfect detachment. I stand. I watch. I analyse. There is nothing but my thoughts in their abstract clarity. I feel no passion, no love for this sea, these elements, this world. It gives a sensation, like consciousness, then is gone, resolving to inhuman absolutes, without dimension, vast and endless, an eternity in which my own existence is no different from the astrologer's postulate, a constellation of signs devised by the mind, sustained more briefly than the time it takes to move an ink-dipped brush across a sheet of blank paper.

PART THREE
Place uncertain

V

Coming ashore they were unnerved by a silence, as to any human presence, the more bewildering for the din of bird cries, rustle of untamed leaves, roll of surf and suck of shingle. When the longboat had been dragged securely up the beach, they proceeded in single file, the first laying claim with step and gaze, the second noting, the third in rapture, following where the others led. The distance across the lagoon was half a mile to a sandy landing stage lined with a colonnade of palms which opened along the edges of a brackish inlet, to a slight rise. Among a grove of spreading trees hung with globular fruit as big as a child's head, and a lesser semicircle of pretty native limes, were two huts disposed according to some idea of civic organization. The stone walls, of pocked black basalt, were thick and low, and their palm-thatch roofing had worn to fibrous black tissue. The sounds of the island rose in their hearing as they strained for audible human noises. There were the neighing shrieks of a kind of parrot; and their own footsteps, squeaking against sand and grass, alarmingly loud, the only footprints that had broken the ground. The huts gave the sign of habitation, but produced no inhabitants. Solomon Truro stepped forward, suspecting a set-up, crunching succulents and tripped by sprawling marrow plants, to finger the doorframe of the first hut. Cursing the silence, the absence of signs, he nuzzled towards the door space with stupid, canine curiosity and entered the abandoned dwelling. There was no mark of occupation – and time continued.

Popple jumped, turning to one side to see a bird, like a giant swan, singular and stately creature, step through the trees in eager gaze at the newcomers.

'Hey!' he called, and the bird came fearlessly forward to within an arm's length. Popple clapped and the bird hesitated, eyeing the men with what looked like amusement. Popple was amused, in any case, at the bird's tiny, stumpy, useless wings, and his laugh rang out, dispelling the last of their apprehension.

'There's no one here,' cried Truro in exultation. 'It's ours.' He set off to explore in widening circles.

At the back of the second hut, Ros found yellow melons bloating beneath the prickly leaves of a rampant marrow vine. And nasturtiums growing from the wall over the ground and draped around the bottle-shaped bole of a palm tree. The orange flowers were cherubs' trumpets among the heart-shaped leaves; and there were bean-plants, decked with tiny dried pods, on what might have been a collapsed trellis.

The trees were older than the settlement. They had outlived the solidity of its masonry. Ros wandered, selecting edible fruit. The yellow globes were so hard that hurling them against rock made no impression. Another fruit she found, on a tree with a shiny black trunk. The spine-studded bough sprang back against her when she pulled free the round green fruit, a kind of stringy, sticky apple. There were finger-sized bananas, and fallen coconuts thickly encased. The limes were the best. When their tough oily skin failed to respond to her teeth, she tore the peel away with fingers and found delicately formed wedges of honey-green flesh. She sucked through strong lips until the tart juice flowed and her throat came alive to it, her body revived.

She took a handful to the men and made them eat. After consuming the fruit, they looked with new favour on their imposed home.

'We are the inheritors,' proclaimed Truro, as he flung away the rind and wiped his bearded mouth with his hand.

The place was habitable, fecund, and was theirs, gratis, so far. Whatever sinister, even pestilential qualities the smiling aspect of their landfall might conceal, it would be churlish not to respond to the beckoning charm that had come their way after the plague ship. So argued Truro, who was rapidly accommodating himself to the place. There were fruits to eat, fish to catch, fowl to take, greens to gather, roots and grains for pounding to flour. There was soil in which to plant the mouldy wheat remaining on board the *Cedar* and in time they would reap a harvest. How much good fortune should they expect? The previous inhabitants might return, despite a desertion that seemed absolute – a desertion that was perhaps well founded.

'Of the Dutch,' said Popple.

'What do you say?'

'We are inheritors of the Dutch,' he repeated. He had been examining the huts, and led Truro to what he had found carved outside the lintel.

'They've scratched their mark,' explained Popple.

'A loaf of bread,' identified Truro, craning to see underneath. 'What they were dreaming of – a great tit, man!'

'It is a broad-brimmed hat, the felt hat of the good Dutchman, his hat of liberty.'

'Then God be thanked if we've driven out the Dutch butter-eaters from this place.'

Truro grew prouder of himself as he grew proud of the domain. They could have claimed the land for England if they had not renounced the flag of England whose king was in exile. They could have claimed the land, not for England but for the true king. But Solomon Truro was no king's man, and Edward Popple, who carried a document with the king's seal, however obtained, true or forged, kept silent. He merely said that to claim was to invite counterclaim, at which Truro, blustering with expletives, announced that the claim was already made – *his claim* – as long as it could be defended. At that moment Truro became melancholy. As they had no idea of the dimensions of where they had landed, island or pseudo-island or peninsula leading to someone else's mapped territory, they had best be prudent. Truro, usually impulsive, voracious, was hesitant and uneasy. A pleasant place was no good if it proved to be a trap. He had never been sole master of anything before, except of himself, a self always in service of other people or other ends. He had never owned anything. To have in his possession a territory threatened to inflate him to bursting point, except that a niggling discomfort with the notion brought him down. Practically, he realized that his dominion was confined; that was the point he fixed on. He could be king, but a castle was no good if it became a prison. To command the situation he needed the means of control. That was the melancholy fact of dependency that Truro came back to. He needed his ship, moored out in the lagoon. The cursed afflicted ship, the rotten *Cedar*, anchored out there with those three weak loyal seamen aboard, was the key to whatever his dominion would be worth. It was essential to be able to leave the place, in order to place it in the world. To sail her he needed those sailors, as they needed him as their captain. By themselves they had neither the strength nor the guts to sail the vessel, and they were ultimately corruptible. He must see them restored to health and bind them to him. So

Truro's great fortune took second place to his ship, and he decided that as long as the ship was sound to inhabit he would live on the ship in preference to the land.

Popple he would order to live on land, where the doctor could gather and assess the medicinal and edible produce of the place, as his best contribution to the survival of their party. The sailors could come ashore one at a time. The boy could stay wherever he wanted. Thus Solomon Truro instituted his regime.

He ordered Ros to load up the longboat with greens and fruit, especially the limes, to promote the convalescence of Vost, Cramphorn and Leary. He got Popple to unload the packs that provided necessities for a camp. Then Truro set to row himself alone back to the ship where his men awaited a report of the discoveries with hope and dread for their own salvation.

Popple and his daughter were left in that strangeness, for the first night, exposed and defenceless, trusting that Truro would return, if only from self-interest. But there was no guarantee. Popple was on edge until Truro left. He did not challenge the mate's order but made sure that Ros stayed with him. Whatever motive lay behind Truro's decision to abandon them in the place, Popple was careful to disguise his glad compliance. As the sound of rowlocks twisting and oars plashing diminished across the lagoon, his shudder at their abandonment turned to a sensation of burdens lifting. The greeting voices of the sailors as they hauled Truro on board carried across the water. Popple feared Truro because he feared what Truro would do to Ros once he discovered her disguise, or stopped going along with the pretence, as inevitably he must. Popple's spirit lightened in having him out of the way. The man was an infernal creature. To satisfy his appetites, Truro had gnawed at the veneer of human behaviour and knew exactly at which point decency gave way. Popple admired the bravery and piercing understanding of the man, and knew the savage power that could threaten those in no position to resist – such as himself and his daughter, entirely in the power of Solomon Truro, who swung a lantern as he walked the deck of the *Cedar*, watching them, holding them even now, across the water. Ros called out to the ship, and her voice faded on the air. As darkness fell, a couple more lamps were kindled across the bay, burning a vigil of ownership. Beyond the huts and the fire, the trees and peaked mountains under a lawless sky, the land itself was claimed in dominion by Solomon Truro.

Staring at their own firelight, Edward and Rosamund turned their backs on the mate. Edward put his arm around his daughter's shoulder and huddled with her.

'How now, girl?'

At last in his heart he could give the place its due, the paradise he had wished for, where they were together alone. The fire was their circle, their only illumination, giving them courage by advertising their presence to the unpeopled darkness of the unnamed place. The questioning, hungry light showed their faces, revealing two people who sat there in a manner of belonging to the space around them as to each other. Beyond the circle there was nothing, or nothing as far as they knew. Without the fire they would not have existed themselves, would not have been there, but lying against each other they affirmed their presence as they fell asleep. At the boundary of the lagoon, where a reef checked the great ocean, waves churned slow and luxurious, lacy crests tumbling then sweeping across the dance floor of water that shone under the moon.

Damp rose through the ground. They slept uncomfortably against each other in their clothes. When he woke to the first greying light, Popple's limbs were stiff and cold, and despite the warmth of his daughter beside him he felt lonely and lost. He wanted to reach for comfort to his daughter's body, to roll her into the hoop of his arms, but he restrained himself, terrified by isolation and responsibility. She was the only woman of their world, the only young person, the life of the future. He wondered what regime he could impose on himself in this new and natural place where the only inhibitions were those laid down by his own mind. Overhead were the rough timbers, fashioned of bent palms the only way the carpenters knew, and the worn layer of thatch which filtered the light of the rising sun. One of their first jobs would be to repair the roof. Popple stared into the space of gathering light, the heart of the world, and shivered at the opportunity given him. Uncoiling his arm from his daughter's flesh, he quietly stood, stretched, and walked out into the dawn.

A fine mist hung on the trees, covered the earth, curtained the sea. He walked towards the shore meditating his task. It was in the nature of a vision, to find the element that dissolved contradiction and reconciled opposition, the key to the door of creation, the philosopher's stone, a metaphor, a method, that would turn dust and seawater to enduring gold. He walked eastwards towards the bestowing of light as the cloud lifted. His two feet on the pebbly shore, his legs planted upright, his arms at his side, his head erect, he made a curious animal to have arrived at this place, as light sent golden fingers through the white mist to needle his skin with warmth.

He felt himself to be immersed in a process of creation. In England things pre-existed him. To discover the world's secrets was to poke in dark corners, to pick scabs, to undress bandages. Here the continuous creation of a world, separate and apart, was gushing forth like a never-ceasing fountain. Another manner, another modality, a quite different performance by the Maker of All Things who was proving multifarious and metaphoric in ways Popple's imagination stretched to conceive, whose truth and righteousness were as speckled as the shell gravel underfoot, as splintered as today's sunrays off the variegated sea. By contrast, the *Cedar* sat like a husk across the water, grey sails furled, her mast a leafless grey tree, her dark shadow on the water making a deeper impression on the eye than the vessel herself.

Then through the quiet shushing of the tide Popple heard robust splashing. As he followed the bay, the sun dazzling over the horizon, the mist disappearing like a film of water dried by heat, he saw Rosamund swimming in a pool that had been shaped by the natural breakwater of rock. He was puzzled. She had materialized there when in his reverie he had her motionless and asleep beside the space he had just vacated in the hut. He squirmed to watch her. She was unaware of him, and he gave no sign of his own presence at a distance there. She was bathing. Water sluiced off the thick cropped weeds of her hair. Light made her pale skin translucent, as if she were a huge shrimp, and her batting arms keen antennae. Her breasts, exposed to air, broke the blue breeze-etched ripples. She revelled in the feeling of cleanness and nakedness for the first time in weeks.

'Hey!' he hollered.

She frowned at the black solitary, her father, striding on the shore, and rolled away. She did not want to be interrupted. Swimming with playful vigour, she ignored him as he drew near. He stood guard, looking modestly away. But when the thump of bundles being loaded, followed by the knock of rowlocks, carried across the water from the *Cedar*, Popple called on her to hurry, and Truro, hearing Popple's cry as if it were magnified by the lagoon, yelled back: 'Good morning!'

Ros waded to the sand and cloaked her body in the smelly clothes she wore as the boy. The salt water dried stickily as she made her way back to the hut. Every eight or ten strokes of the oars she could hear Solomon Truro spit. And her father stood sentinel as the longboat crossed the calm morning water.

'We are lords of the sea and land,' Truro cried proudly as he jumped into the shallows. 'Give me a hand, Doctor.'

Popple smiled sceptically. 'It's a fine morning.'

'Still,' ordered Truro, as together they hauled the boat up, 'today I want to check thoroughly. Will you join me in reconnaissance? We must establish where we are.'

'Do you propose an expedition?'

'A stroll about, no more.'

'Leave the boy?'

'He can come with us.'

'Better he stay. He's tired.'

'A boy like that? His curiosity should know no bounds.'

Truro bestrode the sand of that shore with all the proprietary air of a country squire, his arms akimbo, his head aloft. He turned his back on the sea where he had lived his life and gave his eyes to the grassy approach to the huts, the steep wooded valley beyond and the rise to the craggy little mountain that defined the limits of their vision. Then tucking his head back to earth, twisting his embarrassed gaze to Popple, he became himself again, the wily insinuator.

'You're fond of that boy, aren't you? Necessity breeds weird affections. After a lifetime at sea you forget all that – attachment.'

Popple stared suspiciously at Truro's yellowed bloodshot eyes.

'Smirk all you will, Doctor. I am king of this place. My reign begins today. You submit, do you?'

'To whatever you choose to call yourself.'

Truro laughed. 'There can be no sharing. Let that be clear. This is no commonwealth.'

'I ask only that you permit me to describe and anatomize the place. The power is all yours.'

'Don't try to best me, Doctor.'

'If we return, my findings will be the most valuable thing I bring back to the civilized world. An account in itself of inestimable worth to the Society of Fellows and to my own advancement. If I am not to return, if we are to stay here, I shall need the mental entertainment that the work of collecting and collating information will provide.'

'You're a fool. Commodities – things that we can exchange with other people – that's all that has value out here, and only after they have been transported over the sea in my ship.'

'I feel responsible for Ross, the boy. It was my decision to bring him aboard. He's young. We should allow him to have his life.'

Solomon Truro guffawed. 'Then we'll have to get him off here, won't we? Now come on. I've got some biscuit for your breakfast, then we take musket and knives and set off. Get your boy to keep the fire alight so we can find our way back.'

The pair of stone huts sat in a clearing at a distance from the sandy shore of the lagoon, amid palms and fruit trees at the undulating commencement of thickly wooded hills. To reach the second steep gallery of elevation, Truro and Popple had to pick and cut a way through. The waist-high leaves of the pandani were stiff as boards and spiked like spears. Their elephant-leg trunks, thick and grey-ringed, admitted a way reluctantly. Truro followed a rivulet that ran down from the height, making the red ground slippery, and Popple followed Truro, silently hoping that the man in front would attract the majority of flies. At last they reached the rocky topmost, gaining a clear view of the settlement, the little white bay and its craggy endstops, the lagoon, and the ship tethered inside the reef like a toy in a basin of green wine, her sail furled and the green flag of the black rose limp; some tiny islands littered about, not much more than rocks, and the line of the reef marked by a cordon of thick white breakers beyond which was the great black-blue ocean. To seaward they could see what they knew, but in the other direction they could see no further shore. Below stretched a sea of treetops, shimmering and waving, blooming, into which birds and butterflies dived, and beyond, another wall of mountains, beyond which nothing was visible. Truro was irritable that a grasp of the topography of the place was denied him on the first attempt. He wanted to confirm sole possession of the territory, and was impatient to gauge its size and assets.

Sifting the known, the related and the unknown as he stared drunkenly at all they passed, Popple was more interested in the natural character of the place. It was a warm temperate domain. The valley below was a garden ringed by hills, bishop's mitres, that protected from extremes of weather. Nor had he seen any animals yet, save birds and lizards and the insect host. Did they all hide from the light? He felt sure the Dutch would have had their dogs and pigs and rabbits. And there was such profusion of flowers! He explained to his companion that the life of the place was weirdly selective. Which species was lord of the island?

Truro was king. He laughed to prove it.

The way down was slippery at first, with mosses growing on the shaded side of the rocks, and, as the incline eased, small flowers, like violets, and creeping vines. Then the shrubbery became less dense, with a wild yet orderly array of large trees and flowering bushes, and dappled open space with spongy ground cover. Rivulets ran like open veins off the slope, forming waterfalls, streams and ponds. Birdsong and insect buzz made the air twang. The most common shrubs were varieties of palm and fern, different and nameless, while Popple groped for names like cabbage palm, stink pine and spear fern, and flouncing clusters of massive scarlet and pink blooms, without classification, except as a jungle kind of rhododendron or azalea.

They walked with their broad knives unsheathed, slashing where necessary.

Sweat and insects smeared their faces, and they breathed heavily in the laden air. They had walked for two hours with only water to sustain them, and the intoxicant perfumes of cinnamon and frangipani. They could not stop. At last, where Popple calculated the centre of the great garden bowl they were crossing, the terrain opened into a wide sunlit meadow. They stood to wonder whether it occurred naturally. There were no signs of human interference.

A black parrot about the size of a pheasant shot across the meadow in a line not much higher than their eyes, a flash of coal, and landed on an extended branch of crimson blooms to form a target. Truro took the crossbow from his shoulder sling and aimed at the bird's breast. The bow's twang echoed the whizz of the arrow's flight, and the thwack of contact, and the wingless flopping and bouncing through the blood-matching flowers until there was a thump on the ground. Truro pushed ahead to retrieve the bird, scratching and bloodying himself in his lust. He hung the creature from his belt by its neck, trailing red across the green meadowy grass that closed over his footsteps. Popple made a show of examining the bird. It was no kind he knew. Yet it was a fit sacrifice. Back home Truro might have been hanged for poaching. Here the clean, casual death of the bird was a little act of blood that might exorcise the violence of property. The pair of men stood in the green, sunny circle, he who claimed the place and he who interpreted it, each filled with the inexpressible conviction that they were at the centre of the benign world. Solomon Truro giggled like a kid, and, checking to see that no one was looking, opened his trousers to mark his own territory with his water.

Edward Popple resolved to bring his rose stock here meanwhile, where the ground offered the best conditions for growing things.

The temptation was to continue. Their desire was to look beyond the valley from the top of the ascent on the far side. Yet time was their enemy.

'If we climb it will take us half a day. Then how will we get back?'

'Half a day up, half a day back.'

'What if we're not satisfied after climbing the top? What if a new desire arises? We would be caught. The smoke from Ross's fire is already faint in the sky. It is only the first day.'

'It is the first day, Doctor, and we push on, trusting in ourselves.'

Popple's legs were shaking when they reached the next rise. He was sweating feverishly and feared that, if he stopped to rest, his legs would stiffen irreversibly. The stronger Truro had already gone ahead to the vantage point, surrounded with trees.

'Blue!' he shouted down, peering through the branches. 'Water!'

He saw the other side of an island.

'So that's it,' confirmed Popple.

Truro began to climb one of the tall, straight trees as Popple shuffled to the lookout point. Leaves and twigs fell on his head as Truro shinned up like a monkey. Screeching, a flock of orange fodies burst from the treetop as Truro's big shape ascended, determined to overcome the frustration of not being able to see and know more.

'Climb up and see, Doctor,' he ordered. 'There's a cliff at the water's edge.'

'Can you see over it?' Popple yelled back.

'I can't see past the bloody thing.'

'Come down then, Solomon.'

He crashed down through the tree impatiently. Dangling the black parrot beside his knife, he strapped back on his belt and slung over his shoulders his reloaded crossbow and unused musket. His eyes, black stones set in clay-red grizzled skin, glittered with determination.

'We're going down into it.'

Popple sighed. 'You don't know how far it is.'

'Not far,' grunted Truro.

'There's the way back. We'll have to come up again.'

'I tell you it's not far. Come on.'

They proceeded down the slope through the tightly growing trees. The steep face was swathed with tough, spiky pandanus palms, yet Truro forced a good pace, walking like an engine, numb to pain, in large downhill strides, until abruptly the ground disappeared, and he pulled himself up a fraction before the momentum of his walk carried his large boot out over emptiness.

'Whoah boy!' cried Popple.

Truro might have stepped over the edge of the chasm. The cliff dropped before them in a rough vertical. On all fours they crawled to the edge and peered down to the community of rock forms hundreds of feet below, towers, grottoes, spires, troughs of dark stone knobbled by sea and wind over centuries. A few shags perched in the sun, mere spots from the height, were the only inhabitants. At the bottom a wide ledge ran like a natural wharf along the water's edge, curving with the island, until further off it became a thin strip of beach fringed with casuarina pines.

'Hooray!' yelped Truro, digging in his pocket for a detached brass button to hurl over the cliff. Its tinkle rang out as it bounced off the side. They had crossed the island from side to side. He fixed Edward Popple with his gaze. 'All we need worry about is ourselves.'

'In a place as small as this appears to be it would be possible to know everything,' observed the scholar.

'It suffices, sir.'

The sun was past noon. They had to cross the valley and the meadow of flowers and climb within sight of the fire's smoke before darkness.

'Lead, Solomon, lead along the trail you have marked.'

Edward Popple followed three paces behind, contemplating their isolation, their exile. Around, on the trees, in the air, underfoot, in buds, fruits, burrows and nests, was a newly constituted world. He was servant to the new king crashing ahead, a fake self-styled king with no rule over anything here, a world that existed freely, without dominion or subjection.

Popple could have pushed Truro off the cliff. There had been a moment of possibility, of wish, when with a nudge Solomon Truro and the slaughtered parrot and the crossbow, musket and knife would have dived to oblivion. The doctor could have acted in cold blood. He was capable of that. But he calculated that at this stage Truro alive was more conducive to his and his daughter's survival than Truro dead. They were too few to sacrifice one to the motive of justice, or the impulsion of hatred.

★

When the men returned, Ros took them to the head of the inlet over a bank to a tree, from the grassy declivity of whose shade the roots grew upwards in slender pillars to join the branches overhead. Her father knew at once the legendary banyan tree. Its huge weird architecture created spaces between the flukes of its roots, and in one such cool chamber Ros pointed to what she had found, a pair of creatures side by side like two stone cushions, their shells partitioned into four central plates and ten plates around the side; four fat finny legs with rough scales and six distinct toes protruding from below. Protuberant also was the head, from a loose scaly casing, a pointing snout, a lizard mouth, a double chin and a black eye over which the eyelash blinked.

Truro hissed an ecstatic expletive.

'*Testudo,*' corrected Popple.

'The giant tortoise,' groaned Truro, unable to resist slapping the carapace and making the unhappy head withdraw into its foreskin. The partner emitted a long moan, nodding from side to side until its head withdrew too.

'These must have an age of sixty or seventy years,' said Popple.

'The seaman's salvation,' quipped Truro, 'and our treasure. If there's this pair, there's more. Find more, boy. You've done well. Which one do you want for your supper?'

Ros's eyes widened.

'Tortoise flesh,' Truro salivated, 'and tortoise oil. You've never tasted the delicacy. You don't know what it means to a sailor deprived of meat at sea. You don't know what its odour does to a man. By Christ, she's heavy.'

The two men together lifted the hissing creature whose splayed toes paddled vainly in air. The one not taken, the mate, moaned in a barking rhythm. The chosen tortoise clacked its snout.

'The brute doesn't like to be carried alive,' breathed Truro.

He took his knife and in one swift action sliced the creature's neck. The flailing stopped. The head hung limply, fully extended, dribbling a line of blood back to the huts.

'Precious blood,' swore the mate, 'a damned waste.'

Shell and all, the beast was placed in a pit of dug clay, on a bed of stones covered with red-hot coals, and slowly it baked, the searing flesh emitting a fragrance that compelled appetite. When it was done, they flipped the shell over and Truro cut for its liver, a purple sponge disproportionately large for its frame, Popple noted, and scooped it out. They enjoyed a substantial meal and were soon overstuffed. The doctor was concerned to leave part for the men on the ship, who needed decent nourishment no less than those ashore. He was worried about their condition, and insisted that a portion be put aside for them. Their party could ill afford to lose even one member. But by the end the feasters had eaten the greater part of the reserved portion, sharing guilt. The black parrot, a mere garnish, the mate decided to give to the sailors on the ship, as well as the gull's eggs, shellfish and nasturtium leaves that Ros had gathered and laid on platters of leaves near the fire.

Popple was pleased at the day's outcome. Truro was cocky. He spoke of establishing a tribe if he could get hold of some women, and raised his eyebrows at Ros. 'Eh, boy? Sire a few? Has the tortoise got you going?' Truro mocked. The mate's visions were murky and vague. What was it to be the leader of six virtual castaways? He belched as he insisted to Popple on the need to determine their whereabouts as precisely as possible, so that they could find the place again should they be forced to depart abruptly. Then Solomon Truro stretched out on the ground and slept. He was not returning to the ship this night. Ros, who felt queasy from excess of eating, fetched the kit and spread a blanket over the man where he lay in the open. Popple made a point of leading Ros by the hand to sleep under his protection. He had no trust in Solomon Truro. In the silence, keeping her voice to a murmur no louder than the gauzy rustle of the leaves, she asked her father to tell her about the island.

'It is a fertile island apparently unpopulated by human beings, notwithstanding the mysterious presence of huts seemingly constructed by Dutchmen. Flora and fauna are diverse and wonderful, some having affinity with those of the civilized world, others being new to our knowledge. It will be a labour to catalogue them. Animals are in the minority, beasts of prey unknown at this point. The island affords sustenance, vegetable in kind, and most likely would submit to cultivation. For one such as I, it can be seen as a large, manageable laboratory – a paradise. The question only is how we can survive our sojourn here, if sojourners we prove to be. What are our responsibilities, to physical health and to our civilized existence? We are only six, counting those wretches whom he keeps on the ship. We have few means and utensils at our disposal. Were this island all that remained of the world, this world's centre, we should be the bearers of humanity, the sole envoys of our Christendom. You, my daughter, the Eve. Preserve yourself until necessity determines otherwise. I am too old to be the first man. I am the last god, rather, the cast-out fragment, the bent limb, the wizard. My knowledge will be grafted into the roots and trunks of this place.'

'Who will be our friends?'

'There is no one. We must be friend, colleague, companion, to each other. Together we must form one rose.'

'What about him?'

'Solomon? The mutineer. He must go. He must be encouraged to go.'

'Then there'll be only the two of us.'

Ros smiled dreamily. She saw her father's white teeth, and bent to kiss his mouth.

'My hair shall grow to the ground.'

Flowers were everywhere, sunshine dancing on water, the vigour of unrestrained activity, and a sense that they were the actors of a great new story. But as days wore on, their deprivation became harder to deny. Salt, tinder, soap and other necessities dwindled, and sacks of flour brought on shore from the ship's supply had to be carefully monitored. Life contained a strict measure of routine and toil, and even a degree of futility as attempts to improve the amenity of their existence – the hard ground and rudimentary dwelling – faltered. Popple retreated to mental speculation, Ros would gaze at the sea in a stupor of private fantasy.

Vost brought the flour sacks in, following Popple's insistence that singly or together the sailors come for examination and land exercise. They were as reluctant to leave the ship, for fear of being marooned, as Edward was to set foot off the island in case he be tricked into separation from his daughter. Truro had organized his crew into mending the sails, an overdue job, and scowled as Popple convinced him, out of pragmatism if not humanity, that the sailors might be in need of mending too and must be ordered, one by one, into the longboat.

Vost, the ship's chandler, knowing the limit of their supplies, was gallows-faced as Popple examined him. He was otherwise healthy. While exposed to the doctor's hands he made his own examination of the roof beams of the hut, asking if the wood grew on the island. It was stink pine. He confided in Popple that sea-worms had got to the timbers of the *Cedar*, tiny swimming creatures that amassed almost invisibly to eat away at most kinds of wood. If the attack persisted, the *Cedar* would soon be unseaworthy and useless. Timber that could resist attack was needed to replace the damaged parts of the hull, putrid tropical timber, such as stink pine or teak. If timber that was not to the sea-worms' taste could not be found, it was necessary to have a large enough supply of other seasoned wood to keep patching over the damage as she sat at mooring or sailed. Vost had kept the problem to himself because Truro hated to admit deficiencies in his realm. Vost feared Truro's anger. But Popple demanded the right to pass on the information, and, when interrogated by his captain, Vost turned his chandler's knowledge to good effect by estimating the value of a cargo of the giant tortoises if they were delivered alive to a trading port. There were compelling reasons, by Vost's logic, for abandoning their landfall.

Solomon Truro prowled all night long on the deck of the ship that sustained his dream. Without the means of departure and return, what did he possess in the island? If the *Cedar* decomposed beneath him, he would be stranded in paradise. Nor was there the prospect of building up his subject population. The ship's crew had dwindled from the original thirty to six, and he could not imagine her sailing with any fewer hands. To take all six souls on board was to abandon the settlement, as the Dutch perhaps had been forced to do, leaving the territory open to other takers. According to the reckonings, they were some way east of Mauritius. Perhaps with a favourable wind, the fabled propitious gales of the green ocean, the ship might be carried almost by herself to a shore where they could replenish with men, and the vital women, and a second reserve vessel, to return in state to permanent occupation. It was a gamble, a risk, and also, Truro recognized, a necessity, since what good was it to be stuck on an unknown island with a rotten, worm-infested hulk?

Vost grinned in the morning when Truro ordered him to organize a tortoise hunt to take live beasts for a voyage. Leaving Cramphorn and Leary at their sail-mending, Vost went ashore with his captain, who was inspired by decisiveness, inflated in turn by the grandiosity of his vision of the future. A rat from the ship found its way into the longboat. When they beached, the rat scurried over the prow and escaped across the sand. Vost laughed openly, sharing the creature's impulse. Popple, anticipating portentous news, hovered by the hut. It was Ros who saw the rat dart, stop and change direction over the unfamiliar ground. She chased it, thrashing at it with a palm frond, until the animal found a rock crevice where she could not go. The rat was a survivor too.

Solomon Truro, whose body had endured knife attacks, explosions and shipwrecks, was, like many who count on their physical strength, superstitious about health. He feared any cancer that grew from within. Vost's discovery of the animalcules gnawing away at his ship had worked on him all night, an inward disorder of the mind if not of the body, and by dawn his decision was taken to flee the place with whatever booty could be removed. His attention drawn to the workings of disease, he also found it imperative that the useless doctor be with the ship, in case, in case . . . Claim to the island would be preserved by one of the sailors, the dispensable lifeless Leary, who would stay on the island in company with the doctor's boy.

Truro was a talker, a believer of stories, and Popple saw how simple the man's mind was when he explained his expectation to sail away for a month, two at most, before returning in good repair with reinforcements. The likelihood of such an outcome was small, in a world of storms, errors and hostile beings.

'There's no guarantee of safety off the island, man,' Popple shouted.

Even their bearings could prove false, a quirky wind blowing them not to Mauritius, but to some mythical Cambalu and the icy shoreless pole beyond. Or to the great boreal antipodes, if they were not there already. But Popple turned his protestation to bravado, seeing in Truro's idea a chance to get rid of the man, leaving himself and his daughter alone with the island.

'What is the value of the island to you?' Popple asked the stronger man.

'It is mine.'

'What does that mean?'

'No one can take it away from me.'

'But why do you want it?'

'I have always been someone else's man, someone's hireling, who had nothing of his own. Now I am lord of something.'

'If that something is nothing, what is the difference?'

Truro stamped his foot. 'This? This is not nothing, sir.'

'Its value lies solely in what it is worth to others, not you. What they would give for it, or what you could trade for it, or what they would lend you and accord you on the strength of it.'

'There is treasure on this island.'

'How do you know?'

'You've told me.'

'There may be rare species, medicinal herbs, spices, precious minerals – but until we have knowledge of them, they may as well belong to an island that has never been discovered. The gold may as well stay underground.'

'Gold?'

'Quite possibly. I am tiring my brain with studies to ascertain these things.'

'When will you know?'

'In the two months it would take for a return voyage to

Mauritius, I believe I can prepare an inventory of the riches of the island ready for our exploitation.'

'Do you volunteer to stay? Then I shall stay to help you. I will be here when the gold is found.'

'You send the sailors on the voyage by themselves, what guarantee that they return, and we live out our days with our gold here like pinioned shags? What guarantee that they don't return with arms to seize you, or a crew to claim the island for themselves? You are a mutineer. They are weak men.'

'There can be no voyage. You reason, Doctor, to tantalize me. You goad me. You wish to leave this place yourself.'

'We uncover the treasure of the island. How do we enjoy its riches, with all the pleasures gold buys here? And if the whole island prove to be one nugget of golden ore, how much can we extract with our six poor pairs of hands? How much transport on our worm-infested ship? Beholden to whatever craft should land here to achieve fortune that is rightfully ours. Without population, without transport, the value is nothing, and you are king of nothing.'

'Then we take a bit and leave, enough.'

'For short-lived glory. No. Leave me here, with the boy. We'll prepare for your return. There's nothing else for us to do, nowhere else for us to go. You make the voyage with the sailors, skipper the ship to safe port as only you can, and bring back men and women, your subjects, tools and supplies, and a second sailing craft. Therein lies the beginning of greatness founded on the blessing that has been delivered to us in the chance encounter with this lonely, lovely place.'

'You see around the corner.'

'I am a philosopher. I have left behind my home, my

standing, my life, to seek knowledge. I do not wish the search interrupted.'

Truro scratched his grizzle. 'I understand you, Doctor. You are my prisoner here. Even if, beg pardon, I choose not to trust you, I can leave you here safely and you will carry out your work as obligingly as the worm eats. You must await me, or perish.'

'I shall expect you faithfully.'

'And the boy? Your bollocked beloved?'

'How dare you!'

Truro bared his teeth in a torturer's grin. 'He will come with me.'

Popple sighed patiently. 'You see, I am a philosopher. My work is of the mind. To carry it out involves action, unfortunately, which is where the boy comes in handy. He's practical and agile. If you want progress, you'll leave him with me. We are two parts of a whole.'

'You are the doctor of perversion.'

'I resent your habitual insinuations, but your foul guess-work is not altogether wide of the mark. He is wife to me, providing help and companionship. So leave him with me.'

'The companionship you all crave.'

'It is but a parody of what has been left behind. He helps with my studies, that's all.' Edward Popple looked away, as if indifferent. 'The trick is to find the correspondence between what grows above the ground and what lies below. The visible and the invisible.'

'No blood runs in your veins, Doctor. Well, I shall consider.'

Truro ordered the ship fortified by caulking as far as possible, and the goods that had been unloaded were reloaded. Vost supervised the provisioning: three woven baskets of thirty limes each, two dozen of the large flightless fowl, sun-dried herbs, smoke-dried fish, eggs enough to deplete the season of baby birds, and the giant tortoises which were taken two at a time on the longboat, with all hands assisting, until there were six, and enough fresh grass and leaf to feed them. The intermittent easterlies were settling into a steady force; the currents seemed to flow in the same direction. The sailors began excitedly to recall tales from their youth, yarns heard in distant ports, of the helpful winds of the Indian ocean that carried ships where they wanted to go, blowing with a singing music, monsoons there, monsoons back. The sailors had made a pact among themselves that they were never returning to the island.

On the eve of departure Truro insisted on a ceremony. A bonfire raged on shore, and two of the sailors, Cramphorn and Leary, were chosen by lot to join with the mate – their captain – the doctor and his boy in drinking a last jug of rum. Solomon Truro as king of the island made each man bow and swear allegiance before receiving a cup. He solemnly vowed to serve his people and their mutual wellbeing to his utmost might. Popple couldn't help smirking as he was appointed temporary governor and Ros chief officer.

'These are powers which no man can remove.'

'Pray for our safety,' said Leary.

'There is no God to whom we can pray,' boomed Truro.

'I pray to the one and only God,' retorted the swabber.

'Pray for our deliverance then,' echoed Edward Popple.

'Fear not,' said Truro, his chest broadening, 'I guarantee your safety. Now sing, boy. Let us enjoy your alto.'

'I don't know any songs.'

'Sing a song of England.'

'To the cesspit with England,' cursed Leary.

Dirty, unkempt and drunken, the men sprawled on the ground, including her father, who would share tomorrow's enormous solitude with her. Ros's voice was thin as the sound of a halyard in the wind as the funny song drifted out, rising into nothing with the smoke from the fire. She burned from the rum, and the fire's roar drowning out the noises of the night, the sea, the great dark surrounding space, and the sky bright with numberless stars, receding to the unnamed. A breeze, one of the friendly breezes that would speed the *Cedar*, brushed Ros's cheeks, as she stood to sing.

> *I have a horse called Nelly*
> *She is my piebald love*
> *While I go across the sea*
> *She roams the hills above.*
>
> *No other boy may ride her*
> *She gallops wild and free*
> *But when I am beside her*
> *She nuzzles close to me.*
>
> *Home is in a far wide place*
> *While strange skies cover me*
> *But when my Nelly sees my face*
> *I shall her lover be.*

Cramphorn was sobbing. Edward Popple screwed up his eyes and bowed his head in drunken remorse for what he had done to bring them there. Solomon Truro threw back his throat to the sky, taking the song as his tribute.

'Beautiful,' said Leary. 'Beautiful, boy.' Then he rolled away from the circle and vomited on the grass.

'All that rum gone to waste,' jeered Truro.

Solomon stood and strode up to Ros, taking the soft

cheeks between his rough hands and pushing his bristling mouth against the parted lips. Popple jumped up and tried to pull Truro away. But Truro shrugged Popple off. The man's weight did not budge. He had Ros's lips between his thumbs for a moment and was about to kiss again, when he abruptly turned away from Ros of his own accord and laughed harshly to the stars.

'I don't need . . . companionship. No Nelly for me, lads. Let's go!' He kicked at the fire to roll away the burning logs. 'On your feet. Wipe your eyes. Clean your mouth. We're going. At first light we weigh anchor.' Truro took Popple's hand. 'Do your work, Doctor. I rely on you. Until we meet again, whenever that may be.'

'In two months' time I expect you, sir, and anticipate that you will be pleased with your island.'

'Boy, preserve yourself. Profit from this spot. Heave ho!'

Drunkenly they waded until the longboat ran free. The light of the tallow lantern rocked from side to side as the voyagers were carried across the face of the water to the ship.

At length Ros fell asleep.

Edward Popple sat watch until at first light he saw the shadowy form of the ship with her grey sails hoisted float towards disappearing point. He shuddered in the chill of abandonment, and reached impulsively for the girl. She stirred. Quickly up, she ran down to the water's edge.

'Farewell,' she shouted helplessly, 'farewell!' The silent reply flooded her with loneliness.

VI

. . . withdraws means the tide going down; the *mind* is
less now, but will return, and it is now that one can
see the rock-pools.

William Empson,
Some Versions of Pastoral (1935)

Popple was intrigued by the namelessness of things. For
most of the specimens he identified, there was no name.
He devised names, using English and Latin, on the basis of
a resemblance, reasoned or fancied, between the new discovery and an instance already known to him. In that way he
mapped the fauna and flora of the island to the catalogued
nature of the civilized world, by threads of affinity percepti-
ble to his mind. Or else he distinguished the specimens by
a striking physical characteristic, or a circumstance of the
time and place of their first discovery, a name which was
often quite accidental. So the black parrot that fell victim
to the mate's arrowhead on the day of their first roaming
he named, with commemorative irony, Solomon's parrot.
He attempted to carry out an inventory of the island. On
his rambles he gathered as many different samples as he
could carry. In experimental doses he, and sometimes Ros,
tried each one. At the first sign of digestive disorder or
fever, they would purge.

A time at early evening was devoted to formal conversation between father and daughter, a combination of lesson
and Socratic enquiry in which Popple passed on his knowledge in exchange for the stimulation of her inquisitive
logic. His main investigation was into methods of control

over nature. He was always alert to connections between the exertions of their minds and natural consequences. Since they were the only two humans in the place, he believed it possible to detect the effects of their mental intervention in natural process. For instance, if he carved the word 'yellow' in the bark of a shrub whose blooms had not yet opened, and it then produced yellow flowers, he would be gratified. But that was a toy to the larger power he envisaged over the elements, by which they would one day be free to choose and create their form of life. They would be free of dependency on external agency, including Solomon Truro if he ever returned, if he was ever capable of finding the place again.

A particular task lay in breeding extensions of the rose. The heart of the island offered the perfect spot for rearing the stock, which had survived the journey by ship mostly unblighted. He set the roots out at suitable intervals to allow for variations of soil and weather, and willed them to grow. Obsessively weeding, he cleared the surroundings of local flora to avoid contamination and force growth into the rose sticks. He set up a scarecrow from tatters of a sail sheet, in case the birds should find the novelty to their taste; insects he picked off with his fingers and crushed between his nails. Sun and showers helped, and new tips appeared quickly and shot vigorously, giving Edward Popple a fine sense of accomplishment – and something stronger, a conviction of purpose.

Above all he relied on the discipline of his life on the island to produce a core of power that would emanate outwards. He suppressed passion. He understood that survival depended on a scrupulous self-mastery of which his preservation of his daughter was the centre. He must maintain a protective distance from her, inscribe a circle around her, bonded but kept untouching by the rigour of a fundamental geometry. Thus the island contained his virgin daughter as queen and heart. They had scaled a peak together and stood supreme on the pinnacle. To slip would be to roll uncontrollably down the miry hill into the incestuous behaviour of beasts. He slavered as he thought of what he feared. Her perfection grew, her limbs willowed and extended in curves of milky-golden flesh, supple shoulders and firm arms, thighs of curd and proud strawberry teats that no tongue had touched. He saw her, absorbed in delight as she emerged from the sea with her hand between her thighs, unconscious of him until she felt his gaze cut her like a knife edge.

Ros had kept a boy's dress while discarding the pretence of boyhood. The vegetable garden was her responsibility and quickly showed results. She methodized the household, creating separate areas for herself and her father. She mended the thatch, weaving new batts of palm. She put flowers in the rooms and decorated the doorframes with garlands. Her hair, which had been cropped, began to grow again, caught with a silver clasp that Edward Popple produced from hiding in his purse. When she felt his dark hungry gaze on her, the power that burned in him, locked in him like a black flame that burned without combusting and seemed to eat at his cheeks and bodily frame from inside, then she sought the delicacies of the island to feed him. He never laid a finger on her except, when they talked, to come close and confine her within the hoop of his arm.

One herb they ate produced dreams.

She dreamed of a ceremony, of stone and living matter, ichor and sea-wrack laid at her feet, and incomprehensible words spoken – by whom, she could not see – and she was dancing, with a crown of weeds on her head, a dance of prescribed steps accompanied by wordless song, and someone was watching her, but she could not see him, a protector and a judge.

He dreamed another dance, an abstract coupling of father and daughter that would bring energy and motion within their command on the island, he and she symbols of a pure opposition that must meld if they were to achieve supreme rule.

In time she found herself going on long walks to be apart from him. She preferred to walk along the shore, or climb the crag above their huts to look out at the weave of blue, green and silver that stretched so far, inviting visions into her imagination, as if the figments of her youthful longing would materialize from the emptiness and come sailing towards her. Where her father was content to stare at the sea and decipher nothing, she in her youth could not help expecting a companion one day to cross the horizon and glide to her shore from the infinities of space. She knew the shells, creatures and drift the sea threw up. Purple ribbons and sea-grapes, furry squirting sea-slugs, jellies and mud-crabs.

One day, following a blood-red dragonfly that darted down the steep path from the crag, she found herself disorientated among the lilies and vines. The air was thick with fragrance. The vines, crawling and climbing, made a net between the trees that seemed to offer a way but ensnared her when she tried to pass, light overhead blocked by enmeshing branches. She was alert with apprehension as each step took her deeper. Her energy and venturesomeness exhilarated her, and with each pace she stepped into an original world that was exclusive to her. To get her bearings she scrambled towards higher ground and in no time she was well advanced up the far side of the valley. Even after she knew she was heading in the opposite direction from the camp, she kept going, towards the sheer cliff her father had drawn for her on a rough map. The swords of pandani nicked her. The ground slid away beneath her feet. She came through trees to the highest point and, inching to the edge of the precipice, looked down. She was panting. It dropped to a long, wide ledge of stone against which the water lapped pettishly. She saw the deep sea, the pale lagoon, the narrow strip of beach and baked rock, and the low bush-covered slopes running down to the water's edge. Where the ridge ran down to the sea, the coastline was like a crab's outreaching claws that enclosed a rocky cove under shelter of the rise. The trees formed a screen. And she could see another kind of movement and colour, which looked like the billowing of a huge striped cloth, a canopy that stretched from rock ledge across sand and water to what must have been a boat.

Bands of timber, piles of cargo, planks connecting one craft to another wedged alongside, red and green flags tugging at the bare masts, and the eyes of a monstrous beast glaring from the painted prow, all bobbed in tune with the snaking stripes of the canopy and the rips of fretted foam and tugging current across the shining water.

Snatches of cloth that swept across rock and sand and out of sight under the canopy into the boat appeared like birds as she tried to make them out to her satisfaction. They moved, with their clothes flapping round them, like spinning tops, large yellow discs or glossy black. She was so taken with glee that, leaning forward to see better, she might have tumbled over the edge of the cliff into the scrub below.

She had only a vague sense of direction to guide her along the ravine towards the shore. Zigzagging and backtracking, she beetled along the cliff to a place where it was possible to climb down. What if they vanished? She followed a trickling spring down, rinsing her ankles, and hoped to come out within sight of the settlement while out of sight herself. Should she have fetched her father?

Luck brought her out atop a low escarpment just above the final descent of hills to the cove. She proceeded carefully from rock to crumbly, prickly rock, trying to keep from view while wanting to see as much as possible herself. She was nearer than she expected. She and her father had a pact not to be away from the huts when dark fell. But she forgot about time, and how far away she was. She picked her way further over the rocks until suddenly she had a clear view of the far end of the small cove, the right-hand pincer of the crab, and there was the form of a person. The shadows cast over the escarpment and the hills by the sun to the west, and the dazzle of sunset light over the water, hid her, and she kept down. The young person stood on a high rock above the crashing swell, waving his arms in a slow circular motion, bending his body at the knees and from the waist. He wore loose pants and open shirt that billowed like washing on the line, his back was straight, his shoulders horizontal, his torso flat as a plank, and long black hair flowed down his neck. His face was indistinct and girlish, black marks on a darkened ivory surface. In one hand he held a sword that sliced through air. He appeared to threaten the ocean in a slow dream-like rehearsal. On a rock behind him, she saw a white-haired old man, who stood, out of reach of the spray, bent over a stick, calling instructions to the warrior-youth, and further away, another man, black-headed, dark-faced and burly, sat like one of the rocks, blowing smoke from a pipe. He turned to look sharply in Rosamund's direction as if suddenly aware of her. She crouched low and waited. When she looked up again, all three had gone. She had not seen enough. She saw the back of the old one, curved like a shag as he picked his awkward way out of sight. A longing to call them back seized her; secrecy made her shiver, and laugh with her hand over her mouth.

A turbulence of excitement overwhelmed her, and fear, and confusion, yet she had not seen enough. No, she had seen enough. She must report to her father, withstand his anger and tell him truthfully what she had seen. Or at least warn him that there was something on the island of which he was ignorant.

August the twenty-first, 1652. Popple noted down her report in full, paying attention to the date of the event, an exercise of mind that was increasingly strained and artificial. The strangers may have been callers on the shore whom time would remove, or the product of a girlish imagination. Popple continued his work in the rose garden, but forbade his daughter to go near the place where she had seen the strangers. She itched to make her way across the island to see the others at their landing place, but for the moment she heeded her father's warnings.

Popple was loath to seek them out, less for fear of their savagery or the risk of alarming them than the impossibility of rational communication. Yet he was as curious about what things they might possess, and who they were, as Ros was about the way they lived. Were they visitors, or residents who had been overlooked? He carried a firearm and a knife with him when he set out to work.

Confined to the shore, Ros realized she was not confined. Her stretching logic told her she could walk along the beach in either direction and would soon trace the perimeter of the island to the opposite side, where the other people were and she was forbidden to go. But as yet she would not trick her father. The exploration must be gradual as, mooning and exploring day after day, she wandered far along the shore. She was fascinated by the obscure beauty of the rockpools exposed at low tide, forms of life that were, for her, forms of dreaming, sponges and freckled conches, the shell of a lobster, swarming fish, delicate linings of mother-of-pearl that shone underwater but lost their silver shine when you took them from your pocket later, lace weeds; a silent, inhuman phantasmagoria that partnered her solitude and the immeasurable vacancy of her hours.

One afternoon, in weather that might have been late spring in England, and here, below the line, was a muted hybrid of spring and autumn, with leaves growing sallow and dry, birds scavenging for their nests, and the tide swelling, father and daughter sat outside the hut in their hour of rest, drinking coconut juice, letting a fresh breeze waft their skin, and Popple asked her whether she regretted stowing away.

'Do not regard my life here as limited, Father. Were I at home I should be confined with my mother in service of Lady Brougham, or confined in a schoolroom with other girls and boys of the locality. I should be living in anticipation of your letters, that would never come. I should be sick with worry.'

'You should have your Nelly.'

'In time Nelly should be taken from me and I should be confined even more bindingly as wife to a man.'

'Where here everything has been taken from you.'

'Here nothing can be taken from me. Here everything is mine. Here I enjoy liberty.'

'In deprivation.'

'No, Father, the contrary.' Why did he question her

satisfaction in the natural liberality she enjoyed, a quality to which no conditions were attached? She grew a little heated in response. She was queen of sky and trees, caves and mosses, solitaire bird and parrot fish.

'Still the motions of curiosity draw you to things new,' he insisted.

'As you taught me. To seek improvements. As I do in many things, including in these flat loaves I baked, of which you have managed to eat two!'

'The question is whether newness – the undiscovered – lies within or without.'

'Are there not angels that descend from heaven? What do they look like, Father? Do you not believe in God?'

'I hesitate to pronounce, not simply nor solely. Now, here, other gods might be possible. We learnt: "Thou shalt have no other God but me".'

'Is there no Goddess?'

'Except you, dearest.'

'Look –'

In the shallows, wading round the rocks at the point of their beach, the shape of half a man appeared, visible from the thighs up. He was followed by another. They looked like moving rocks, squat and solid, miraculously floating rocks, dark against the pale blue mirror of the late afternoon lagoon. Father and daughter watched them move closer. Intent or poor of eyesight, they failed to notice their observers. They had round heads on short necks, golden skin, the one in front a black mane and beard, the slight one who came behind wearing a conical hat. Tied up round their waists, their pants ballooned on the surface of the water. A knife dangled on a strap from the neck of the bearded fellow. From time to time he reached underwater for something his toes had found and used the knife. He handed what he found to his companion, who put it into the sack that trailed over his shoulder.

The English pair watched in silence as the two strangers came round to the beach and walked up the sand, water sluicing off them. Popple turned to his daughter, raising his eyebrows without a word. The longer they went unnoticed, the longer the moment of confrontation could be held back. Holding his breath Popple faced his daughter for a last drawn-out moment of tender cherishing, as if their world together was on the brink of extinction. His head was precisely upright, his lips closed, the scorings of his concave cheeks running down the regular growth of beard that tapered to a handsome triangle, the bird's feet of his eyes splaying to his temples in humour and enquiry, his coal eyes, deep still pools, holding her steadily, beneath the ripple of his frown and the dirty mat of hair, interrogating her and loving her, wishing to turn to crystal the freighted moment of their solitude together. Yet apprehensive, generous, seeking her assistance to harmonize the intervention, so that a higher power, a greater dominion, would be theirs, he prayed for victory, and reached for his musket.

There were no lines on Rosamund's freckled pink and orange skin, which the sun had ruddied. Her cheeks were chubby, her lips full, like fruit, her eyes green jade that sparkled with light from the sea. Her high smooth forehead had bumps that identified a striving brain, her hair was a thick curly fleece of sun-bleached gold, greasy and fragrant. Her eyebrows, eyelashes, the fluff on her upper lip, and lower chin, were wispy growth. She concealed her excitement in deference to her father, her anxiety turning the held moment to one of exquisite anticipation.

Any instant there would be a sound or a gesture, strange to interpret. Until then they were king and queen indeed, observing subject activity, or god and goddess noting the intrusive consequences of creation, or lovers watching the unexpected fruits of their activity draw ever nearer.

The island was hushed. Popple stood to his height on the grassy knoll, the quiet motion catching the attention of the gatherers on the shore, the hatted one turning his head to emit a sharp moan. The bearded one muttered inaudibly. Planted to the sand they stared. A flicker of over-the-shoulder glance suggested an impulse of retreat. The impulse of attraction, of friendliness, was frozen by caution. Were they the same species? Were there more? The second one stood beside the taller. There seemed to be only two. They took a step forward, then another, then the tall one made a gesture with an outstretched arm, moving it slowly through the air above his head in a signal.

The gatherers' feet dug into the sand. The prey in their shoulder sacks scrabbled and clawed.

The bearded man unbuckled his knife. Popple had his musket in his hand as he walked forward, signalling to Ros to keep behind him. But she walked abreast of him.

'They look like Tartars,' whispered Popple, before he shouted, 'Come over! There's nothing to fear. We are friends.'

The eyes of the Chinese whitened. The incomprehensible sounds made them shiver. The strangers kept moving towards them. Soon they would be right before their eyes. If they were to act, they could only do so with a concentration of surprise and unleashed energy, rushing, leaping at them, overwhelming them with suddenness and stabbing them to death. But the order had not been given. The decision was not theirs. So they stood their ground as if paralysed, until the foreign man got so close they could see his horrible grin and staring eye-sockets, and hear the flow of jabber so like the sound of the importuning monkeys on Mount Emei – those that steal your brass belt buckles from round your waist – that Huang, the bearded Chinese captain, could no longer stop the tickling in his throat, the clattering of his teeth, could no longer push down the peals of laughter that burst from him at the two clown-devils. And the hatted man joined him with a dry rat-a-tat of mirth.

Popple was taken aback, his grin turning solemn. He was angry at the failure of communication. Rosamund smiled with welcoming sweetness and began to laugh. She curtseyed, and the Chinese men bent their heads in a little bow, at which Popple bowed more deeply, put his musket down, and opened his hand. Huang passed his knife into the left hand, disclosing his right palm to scrutiny, then wiped it on his smock and copied Popple's gesture. The two men stood with right hands outstretched. After a pause, Popple took the tawny hand in his and squeezed it. Huang squeezed back, with a wrestler's grip to which Popple civilly submitted until he could extricate his fingers.

The hatted man slung his shoulder sack on to the sand and opened it for the foreigners to see. Whether a poacher was laying bare his booty or a hawker offering his wares was uncertain. It was weighted with shellfish, oysters and clams, sea-grapes and fleshy black weed, scratching, scrambling crabs and shrimps.

'So many creatures!' gasped Ros, plunging her hand into the sack.

The hatted Chinese grabbed her wrist.

'Yow!' she yelled. She had a crab dangling from her finger. The Chinese collector of such things took the crab with one hand and prized open its claw, while Rosamund panted with embarrassment rather than pain. Her finger was deeply indented, but there was no blood, and they laughed.

'How did they get so many?' asked her father.

Popple took an oyster and tried in vain to open it with

his fingernail. Huang reached over and deftly inserted his knife, opening up the plump slate-green flesh. Huang held it in air for Popple to see, and Popple put his finger into the shell, scooped out the flesh and swallowed it in one gulp. The Chinese cried out in horror, shaking their heads and their hands, patting their mouths. They mimed cooking. But for Popple it tasted delicious and he bowed in gratitude.

There were more oysters in the bag. The polite thing seemed to be to invite the visitors into their dwelling. Concluding his bow, Popple stretched an arm towards the huts in the distance and indicated that they should go together. The Chinese stood their ground, smiling.

'Come!' instructed Popple.

The Chinese wondered to what they were being invited. Would they be outnumbered? Were they to be seized? What were these denizens of the island?

Rosamund joined her father's efforts to encourage them. She was curious as could be and saw these two forerunners as manageable entry into the strange larger presence she had been imagining since the first day she glimpsed their camp. Popple would have preferred the island to himself, but since there were new arrivals he also saw that it was best to avoid hostility. They would not move, so Popple turned and walked steadily towards the huts. Rosamund waited, then skipped after him. The Chinese held their ground. Slowly they untied the straw sandals hanging at their necks and bent to slip them on. Then in a helpless surge of curiosity they shuffled forward. They could not lose the privilege of reporting back what they would discover.

Expecting to find other people, they entered the enclosed space of the hut warily. They surveyed the rudimentary solid structures that held little to impress them. Prepared to acknowledge the achievements of an alien race, they noted signs of considerable labour, but the place was unimproved. Improvised tables and chairs, baskets, leather trunks, unrolled bedding, and some weird cooking utensils. They waited for their hosts to offer them tea or ask them to sit. There was no way to convey what was wanted.

The girl returned with fruit and gave one to each. They lowered themselves on to the dry sandy ground and began each to peel the fruit. The Chinese took it as a testing ceremony – and wondered where the rest of their people were hiding. At length, unable to express himself, Huang allowed his eyes to rove. Popple's place of study was set up in one corner under the window, with a stack of books and a pile of papers weighted by a shining transparent disc. It looked like a smooth, shaped piece of crystal. Noticing Huang's attention, Popple fetched it, peering through it as he offered it to Huang, whose expression showed his consternation as the great floating eye came towards him. It was a magnifying glass, and once Huang grasped how the toy worked he was enchanted. He brought it close to his hand, the skin of the lime, his companion's face, delighted as he watched the transformation of size, detail, colour. But when he touched the enlarged object it was no longer there.

Popple showed how he used the glass to read small print, and Huang examined with great fascination the way the little books were assembled, and the page after octavo page of indecipherable marks.

They stood, anxious to get away, once they had devoured the fruit. They had seen enough on which to report. No further steps could be taken without consultation. Huang ordered his companion to take three or four of the oysters out of the sack as a presentation. Then the neck of the sack was drawn tight and it was flung over the man's shoulder and the hat donned. Popple looked around for a reciprocal gift and found a loose folding of a pamphlet on the circulation of the blood, its text in Latin, with a fine anatomical engraving of the heart. This he solemnly offered to Huang, who accepted with equal solemnity, bowing before he stuffed it in his breast.

Once outside the hut they strode almost at a run across the grass, their straw sandals flapping softly, back to the water's edge where they waded in without a break in their movement, and, up to their waists in water, rounded the rocks out of sight.

Lord Lou sat on a three-legged stool in the prince's cabin with his knees wide apart and the worn gown gathered into his groin. The skin of his bony legs was marked with white blotches, his toes, splayed and bent, clawed over his old slip-ons. His arthritis had worsened in the months of confinement to the boat, and, with pleasing mortification, he adopted positions that strained his joints. His white hair was thin and long, like a maiden's, his smooth skin had tightened with leanness.

'To have found this shore is a sign of favour,' he said, 'but which shore is it?'

'It is your skill that brings us here,' said the prince sweetly, who stood gazing out the window. The bobbing waves transported him, they made him calm, they made him vague and forgetful, floating weightlessly through a world of dreams. He had grown a little more solid, but his bloom had turned to pallor, a dietary problem combined with the strict ritual of his days, which was a form of asceticism: exercise, meditation, study, vacancy. His only interlocutor was Lou Lu. The rest of the crew had come to consider him a kind of ghost and drew a circle round him. But he was still the emperor.

'I directed the rudder as I threw the divining sticks,' commented the eunuch drily.

'How near are we to Rome? This is perhaps its outlying shore?'

'Rome! We journey without maps, without experience.'

'You have used the compass according to your understanding. You cannot be in error.'

'If not Rome, then a stepping stone. We must rejoice to have come ashore after days of sailing across endless water, to have come ashore before drifting into the realms of ice and monsters. We have crossed the green ocean. It remains only to pass through Africa and we shall reach Rome. Meanwhile we shall stay here. There is abundance here. We must discover what place it is.'

Old Lou looked at the prince affectionately. 'It may be part of Your Highness's empire.'

'I should like to walk around it.'

'When it is safe, you shall.'

'How can it not be safe?'

'Wild animals, hostile tribes, deceitful elements of nature.'

'Are we the first from my empire to visit here?'

'I expect so. These are the western isles that lie beyond the western seas. Beyond the beyond. It is here that you will find proof of your divinity.'

The prince frowned. In months of travelling solitude his claim had not once been questioned. He could not understand the need for proofs. 'How so?'

'Miracles. Wonders,' croaked the eunuch.

'Are the Immortals here?'

'No, but perhaps what makes immortality.'

The prince turned to the porthole overwhelmed with a boredom so profound that he could neither feel nor recognize it. He threw himself down on the brine-smelling greasy quilt. 'Tell me, Wise Man.'

'Where the rarest things are found, the freaks of nature, the chance creations of the gods, there shall be the unique being, the one who can appreciate them, who comes once in time, standing apart from the far-stretching ranks of humanity, to see and know the precious wonder that the world has produced. That being has the mandate of Heaven. That being is you, my dear prince, and you have come to this place, wherever, whatever, it is.'

Outside the cabin gulls cawed, the moorings groaned, the planks connecting deck and shore bumped up and down on the rock.

'There is a legend from the south,' continued the commissioner, 'of a black flower, a bloom of no colour that combines all colours, for what is black, is it absence, or is it everything under heaven? Without the sun, everything in the world is black. Pure, deep blackness survives in the lines of ink that soak into white paper, creating indelible meaning. Black is final significance. Is mysterious power. Where the black flower grows, a rose it is said, one finds the endorsement of the superior being. Whoever has it is undisputed emperor. They say the black rose grows atop a mound that conceals one single nugget of gold ore, a mountain of gold.'

The prince spoke in hushed respect. 'Does the black rose grow here?'

'I believe we will find it,' said Lou Lu, allowing his eyelids to sink over his eyes.

The prince placed a soft hand on the old man's shoulder.

Then the gangplank clattered, and there was the sound of steps pattering across it, the balance of the timber twisting as bodyweight shifted.

Huang called. He was in a quick low kowtow at the door of the prince's cabin.

'Sir −' He lifted his head as the prince himself opened the door and Old Lou, who could not move in haste, opened his eyelids, yet failed to rise from his bent knees. 'Will the Lord Lou receive his humble report?'

Lord Lou nodded slowly.

'There are inhabitants,' Huang blurted, 'a man and a younger one. Strangers.'

'Of what manner?' The sounds rolled from Lou Lu in bass vibration.

Huang pushed the folding of printed paper into the eunuch's hand. Lou Lu turned it before his eyes, upside down, then upside again. After a long pause, in which Huang gaped at him as if making a plea, the old man spoke the nonsensical sounds: '*De sanguinis circulatione motum cordisque.*'

'They are Christians,' he pronounced. 'And wizards. I recognize their pig language. Latin.'

VII

. . . the wise Chinese in the fertile wombe
Of Earth doth a more precious clay entombe . . .

Andrew Marvel,
*An Elegy upon the Death of
my Lord Francis Villiers*
(1648?)

The unknown was a gamble, a throw of the sticks informed
by interpretation. The only avoiding of encounter lay in
flight, to turn their backs on help that might be proferred
and information gleaned, to sail again across the empty sea.
Contact was better. If they were near to Rome, as seemed
likely, how unwise to leave without asking the way. Lord
Lou shrewdly followed each chain of transactions to conclusion with a perspicacity deeper than the most devoted chess
player's, with foresight more probing and calculations more
predictive, after a lifetime of dealing in human affairs.
Ignorance was their vulnerability. They knew neither the
nature of the terrain nor its social constituency, and nothing
of the status of the inhabitants they had met. All was
projection and guesswork. Yet their ignorance should allow
immediate and undetermined responsiveness to whatever
situation they found. The largest practical matter was the
power of the other party. If the power were great, being
weak in contrast they posed no threat. If the power were
limited, it would respond with hostility to potential danger.
The trick lay in powerlessness, along with independence
that asked nothing and intelligence that offered prospects
of gain.

Lord Lou went to meet the strangers unarmed and unaccompanied except for Captain Huang, and Jia, the boatman who had made the first encounter. The shallow boat followed the shoreline, the sailor poled with a single oar while Huang kept watch, the travel slow and stately. His gown gathered around his bent knees, his back straight, his head covered, concealing his gaze as it played over the expanse of lagoon, glassy and glittering, Lou Lu sat low to the surface of the water. He read the signs with authority to confer his own meanings, and found them favourable, as if to justify the curiosity that drew them on, and a deeper impulse of kinship in that lonely place, of hope checked only by the webbed layers of caution, prudence, timidity, wariness, and passivity in the sage's mind.

So low was the boat, the bamboo hat so large that it dwarfed the wearer, his face lost in its cone of shadow. Lord Lou might have been a prisoner to be delivered over to a foreign shore, or an elder of the tribe to be cast out in sacrifice, his usefulness outlived, as the load came into clarity. Outside the hut, Popple stood sentinel to watch their approach. Proud apprehension rippled through his guts as he perceived the elevation and dignity of the hatted old man who was sent to him.

'Hail!' he shouted, raising his arm in the antique gesture that he took for universal. '*Ave!*'

Popple strode down the grassy mound like a priest greeting the stragglers of his congregation, paces long, straight, purposive, brows raised in a parody of welcome, arms helplessly outstretched. He recognized in the slowness of these visitors a degree of civility. So benign was the ocean that day, smoothed to little more than a meniscus along the sand, its currents swelling, bursting in mild froth, subsiding in fizzy exhalation, breathing again. So empty was the distance, so airy and blue the unclouded sky, the faintest scar of a wake left by the steady travel of the boat, the ingenious to-and-fro of the pole-oar a skill Popple saluted, a subdued disturbance of water, the principle of the fish's tail well-adapted to the element. Their mission was tentative, not urgent.

A solitaire bird under the lime trees squawked in the direction of the hills as the skiff scraped against shingles and the boatman leapt nimbly ashore.

Their narrow half-closed eyes appeared at first not to see, the burden of the boat stayed seated and hunched until the anchor, a disc of metal, was embedded. Then the boatman picked the old man up in his arms and carried him ashore where he straightened himself before facing the oncoming stranger. He called out no greeting, but bowed, not a deep bow, arms at his side.

Popple halted in his tracks, grinned, returned a clumsy nod. He felt bareheaded, since the visitor had not removed his hat. Ros hastened to catch up with her father, standing behind him, panting a little wildly. Her eyes twinkled at the two boatmen, acknowledging old friends. They rolled staring eyes back at her, as if this were a manner of salutation.

The silence was broken by a barrage of full-voiced high-toned sing-song speech that resonated from beneath the bamboo hat, a liquid sound in which not a word could be identified, followed by a further flow, and another, each ending in a pat and a sigh.

'Ah!'

So Popple responded: 'Ah!' And nodded: 'Ah!'

'Ah!' returned the old man, reaching for a concealed pocket in his shirt and pulling out the printed page of Latin.

'Ah!' exclaimed Popple, and pointed to the hut where the rest of the book was. Huang knew his meaning and appeared to interpret for his superior, indicating that the invitation should be accepted. They walked slowly, disconnectedly, forward to the house, eyes skinned for any other people.

Before the door they stopped and waited for the host to usher them inside. After the direction was given, however, they resisted, protested, waited again. Popple repeated the invitation, urged them, and set the example himself. Still they waited, like mules. Were they scared of a trap? He dared not touch their persons to manhandle them inside. At last the bearded one took the decisive step and Lord Lou followed, the younger boatman behind to protect him. Popple ground his teeth, quite unable to construe the charade of ceremony, caution and misunderstanding.

It was Ros who understood the complexity. They were thirsty and, with great formality, she offered pewter mugs of boiled water. The young boatman tasted his, testing it, before exchanging mugs with the old man, who, to sip, grandly removed his hat and exposed a bare shiny head that had the tone of smoke-yellowed parchment. White hairs, individually countable, grew in a distinct circle down his scalp, becoming a patchy mane over his neck. As Popple and Ros stared at him, he looked up with a gap-toothed grin, eyes twinkling, and giggled.

'*Aqua*,' he pronounced.

Popple was startled and instantly mimicked him. '*Aqua*.'

Ros chimed the sound, which might have been a nonsense until Lord Lou added: '*Aquam bevimus. Latinum dicamus.*'

Popple could not restrain himself from grabbing the old man's hand in an exuberant shake. 'Yes! Let us speak Latin! Pig Latin! Let us drink water!'

Lord Lou pulled his hand away with a shudder, at the same time signalling his escorts to relax.

Popple took the book from the shelf and laid it on the trunk that served for their table.

Slowly, in an agony of elocution, the guest read: '*De sanguinis circulatione motum cordisque*'. He dipped his finger in the mug and inscribed a wet trail on the trunk's surface. Ros watched the pearly moon-nail on the shrunken tawny finger draw pictures that the old man named, one by one, until there were four.

'It is their language,' pronounced Popple, 'the script of Cathay.'

That first painful language lesson threw up some basic information. They were journeying from China in search of Rome. The others were from England, which was not here. How far from China, how far from Rome, could not be conveyed, nor whether they were representatives of their states or merely samples of their kind. None of the parties to the first formal meeting at any rate was native to the land which formed a curious backdrop to their faltering dialogue and partially expressed concerns. They wanted to know about the land, which the Englishman, to the surprise of the Chinese, conceived as an island. The Chinese feared that what lay interior to the island – people, dangers – must make it advisable to get away. The English were concerned that these calm, well-organized visitors might be an advance guard for something greater and more implacable. If Rome were the issue, a world map could be drawn to show how far there was to go. Lord Lou wondered how Popple could draw such a thing since the evidence suggested he had not reached the present place by any rational design and only as a fabulist knew the way from Rome to the island. Or if he had been unceremoniously, punitively, flung ashore, his knowledge had not been put to use. In which case they were all in the same stew, or almost.

Popple looked at his drawing and caught Lou Lu's laughter. Their knowledge and their clumsy attempts to ascertain answers were absurd. Their knowledge, given their situation, was so hypothetical as to be merely a gracious entertainment offered by each side to the other.

Without introductions, without social language, it was impossible to gauge who they were, in terms of class, standing, commitments, grievances, or what other force fitted people for their place or impelled them through life. Another form of knowledge, however, proved uncannily possible and Lord Lou and Popple, standing before each other as in a mirror, recognized their reflection as outcast, explorer, idealist, obstinate loyalist, deviator from the times. Popple's streaky beard, Old Lou's white wispy mane, eyes that penetrated more than saw, practised hands that grafted the stock, played the tiller; two men who quickly surmised that they had much to exchange. Much to learn. Lord Lou wrung his hands, Popple squeezed his beard, in frustration and desire.

Popple prodded himself in the breast and said his name three times.

'Po-poo,' came the wavering echo. 'Po-poo.'

Then the finger poked the old man's chestbone and he said: 'Lou.'

'Lo!' came the answer.

As prelude to further hospitality Ros produced segments of lime which they refrained from accepting. The matter of her sex was not easy to clarify. Her shape responded to nothing Chinese. Popple put his arm round her in owner-ship, highlighting a resemblance that made them look like early and late developments of the same form. But when Ros kissed her father's cheek to display their relationship for the strangers, their respectful giggle showed that they understood her to be a creature of the opposing gender, a mate. Their dark eyes darted as if light were flashing off oil.

Lord Lou sat on the stool and took the refreshment, the wedge of fruit. In Latin Popple struggled to lay out the fundamentals of his cause. Ros rocked, hugging her knees, restless for the barrier of tongues to be dropped. Then it was Lou Lu's turn to explain. Captain Huang strolled outside to look around and Ros ran out after him. In a sign and grunt language she showed him the workmanship of their dwellings, and the features of the trees and the rockpools, regularly flushed by the tide, where sea urchins congregated. With a joyous exclamation he took one in his rough scaly hands and allowed its spines to roll gently over him. Then he took his knife and sliced it open, offering half the palpitating orange heart, an aureole, to Ros as he swallowed the tangy other half himself.

He yelled for the boatman to join them, but young Jia stayed guard, bearing responsibility for the protection of Lord Lou, their source of understanding, their fount.

As he prepared to depart, Lord Lou stood on the bank and pointed at the sun, imitating its movement to show that he would return. Ros loaded up their boat with living sea urchins. Popple signed his arm not at the sun or out to sea, but back over their heads to the mountain. His arm was like a dial. That was the direction in which they would travel next time, to the Chinese camp.

'They are accomplished people,' mused Popple to Ros when they were alone, 'knowledgeable. Yet I have no access to what they know.'

'Did you notice how delicately they held the segment of fruit with their right hand, then how like animals they chewed it?'

'I do not understand their high and noble mission. The old man journeys not for himself, not solely, but for another figure of higher standing or higher order. They seek nothing but confirmation of the order. He told me that the world was a disc spinning between firmaments of water above and below. He travels to Rome, not as to a centre but an outpost where he can restock himself. He does not seek wealth. His interest was polite when I explained that I was a gardener, a maker of new specimens.'

Ros burst out at her father. 'You are a philosopher, no ordinary gardener.'

'I could not have said so to him. I doubt their philosophers tinker with the natural world.'

'Then show him. Take him next time to your garden.'

'I am a deviser of possibilities.'

The man was lost in his elaborate weave of facts, words and images.

'Father, they have a boat. A seaworthy vessel. Father, we could sail with them if we needed.'

'When there is no need, since we have travelled far to find this blessed and pure island. We must stay for the results of a season.'

'What strange eyes they have. What do they see, Father?'

'They see what we see.'

'I see that their faces are like smiling masks. Is that what they see?'

'You cannot read them like a book any more than you can read their writing. Any more than they can read our books or our faces.'

She walked in a quandary about the place where her father was seated.

'They are familiar,' she decided, 'yet unfamiliar.'

'We will know them better,' he confirmed. 'We will acquire their knowledge.'

★

The prince hung one pallid arm to the floor as Lou Lu made his report.

'The place is no part of an archipelago. It is isolated, with no neighbours. The inhabitants are two, a man and a womanly creature. Castaways or border guards. This civilization is not theirs, furthermore, and their own civilization remains unclear to me, although of Europe and the western world. What channels of communication they have, what reinforcements, I am unable to determine.'

'What manner of beings are they?' asked the prince, amused.

'Coarse in their conditions, but rational and amiable. A sturdy, hair-covered man and his kin, who resembles a ginger root with hair, eyes and eyebrows of no colour at all.'

'A freak?'

'Unpleasant to behold, certainly.'

'How were you entertained?' continued the prince, laughing at the discomfiture the commissioner experienced in this primitive exercise of diplomacy.

'With what they had. Sir, they are useful to us. Their geographical and maritime understanding, their navigation, superior to ours. They are here on purpose, unlike us. They have an idea of where they are. They find this barren place important. Why?'

'What do they offer?'

'Converse.'

'Then we must respond sweetly.'

'For certain.'

The prince gave a long nerveless exhalation. 'The commissioner's gifts of language are found to be more valuable than ever. What is the worth of novelty?' he inquired of the old man.

'Apart from gold and precious stones, the indestructible things, novelty is desired above all else.'

'Above power?'

'Novelty draws people to itself, thus conferring power. When the ruler appears among his subjects, the world must seem to be made new. Invention, hope, promise, advancement are essential accoutrements of the leader, the true heir no less than the usurper.'

Bored even with this new diversion, the prince rocked his hammock, sighing to the roof of his cabin. 'Let us become their firm allies and empty their minds of their treasury of new skills and new devices. I order you.'

The old man's eyes glittered at the prince's subtle, trusting counsel. His ambition, nothing coarse or lumpish, was refined to a slender probe. He understood instinctively the rare politic art of how he must show himself, transformed and empowered, on his return from wandering.

'Your Highness must not invest too much hope in the two unlettered barbarians. Their allegiances are all unclear. They are in probability neither scholars nor officials, by their conditions certainly not merchants. Marginal people. They may not reliably guide us to any centre of empire or learning.'

'The centre is with us. We merely absorb them.'

'To do so may not be to our gain, if they are floating bodies, debris, waste matter.'

'Bring them in.'

'They may not come.'

'Find a way.'

An energetic intelligence ran through the lines of the old man's face when he was engaged in the semblance of debate on high policy.

'Sir, do not erect your hopes on this random encounter. How have they got here with no vessel? When will their ships of confederates return to overpower and enslave us?'

'Uncle, your caution prevents that outcome.'

'Already the boatmen are talking. The alien brings fear and blame should mishap come among us. Fantastic dread is in their nature. So we must go with care, show resistance, close our eyes, turn our backs, until a space forms into which the alien element can be received.'

The ropes of the hammock groaned with Taizao's rocking. He seemed to be gliding on eternity like a seabird. Lou Lu gazed on his youth, his beauty, his majesty; a kind of perfection impervious to blemish of change, that would be gone like a mask dropped, like dew, leaving no trace except in the twisting, spider-spun caverns of an old man's memory. Taizao's sooty eyebrows, his waxen skin and budding lips, were as marks on the surface of unbroken water, an evasive answer to the onlooker's desire for a human sign. His young beauty was a specific and transient illusion. A calenture. A mirage. Yet he was the emperor, Son of Heaven, before whom Lord Lou enjoyed the performance of a deep bow as he left the presence.

'Commissioner,' Captain Huang came tugging at Lou Lu's sleeve. 'The men want to swap things with those people. They want their treasures.'

'No!' snapped Lord Lou. 'By exchange they intend petty thievery.'

'We have weapons. The men are tired of waiting.'

'As may the others have hidden arms. The men must live in daily patience, to find out what can be found out, before we are in any position to act for short or long-term gain. Tell the men not to be misled, Captain. It is no ordinary situation.'

When the Chinese failed to return the next day, and the next, Popple began to worry, filled with devastating anticipation of their never coming again, so intense was fleeting human contact in the unpeopled place. More likely there was an issue to resolve before they could make good their promise to return. Who knew what hierarchies and forms they observed?

On the fourth day Popple and Ros took the initiative and set off. They climbed the mountain behind their dwelling with agility and descended the other side following what was now an identifiable path through the hazy morning to the garden. Whether to claim ownership or keep out hypothetical marauders, or simply in an aesthetic impulse to frame his work, Popple had built an octagonal wooden fence around the plot inside which, planted in a well-spaced pattern, the rose bushes grew from the tilled black loam in splendid profusion of tender pink-tipped leaves, the more remarkable for their northern exoticism amidst undifferentiated southern fecundity.

'What a master you are,' said Ros, 'to revive such life from those miserable sticks.'

'Cuttings,' he said. 'They have no problem in taking.'

'Will you show the Chinese?'

'When we know their aim.'

The way was less distinct, arduous in its last stages, as they climbed the rocky heights to a vantage point. Ros, the more lithe, feared that her father might fall. They lay flat over an edge of rock, to observe without being observed, and as they stuck their heads out, like tortoises, they grew dizzy at the drop. Below lay the structure of canopies and awnings, boat shells and connecting ramps, rising and falling with the mild swell. A sailor on guard on a pedestal of rock lifted his gaze in the direction of their movement, fixed their position and waved.

'Ssh!' whispered Popple.

The guard called out, and others ran to join him in staring up at the cliff.

They retracted their heads but were seen. Popple argued

that they might have been mistaken for a bird. Ros laughed. 'Then they would shoot. Father, we mustn't alarm them, or let them think us spies. We must go down at once and explain.'

Popple hung back, his impulse all for retreat.

'Father, I shall show you the way,' she pouted, cheeks flushed.

He followed with lingering unsteady steps, his head erect for dignity.

'Bow,' she ordered him, to pass through undergrowth.

They emerged on a rocky plateau a little beyond the Chinese camp. Lord Lou was expecting them, his face creased in a cold smile of greeting. Popple wiped his brow with a kerchief and Ros edged close to her father. A group of men gathered behind the elder to leer, scared to approach, unable to resist, the two ill-featured strangers.

'We waited and you did not come,' boomed Popple in his Latin, 'therefore we have come to find you. I wish to go on talking.'

The lines around Lord Lou's mouth tensed and relaxed, like the legs of a spider at the centre of its web. 'We are unprepared. Our house –' he indicated coyly, not having a word for their dwelling, '– our boats, are small, unworthy to welcome you.'

The two men were immobilized in each other's presence by inarticulate desire.

'Come.'

In a decisive gesture Lou Lu led the visitors under cover, sat them on stools, and had tea poured; steaming, fragrant liquid – the green of mountain-water as it tumbles over flinty pebbles and jade shards, an extraordinary delicacy of gratification to the palate.

Impressed by the tea, Popple embarked on other matters of civilization. London? The world was a globe bisected by the equator and sliced by meridians that started from a zero point at London. If the night sky was visible they could know precisely where they were with respect to London. But where was London? A journey of two months away.

To Lord Lou the fantastical talk had no relation to experience. When Popple waved his hands as if to conjure the spherical world, and talked of winds blowing with the season across the green sea, then Old Lou might have understood. They had been blown hither by one wind, and would be carried hence by another. When would the wind blow that took them to Rome?

Would the foreigners consider guiding the Chinese expedition to their home, their destination?

'We are not going home. We are to find a new world.'

'Not Rome.'

Popple bowed his head in acknowledgement. He was no courtier, he explained, he was a scientist who sought knowledge.

'To what end?' asked Lord Lou, repeating the question pointedly. 'To what end?'

'Knowledge is its own end.'

'Only for the private man who refuses to serve the public good.'

'Whose good are you serving?'

'I serve our people. I serve the just and right way. I seek to include the foreigners and their popes of Rome in our great enterprise.'

'Then your strength is limited.'

'It does not change the right way.'

Popple wondered at the man's dignified conviction. It was some complex invisible spirit these people worshipped. He would judge with his own eyes.

Meanwhile Ros stole away. Her Latin was rudimentary.

The mobility of her face was her best language. Food preparation, hygiene, sail-mending: there was a high degree of organization, she saw, and no one was idle. No one dared to stop her as she wandered round the camp.

She ventured across the plank that joined the boat, where her father was with the old man, to another boat, the largest, that lay silent and enclosed alongside. A man sprang on to the plank to grab her, in the scuffle almost pulling both of them off balance. He let out an abusive volley that was subdued at once by a low order from within. Her assailant's tight grip marched her across the deck towards the cabin.

The hanging opened into a dim chamber smelling of rough fibre, close bodily warmth, bedding, unmoving air and a faint rank oily whiff of garlic. The light of a window shaded with bamboo mesh outlined the head and mane of an indiscernible person there who could see her clearly with fully dilated eyes. He gaped, he beamed. 'Oh?' She heard him give an upward nasal inflection of surprise. He was laughing at her.

'Excuse me,' she said.

He laughed uncontrollably, slinging his legs out of the hammock and marching towards her. She thought he was going to poke her bosom so she made a face at him, and he jumped backwards in playful alarm. He was unclean and inactive, she could observe, with prettily shaped eyes. With a glance over her shoulder she noticed that the fellow who delivered her there had vanished. She gathered herself. She recognized the young warrior she had espied from the clifftop on her first visit.

'You probably do not understand a word I say. I wish we could talk but, whatever you are, you are not inclined that way, so good day, sir, I await our further acquaintance. Pardon my ill manners.'

Taizao twitched his head like a rooster as she backed clumsily through the door hanging and was gone.

He followed her to the threshold and watched as she skipped across the plank to the adjoining craft. Her smock was dirty, torn in places, and bundled around her bulbous form that was round, fleshy and curving, like a ginger root, as Old Lou had said. Or were her clothes padded and stuffed? Her wobbly form was unlike anything he had seen before; her pale gingery hair crawled in thick tangles over her head, springing as she moved; her pale dotted skin revealed colours of blood moving beneath the surface. The intriguing creature turned to peep back at Taizao before disappearing. Goosepimples covered him from top to toe.

★　　★　　★

Popple unbent his legs from the little stool and rose with effort, reflecting the old man's frail formality. Every movement was slow, as speech had slowed to the careful placing of language stones. Neither man was typical of his place and time, and each was enveloped by his own culture as if by the womb. Each move in their dialogue was an impulse towards birth. The need to maintain dignity impeded their interaction, however, resulting in a balanced rhythm, a stately, strategic dance of conversation. Popple discovered that the old man came from the centre of the world, whereas he, Edward Popple, came from the moving point of history. The Chinese lived in space, the European in time, the one centred in a spiralling stasis, the other riding, or impelling, the crest of a wave through the void. The Chinese had heard of Jesus Christ but did not understand that He claimed to join matter to eternity, humanity to God. The European had heard of harmony but did not understand that harmony was achieved by subordinating the lesser to the greater; he knew fate, but did not see that fate's course offered the natural way.

'You worship God,' said Old Lou, 'and want man to be master.'

'You follow tradition – the world changes and you suffer,' countered Popple.

'Our tradition is as broad as the sea. Carries us everywhere. Can absorb everything. Now forgive me, I am tired.'

Lou Lu yawned. Popple saw his blackened teeth gape like a horse's jaw. His slender hand touched Popple's elbow with the lightness of a falling leaf and ushered him forwards.

'Come.'

They crossed from the floating space to the solid rock of the island and an awning-covered storage area. Baskets, buckets and trunks were stacked or lashed together. Stupendous earthenware urns with stoppered mouths stood in rows, plump and shining.

'Oil, vinegar, rice, wine, pickled vegetables,' enumerated the old man. Their colony was far better equipped than the hermit-crab existence of Popple and his daughter.

At the end of the storage area, in a sheltered, half-sunned and half-shadowed nook, Popple saw the pots. In close formation red clay vessels filled with black loam, seaweed and tealeaves stood on red clay saucers. It was a nursery where plant specimens grew in pots, sticks in leaf, severely pruned, nipped and forced, some with buds and flowers.

Bending his knees, Popple delicately ran his fingers down the stalk of one of the plants, over the spines, unfurling a bud. Lord Lou frowned at him.

'Rose,' said Popple. One word.

The old man echoed the sound.

'A member of the family at any rate,' continued the naturalist, 'although quite unlike all our others.'

It was a small bloom with double, tightly packed rows

of scalloped petals, a tiny bunch of screwed-up muslin, as Popple pried open the whorl to inspect the reproductive organs within. It had no fragrance, and a colour of no rose flower he had ever seen. Bright yellow. It was, to Popple's expert eye, the most remarkable rose specimen; a rose, and yet not; *could* not be. His puzzlement accounted for his compulsion almost to ravish the diminutive form in exploring it. At the same time he deferred, each moment, to the Chinese elder, hesitating, holding himself from jumping to conclusions.

'The flower of young love,' said Lord Lou. 'We carry with us numerous such things as an essential part of our mission.'

Popple needed no larger explanation. 'What we call a rose is not this. The head is flat, not bunched. Its face is open, permitting a sweet fragrance to waft in the air. Red or white or in between. The rose cannot be yellow. Yet this one has thorns, and the subtler armature of prickles and glands, and –' he was rubbing the downy underside of the calyx, '– a soft, sparse pubescence.'

'It's a common flower,' Lord Lou responded. 'Like young love, everywhere, profuse, short-lived, having no special symbolic value, no duration, one bloom replacing another the year round. Growing wild, or for planned gardens, or in rocks, with educated people placing no store on it. An ordinary, vulgar flower, held in contempt, always available, needing to be sold during its short prime, like a girl. Its fruit having medicinal uses. Its hips making useful tea.'

Popple listened, aghast at the devaluation of his flower into little more than a street whore, if the peculiar bloom were really the rose. A distant cousin perhaps.

'Then this is not a rose.' He forbore to explain the high spiritual nature of the flower, the queenly beauty, the amorous essences. The Tartars evidently had not found the English rose.

Old Lou indicated one or two other plants with the rose's characteristics, thorns on their stems, but no flowers yet. Aromatics too and medicinal herbs, to which he directed attention, Popple passing over them out of concern for the one possibility that he did not know how to broach.

He wished he could carry the rose pot away as a trophy, but fearing such an action would inflame the new concord, Popple pulled an exaggerated face to show that it was time he returned to the other side of the island if they were to be home before dark.

Rosamund was bouncing between the boats, laughing with the sailors, noticing every detail of their different objects and methods. She was exhilarated by the return to a kind of human society.

'Come!' boomed Popple, emerging from the awning. Her cheeks were red from laughing at the sailors' mimicry of birdsong, a shrill chirrup that set the seagulls wheeling in the late-afternoon sun.

'Listen, Father.'

The sailor puckered his lips, hollowed his cheeks, and with extreme concentration became a songbird with such verisimilitude that Popple was forced to laugh too. Then he put out his hand to lead Ros away.

Lord Lou bowed and Popple offered a handshake in Christian fashion. Within his large grip he felt the cool unresisting extremity of the old Chinese. He released his grip without relish.

'*Vale! Valete!*'

He wanted to bud the putative rose.

'Farewell!'

VIII

The laws of the vegetable kingdom are themselves governed by other laws increasingly exalted.

Marcel Proust,
Sodom and Gomorrah I (1921)

The low oil lamp cast high agitated shadows into the corners of the roof of the hut as Popple wrote – great shapeless figures with billowing, darting bodies, massive headdresses spiked with feathers, or voluminous beards and wavering veils; homeless heroes and great ladies acting out their tormented drama in an obscure nook of the world. What Popple recorded with eloquent precision was of nature, however, and had nothing to do with fantastic human projections: 'A small flower, yellow as intense as the buttercup's, with a golden flush, as if seen through lightly caramelized sugar; veined petals, loose as goldfish tails, styles free and rising about half the length of the interior stamens above the disc, finger-nail olivegreen leaflets, a miniature, a dwarf, in flower today, the ninth day of September, *anno domini* 1652, which according to my observations must be the spring season in this place.'

From his records of the days, month after month, temperatures and climatic changes, and the behaviour of plants, his own and the native ones, Popple had established a more or less inverse correlation to the seasons of home; a phenomenon widely noted below the line. On this reckoning the little rose flower bloomed not unseasonally, but a little late, as if clinging to an original schedule yet holding back out of response to local conditions. Or was it not the first flowering? The remarks of the old Chinese indicated nothing noteworthy, in his eyes, about a rose bloom. When one died, another appeared, behaviour quite contrary to that of the European rose –

Popple scratched his head.

Ros, asleep, tossed from front to back, emitting a small moan. Her discomforts stabbed at the father in him. The bed, a mat on the floor, was too low and hard. Without waking she groaned again, her hands unconsciously reaching for her stomach. A dream, perhaps, that perplexed her, disturbing sleep.

Laying down his quill, Popple went to her. Her mouth was clamped shut. When he placed his palm on her moist forehead, she opened her eyes with a start, a flash of terror seeming to roll inwards before she recognized her father and smiled. Her hand came up from her belly and pushed away the pressure of him.

'I have a pain.'

'Our diet takes its toll. No one knows how we suffer.'

'Don't worry, Father,' she said, reaching now for his hand to kiss it. 'It's only a condition. It will pass.'

'Sleep.'

In the morning she placed pretty beach shells along the window ledge. She asked her father when they would visit the Chinese camp again, or whether it was their turn to extend hospitality.

Popple sighed: 'What fine hospitality can we give, we who have made austerity and abstinence our sustenance!'

Ros's face was puffed up, her eyes pale and swollen. After she had talked to her father, she lay down on the bed. She had little strength to prepare the meal, no lust to consume the weak gruel of bird-bones and wild leaves. The light off the sea stabbed her brain.

'I'm sorry, Father,' she said, 'I need to sleep.'

And she lay down on the ground.

There were two methods for crossing the Chinese rose: to graft or to cross-pollinate. The former was a method of propagation. By implanting a bud from the Chinese specimen in the wood of his stock, he would grow it as his own, gradually absorbing characteristics of the host in a process of acclimatizing by adaptation that would take several generations. The latter was an act of proxy intercourse performed by the gardener go-between, the ripe pollen of one brushed on the sticky stigma of the other, Nature entreated to do her irresistible work of seeding and fruiting in a process of creation that could be repeated time and again to produce the unknown, disappointment and miracle tumbling together in the garden of possibilities.

For both experimental methods, healthy understock must be prepared and Popple embarked on a systematic programme, kneeling on the ground to clip, dig and root. He needed ten distinct, vigorously growing plants of each variety ready to be budded at the time he identified as early summer on the island.

'It's the female's curse,' Rosamund murmured wanly to her father when he returned to find her pain continuing.

It had never affected her as severely before.

'Can I rub you?' he asked.

She turned her head to the wall.

He prepared a pan of heated water, wrapped in a cloth, which she could rest on her vitals to ease her pain a little.

'You must go to the Chinese again, Father,' she instructed. 'Do not arouse their anger by standing apart.'

He was grieved that she should crave their presence. The desire for human contact, if a natural instinct, was paradoxical, since encounters with other people led invariably to discord. The perfection of Popple's dream was that he should be quite alone on the island with his darling daughter. The faith in such completeness had all but stilled his other ravening lusts and motions, the vaporous products of unacknowledged despair, perhaps. Replete emotionally with Rosamund as the only partner in his world, he the only partner in hers, he wanted now for nothing, for ever. To be with her, and no one else, on this benign island, where no beasts preyed, was the realization of a dream which would be crowned in time with the discovery of the power that comes from perfect harmony, the alchemy of nature's rarest creativity, the key to the orb.

Ros turned to her father, her eyes red from silent tears. 'I'm going to burst if the blood doesn't flow. My brain will split asunder.'

'How can I help?'

'Those strangers on the other side of the island.'

'They won't understand. I saw not one woman among them.'

'Ah!' groaned Ros. The baby face of the young man with diminutive features lolling bonelessly in the hammock, what was wrong with him? His eyes fired with such amusement when he looked at her, she had nearly wet herself. 'Father –' she grabbed Edward's hand. 'Invite them here!'

'We must not seem too hasty, my darling. We know nothing of their intentions, their plots and factions, the desperation that has impelled them to this place. We cannot count on their honesty, or their integrity, and not at all on their Christian mercy.'

He could offer her no help. The menstruation had no use where they found themselves. She must endure alone and prevail without the companionship of women. He pitied her, but was stern.

'Unless it suits them,' she qualified. Her body was painfully distended.

Night came, and she did not eat. Popple partook modestly and sat again by the lamp to inscribe his words of power, drawing them from memory, from his studies, from earlier theories and formulations. His texts were classical and modern, the natural philosophers, occidental and oriental, modified by his new understanding that the solution lay in matter. The task was to combine the elements in an exactly proportioned and immutable state. He paused when his mind could remember no more, and untied his purse to take out the carving of green jadestone from which grew inseparably the black rose, like a birthmark. Should he show that to the old man? He wrapped his palm round the warm object, swallowing it completely.

The moon in the night sky was half revealed, a semicircle of pearl lustre, and half hidden in a consummate illusion. In a sky crowded with stars and stained with rags of cloud the moon bodied herself only partially, exquisite, outlandish, piteous, the greater reality of her roundness concealed as she rode, an idea only. Blanketed, unobserved, Ros looked to her as a friend, sharing pain and loneliness, in her changeability and her deep secrecy. She piled the moon with her desires. She wished that the moon might pull the stoppered blood from her body and start the flow again, even as in the small hours of the night the neap tide uncoiled on the sand.

But in the morning there was no alteration and the coagulation of her vital essences turned her to stone. Ros's head pounded, her cramps like twisting knives.

'I shall die of this, Father.'

Popple was scared. 'If only we had some medicines.' His face was long, his eyes sunken from sleeplessness.

'I can't help crying. Give me water before I dry out.'

'What makes you cry? Tell me. What is it?'

'I cry for nothing, for no reason. For sadness, for birth and loss. I cry so that my salt water will flow with the currents of the sea.'

'You're raving, child.'

She smiled. 'Leave me, dear Father. Ignore me. I will change with each day. I only wait to become part of my body's change. Ah!'

Popple felt removed from the suffering girl in her helplessness. A deep voice rolled from his chest. 'And my body,' he stated, 'cannot participate in the processes of change.'

Frightened by admission of his failings, he turned away, burying his head in his shoulder.

Edward Popple wore no shoes and the grass sprang beneath his bare soles, tartness on the air as he walked down the slope from the dwelling towards the shore. The beach, washed of footprints by the tide, carried random messages as the daily post – roots, plants, cuttlefish and bird corpses. Removed so far in space, they were removed from existence also, where no language made sense entirely. The principles of understanding referred directly to the world around them, no philosophy explained, and yet, he insisted on attempting such connections to produce the meanings which could ultimately be taken home and laid before the Society of Fellows, at the feet of England. Was he losing his reason? How could he even tell? Was his poor girl going mad? Was he condemning Rosamund to that? The woman, and he the man who kept her as his princess to intensify her female power. Must he become as husband to her, taking that risk, to bring into being the life that otherwise would turn inwards? Her blocked, swollen condition a form of hysterical pregnancy, demanding the real thing which he alone could provide, breeding his seed on his own seed.

The crisp sea into which he waded to splash his face chastened him. He must put aside such obscene analysis. But his anguish at her distress could lead him to anything – even to abandon the island, if there were means.

He stood calf-deep in lapping sea, the ropes of his black mane bedraggling his dirty collar, his beard dripping, his bushy eyebrows lowering over the haggard eyes, his frayed sleeves unrolling over his wrists and large hanging hands. A lunatic visionary, stranded in the diaphanous light of a gentle morning.

So Lord Lou saw him when the skiff, poled by Jia the boatman, rounded the rocks of the headland, Old Lou as still and hunched as a stained ivory carving, all knobs and striations, floating over the smooth surface to land. He raised a hand in acknowledgement of the foreigner – who was fishing, using bare toes to gouge cockles from the sand.

'Hall-oo!' called Popple, glad of the disruptive splashing as he waded across.

Lord Lou bowed with customary grace, revealing no reason for his call. With a muddled air of hospitality, Popple led Lou Lu and the boatman towards the hut.

The girl called out, and the urgency of her voice caused Lou Lu, uninvited, to look in to her. Her head lifted from the bed to smile at him. He collapsed beside her, speaking agitatedly in his high wavering tone. For several minutes his fingers read her pulse. She stuck out her tongue: scarlet, covered with brown-green moss. He looked closely into her eyes and sniffed her skin.

When he rose, he gave a command to the boatman, who ran to the boat and set off by himself. Only then did Lord Lou accept the boiled water Popple had prepared for him.

He squatted on the floor and in his gelded voice, disgusting to Popple even as it compelled attention, the old man began again to explain the purpose of their voyage, for they were far off course. Their emperor had taken his own life, besieged by enemies and traitors. Usurpers held the throne, brutalized the country with their new order. A few loyalists, confident in the cause of the emperor's true heir, fled southward and rallied their forces. Perhaps the movement to regain the throne was gathering. A band of faithful, under the guidance of Lord Lou, the emperor's erstwhile advisor, was making the journey to Europe to convey the true state of affairs in the Bright Empire, to rally barbarian support in exchange for promised favours from the restored emperor.

Lou Lu was heartened as he explained to Popple their predicament. There was no sign that he would give up, or ever admit defeat. He entreated the support of Popple, a European whom he took to be equally marooned on the nameless island. Such were the deductions of the wise Chinese, the telling of the story his decisive act.

Popple had difficulty following as each intricate stage was summarized. The account was all-too-familiar, the effort to bring about renewal, loyalty to a losing cause, exile; it paralleled Popple's own circumstances. The chief difference lay in the nature of Popple's support for the redeeming order. His king was a symbol who might be given substance by the specimens and discoveries their journey would bring back. They had not killed the king, but only a man, on the instant of whose death a king of another form came to power. For Popple it was from the abundance of the infinite spring of the world that the true ruler must arise. The Chinese mission was tactical, a journey designed to intimidate the false ruler and reinforce the true by bringing to bear the supposed weight of an outside world. A counter in the game of history played out within courts in exile and palaces at home.

He nodded with deepening comprehension. It was the purpose of the old man's story to seek Popple's help as middleman with Europe.

'What do you imagine I can do?'

A smile glimmered across Lord Lou's mouth. 'We cannot go by ourselves to Rome. We need a guide. An introduction. We need a person to explain us to them and them to us. We ask you to join us.'

It could not be so simple.

'To return to Europe,' stammered Popple, 'when we have taken such lengths and such risks to leave Europe behind. You ask us to join you.' The dumbfounding proposal part honoured, part offended Popple. 'If we take you to Europe we will not seem to belong to your party. The inevitable interpretation, rather, is that you will belong to us. You will be our captives, our display, and none will heed your cause other than as an amusement.'

Lou Lu's careful, equitable mien was ruffled by violations of order, the greatest of which was the thought that he and his people should not be afforded their rightful supremacy. The mere thought. He sniffed in anger. How could anyone who compared their dignity with the two bedraggled bignoses consider for a moment that the Chinese were subordinates? Tribute enough for the Europeans to be invited to join the Chinese party, a magnanimous alliance in itself for the attention of foreign kings and popes.

The highest dignity of the Chinese mission, the young emperor of Ming, Taizao, Prince of Yong, Lou Lu concealed of course. That identity could not be let known to Popple. Whoever was called on to assist the mission, hierarchy must be preserved. If the foreign pair favoured the Chinese with their help, it was the Chinese who had shown greater favour in asking for their friendship. So knotty perplexities of etiquette, the more stubborn for being as habitual as breathing, braked the dialogue between the two men.

It was afternoon when boatman Jia returned with the physician, a short lean man with a head as round and shiny as a dried red date. With scarcely a reference to Popple, Lord Lou led the man to Ros's bed where the basic examination of tongue, pulse, eyes and smell confirmed the diagnosis.

'How old is the girl?' was the only question, interpreted by Lou Lu.

Popple answered: 'Fifteen now.'

The physician took a cloth packet from his coat, opened it and extracted a length of fine silvery wire. He twiddled the braided top between his fingers. Ros's eyes widened as the long needle approached her, the physician's face set in thoughtful calm.

Popple asked for an explanation and was ignored. He grabbed the arm that held the needle and yanked it back. The physician scowled.

'It will not hurt her,' explained Lou Lu.

'What weird science is this!' exclaimed Popple in his own language.

Ros held her father's gaze. 'Let them,' she said.

The physician reached for her right foot under the coverings and worked up until he found a point on her lower calf. With the needle held like a pen between his fingers, he inserted the fine point into the flesh. There was the merest prick, then a sensation of spreading pain that made Ros's eyes become white moons. Twiddling, the physician sunk the needle deeper. Popple sucked in his breath in unrestrained horror at the operation. Half the needle's length was in Ros's calf.

Then with shorter needles from the pack the operation was repeated on the tender area of webbing between thumb and forefinger of both hands.

'Rest,' said the physician.

'Rest,' translated Old Lou.

'Rest,' said Popple comfortingly. The needle stuck out of the calf, wavering. Ros lay passive. Popple took out his watch. They sat back and waited. It was five minutes.

Popple's watch was chained to his trousers. Lord Lou reached out his hand and took the device, weighed it in his palm, chuckled at the turning hands and returned it with cheerful reluctance. On the face of the dial he drew a circle to indicate that the girl must wait until morning before any change could be expected.

Old Lou was carried to the boat in the boatman's arms. The physician waded, clumsily hopped aboard. With a shove and kick, the boatman set the craft in motion. Day was closing. Popple waved in silence, then returned to the vigil at his daughter's side.

She breathed with greater ease, the swelling around her groin easing. She no longer had the impulse to cry. Popple took her hand from time to time, talking erratically of home, of the family abandoned, Delia and Henry, wife and son, mother and brother.

'We are set afloat from them now,' murmured Ros.

Then Popple, fitfully nodding, wakefully fretting, almost toppled to sleep.

Ros lay in solitude, in darkness. The half-moon, a little leaner amidst the freckling of stars, drew her gaze. She was no friend, but a cheating companion who gave lonely distance for love. The moon who should remind of home, the same moon as at home, the same focus of wonder and longing. Yet there was no proof, no substance to the notion that she was the same one, or if she was the same, unattached, uncommitting, night after night, month after month, for centuries, what a banal thing she was. Unworthy of worship, thought Ros, compelled despite herself by the half-rounded form and her ungainly dominance of the sky.

As she listened to the water's regular fall, she became more comfortable, attuned to the night's pulses of sound and movement. And she felt the blood begin to flow between her legs, warm, wet, sticky, once again. She was eased. She got up from the smelly bed and walked out to the night. She splashed herself with fresh water from the barrel, a cold clean stinging. The pain had gone. With suppleness and fluidity, she prepared her cloths. Released. She surprised her father when he awakened. Wellbeing returned by the fibre-thin Chinese needles.

The physician was complacent about his success and Lord Lou modestly accepted Popple's thanks. Popple was impressed by the efficacious wisdom of the old Chinese and wondered, after all, about joining forces with him to travel in triumph to Europe. But the rose-breeding remained. He needed Lou Lu's help, and, trusting sufficiently, asked the old man whether, as a kind of thanks, he might share with him his secret.

A bank of charcoal clouds capped with snow-white spume had appeared over the spine of the mountain. The Chinese physician indicated that it was a warning. The blue of their heavens was troubled for the first time; for the first time there were signs of turbulent change. Lou Lu and Popple, sharing the faith of savants, were excited by the prospect. In changing winds and changing conditions lay their hope.

They set off together, lingering to note curiosities, to debate the use or reason for strange formations of the island. Popple wanted Lou Lu's explanation for the absence of mammal life.

'It is an island without teeth,' argued Popple.

'Not so. Birds devour tiny frogs. Fish's teeth swallow flies. We eat everything.'

Popple laughed, baring his blackened teeth. 'Then we are needed here.'

From the peak they could see the roiling weather approach a sea of turquoise-green woof and slate-grey warp, like a dyed silk, that stretched without prospect of land to a veiled horizon. Then down they descended, the old man treading carefully, maintaining stamina, as Popple led and the physician followed.

The light was softer when they reached the basin where the roses grew, miraculously profuse in upright chest-high rows. The cloud canopy seemed to wrap the hidden garden and its gardeners as they walked in a complex pattern between the rose trees. Open pink faces shone in the greyness, and white, like powdered ladies or lost souls, and dense blood crimson, with golden inner furniture. Their fragrance sprayed on to the air, mixing and circling in a dome over the tilled earth, sweetly filling Old Lou's nostrils, causing his skin to soften and his eyes to light, the most exquisite, enchanting, intoxicating perfume.

'They are sisters to your plants,' explained Popple, 'or cousins. Transported from England and flourishing here for their brief flowering.'

'They will flower again.'

'Not for another year. Sir, I ask you. Please allow me to introduce these plants to your yellow dwarf, your eglantine.'

'You wish to breed?'

'To create a new crossing.'

Lord Lou beamed. The novelty of the proposal attracted

him. He liked the ingenuity of horticulture. 'It would be the first time.'

'I think so.'

Lou Lu chuckled. The resultant progeny would be a rare treasure. He thought of Empress Wu who ordered the flowers to bloom. All obeyed save the peony rose. This time roses would follow the imperial command too. It must be tried. It must be done. What better omen could there be for the cause, what better evidence of the superior being?

He clasped Popple's shoulders with shuddering intensity. 'Let us work together. Let us share this venture. I shall order our stock to be carried here. Are you content?'

'You have a large understanding. Thank you, sir.'

Loud and single, the first drops spattered the garden from the thickening clouds, slapping the faces of the roses, making leaves spring.

'Let us return,' said Lou Lu, tilting his head anxiously to the sky.

'Are we agreed then?'

'We are agreed.'

The physician opened a paper and bamboo umbrella over the old man's bare head.

'Excuse me,' the eunuch said, taking himself off a few paces between the roses, the umbrella following, where he squatted to the ground and pulled away his clothes. The trickling sound of the old man's relief was heard like a whistle through the drumming raindrops on the taut umbrella. Popple considered the old man's unusual posture. If he was a man. Or was he differently formed? A frown deepened across the bridge of Popple's nose. The strange act displaced the sense of agreement and identity he felt. Uncanny, what was common, what was different.

Drops fell with tense, painful slowness. 'I have only one

umbrella,' offered Lou Lu in his weird quavering voice. 'You take it.'

'No, you, old man.'

'You.'

'YOU!'

So age conceded its deserts, and Popple led the way up the far steep track through glossy batting foliage until they reached the Chinese settlement tucked against the rock ledge. The cloud darkened the boats, closing them as if they were sea-anemones responding to touch. The bamboo awnings and blinds were closed tightly as the rain began to lash. All was battened down.

Boatman Jia's return without Lord Lou had alarmed the Chinese camp and Captain Huang kept an anxious look-out. With a shout he ran to greet his master, solicitously ushering the exhausted old man to his cabin. He paid no attention to Popple, who was left outside. No one else would venture into the rising storm. There was no sign of human occupancy. No opening. All entrances were closed. Everything was stowed in craft that, to all appearances, had been deserted. Offered no shelter, Popple stood in the pounding rain cursing their forgetfulness, their negligence, their indifference, as if he were invisible. No one showed the slightest concern for him as he faced the troubled crow-black sea.

So he found his way to the nursery where the plant specimens were kept, and with his knife cleanly sliced off the buds of the miniature yellow rose. Carefully he wrapped the buds in his handkerchief and nestled them inside his shirt, spiking and tender against his skin.

He was gone quickly in the virtual darkness and spasmodic rain, until stumbling and exhausted he reached his rose garden again. Barely able to see what he was doing, he found among the flush of blooms, lifted in the rain, his prize specimen, the blood-dark damask. The buds were not yet open that would receive, when it ripened, the pollen of the faraway species he had seized. The buds were the elect, to which he took his knife, slitting the petals, removing the stamens, preserving the pistils. He removed his shirt and ripped the sleeves into pouches to wrap around the buds he prepared. Their vulnerability must not be exposed to self-pollination. Rain, insects and wind would bring the pollen of their own kind that they desired. But they must await the stranger. The more remote the habitat of species intended to hybridize, the more difficult the receiving plant finds it to take the foreign pollen, the more powerfully operates a resistant affinity for its own kind. They must be entirely isolated. Styles, pistils, pericarps, ovaries. He tied a damp rag around each bud from which he had cut out the stamens. Each was encased in a torn part of his shirtsleeves, giving an impression of segments of amputated limbs growing from the bushes.

The Chinese rose was to be the male parent, providing the colour.

Back at the hut, Popple pulled the petals from the buds in his handkerchief and observed the stamens, covered with bright yellow pollen. Gazing through his magnifying glass he swept the anthers with a camel's hair brush to gather the unripe pollen. He turned the brush's head in the dry cavity of a solitaire bird's feather to remove the pollen, then stoppered the feather tight. There inside, the fine particles of dust would slowly ripen to gold.

From the sprays in the rose garden he prepared additional buds for pollination when the rain stopped. Daily he checked the stigmas of the covered heads as the flowers became blown and stickiness appeared, showing they were ready to accept the pollen. As the season of cyclonic disturbance eased, clouds and damp were expelled, and the genial warmth of the island returned for stretches of days to charge the atmosphere tenderly. The balmy air was almost elastic, and on the day the pistils of the seed-bearing English roses in the garden were ready with a viscous exudation in the sutures of their stigmas, all nature felt instinct with joyous life. The reserved pollen was powdery yellow gold, Popple noted with pleasure through his magnifying glass. Calmly, with the most delicate touch, he applied the pollinating brush to the stigmas, then sealed each flower in a muslin bag. Twice more in the course of the day he repeated the operation. The conditions of the world, warm and sunny, electric with the attraction among all natural kinds, wanted the hybridization. The circumstances were as perfect as the two rose strains were remote, the higher affinity of perfection reversing the desire for like. Tiny grains glued to the pistils, which Popple cupped in his hands, willing the fructification with all his philosopher's power. He would not leave the garden. In the globe of nurturing warmth created by his hollow palms the mystery worked.

IX

An occasion for ceremony conferred a sense of purpose, called out puffing-up, as the Chinese prepared for Lord Lou's visit to the garden. Three men were sent to clear the path and, when it was decided that the old man could not walk, the best litter was repaired and bearers nominated. The silk robe of rank, serpent-coloured damask, was unfolded for Lord Lou, and its wide black lapels spread around his skinny neck. The ranking hat with pert ears was unwrapped and placed on his head, and the lordly boots of soft leather slipped over his old feet. Only his badge of rank, the embroidered crane, was missing, left behind when he fled the palace so many years before. He swore never to wear a replacement until he returned to his position behind the screens of the imperial throne.

The litter jolted up and down the path, whipped and slapped by strange fronds. Old Lou forgot that he was not going to a court audience. As he nodded, fancies ran in his brain. He was being carried in state, with people craning to see him or bowing, never low enough, to honour him whom they feared. Lord Lou Lu, old cockerel, spoutless teapot, the one among the many whose reward of power outbalanced the purchase price of his nobility . . . He was being carried, in his father's arms, a boy of ten, to the low mud house of the knifers by the canal, where for generations outside the palace walls the knifer's family had prepared young cockerels for the game, lifting washing water from the canal into which the bloodsoaked bandages were thrown. He was being settled on to a low bed, his legs split apart, tourniquets round his thighs, his waist pinioned by a man's arm, strong as a hoop of iron, and spicy pepper tea dousing his little precious, and a nerve-numbing potion poured down his throat. With a small curving blade the knifer sliced off the parts sheer to the pelvis. He had screamed. The hole was plugged with a brass stopper and he was bandaged, candidate for high office. For three days, reeling and weak from pain, in an agony of thirst and denied all liquid, he was helped around the room by the knifer's assistants, forced to walk on his own legs. From that time on he had held his thighs together when he walked. After three days he was unbandaged and the plug removed. Would he flow? If his urinary passage was blocked by tissue growth, he would die of self-poisoning, like the boy before him, who was carried out on a hand-cart in case his extreme groans put off the other candidates. It was the deciding moment. The urine trickled, and gushed. The knifer gave his congratulations, satisfied to be an agent of fortune, and pronounced the child thoroughly sexless, thoroughly pure. The boy's little precious was pickled for presentation in a crystal vessel. At the time of death Lou Lu and the tiny organs would be reunited in the coffin, to present him as a whole man to the gods, who might otherwise reincarnate him as a she-mule. The precious was all Lord Lou had saved of his personal things when he fled the palace, the precious and young prince Taizao, whom he carried in his arms . . .

The litter came to a halt and he heard the bearers debating whether they had reached the right place. There was an absence of ceremony about the arrival that worried them. A dark, hairy man in grubby woollen clothes, torn and worn, stepped forward over the turned earth like a farmer across his land, slow, unenthusiastic, drawn from his work by the irksome distractions of curiosity, politeness and aggression. He stopped by the set-down litter and watched with amusement as the bearers helped the frail old figure in sumptuous robes from that unsatisfying contraption. At last, after puffing and patting and adjusting, Lord Lou erected himself and bowed to Edward Popple with their now customary greeting.

'Old friend!'

The Chinese's eyes, quartzy grey, not black, twinkled into Popple's heart. They were truly kin, each ennobled and rendered shy by the peculiar coincidence of their lives in the gentle centre of a remote and unknown place. But the twinkle turned to hard deflecting glitter as Popple, behaving as a host receiving guests on his property, added an expansive gesture of his arm towards the fenced garden. The litter had stopped outside the gate in the fence, and as Popple prepared to usher Old Lou inside, a commotion broke out. A second group of men came pounding down the slope. Popple looked up in perturbation. More people, and another litter. He could defend nothing if the enthusiastic numbers of the Chinese challenged his claims to ownership. A second litter came to a halt behind the first, but no hand reached out from inside. The bearers, slighter figures than the sturdy, supple men who had borne Lord Lou, calmly opened the door and exposed the flowering rose-plant, a dwarf bush in an earthenware pot bearing a few yellow flowers – and bees buzzing devotedly among them.

Popple smiled with emotion as the pot was carried towards him by the two bearers. He ushered them forward to place the rose-plant among its larger flowering fellows from the other side of the world.

'Thank you!' he exclaimed, clasping the old man's hands.

Old Lou nodded and trailed his sashed robes through the gate.

The yellow rose was diminished on the ground. The bees that had arrived with it made wider orbits in the mild air and gradually departed, perhaps to find the larger roses, attracted by their more marked scent if not their muted colours. Buzzing and dipping they would carry the eglantine pollen promiscuously to other plants. The bees could not be relied on, nor the flies, wasps and butterflies that came around. To engineer the desired encounter required human fingers.

Lou Lu wondered why Popple was mute and unceremonious, his rough hands stained with dirt and sap. The old man had not conceived that they would do the work themselves. The technique, as a practice, was for artisans. It was in the theorizing, the decorum and the prescription that he and Popple had their roles and their duty. Lou Lu's skinny fingers were less adept than his mind. He had imagined somehow that Popple's partner, the girl, would do the work. Why was she not in the welcoming party?

Sunlight filtered through dancing leaves and bounced among the rose bushes. The fragrance reaching the old man's nostrils fascinated him: so delicate, so elusive, so purely invigorating. There was not this scent in China, lighter than the drugging power of sweet osmanthus, the hyacinth or the ginger flower.

The visitors talked loudly, laughed and grimaced. 'Ha! Heh! Yoh! Ai-yah!' They strutted about, tramping voraciously over the novelty of the place. Ros hung back out of sight, hoping they would not discover her. She had no feeling for flowers, or for botanical specimens. She found their way of life too riddling, rooted yet effete. Plants were insubstantial, things of air and water, colour and light. She was *animal* and preferred beings that could move of their own accord, zoological creatures that she admired not as carnivores but for their power of energy and their motor capacity, their engines that burnt sustenance to create heat, action and change. She found herbivores the most compelling. By eating grass and seeds to be able to fly, to dive, to climb, to leave warm footprints and steaming traces, to drop offspring that satisfied their needs by sucking a mother's body. Such transformations thrilled Ros. To feel Nelly munch damp grass then race like a burning chariot down the corridor of trees at Brougham House ... But preferring beasts to plants, she did not include men, not even the visitors. She suspected their eyes. She wanted to barber them decently. Their lumpy earlobes and flat noses she found unpleasant, and how she disliked their loping and wriggly gait, their bulging clothes, their grinning joy.

Birds were chief among the island's creatures, and of birds, the solitaire stood out as the main actor, until the human beings came along who had caught and cooked it from the first day, not realizing its lonely status. One of the clumsy solitaire birds came pecking over the ground towards the edge of the garden where Ros lingered. She dived to catch it. The useless wings flapped. Their bullet-like tips pummelled her. She gripped the plump breast and, stroking the long neck, quietened it with a sweet rose-hip from her fingers. She cooed in the sun, hidden from the visitors as they prowled the garden on their investigation.

Surrounded by hills and crags on all sides, the garden was in a bowl, yet not a sink. The spot where Popple established his plantation was a rising mound of richest earth that made a convex shape within the concave, a swelling within a declivity, a sun within the moon. The spiky bushes were luxuriant hair on the mound, exuding moist odour, while sunlight shafted and gardeners fingered the flowers. Lou Lu observed the harmonious confluence of elements and forces, conducive to generation and gold below the black earth.

Popple introduced each bush by its Latin name, adding the common English for the pleasure of its poetry on the tongue. The Summer Damask, the Holy Rose, the Rose of Alexandria, the Phoenician Rose, the Striped Provence, the White Moss, the Apothecary's Rose, the Rose of Lancaster, the Rose of York, the Rose of the World.

Old Lou, recoiling from things incomprehensible – not words, sounds only – smirked at the man's enthusiasm. The growth provided good breeding stock. The plants would reveal transformations occurring underneath.

'The greatest rose is yet to come. Its existence lies with us, here in this place.'

Lord Lou chuckled.

The bearers of the rose carried it, on Lord Lou's instructions, around the receiving plants. Popple held open the English rose while the yellow blooms were shaken, brushed, or thrust against the other flowers to release pollen. It was a crude, casual process, the results entirely unpredictable. There might be no success at all; a mismatch.

Unlike Popple's careful secret cross-fecundation.

Ros bowed to Lord Lou, Captain Huang and the physician, when her father brought them over, but did not participate. She continued to pet the solitaire bird distractedly. Her sultry behaviour irritated Popple, detracting from the triumph of the day. It was necessary to share with the strange people, as Ros herself had taught him. But on this occasion she resisted his will, of which she was part, and thereby sapped his power.

When the work was finished, the Chinese retreated as

they had come, in state, promising to return the next day with another of their plants.

Lord Lou's eyelids drooped, his head nodded, on the return journey. Exertion, heat and interaction, the immediate things, exhausted and emptied him. His mind resorted to his grander dreams, arching across time and space, the Ming, like a mighty rainbow over the restless waters of the ocean, and he was replenished.

★   ★   ★

In the evening, in their hut, Popple asked Ros what was the matter.

She turned to him blankly, sourly, her cheeks curdled, her thick locks like a straw helmet. Her green eyes stared a little tearily. She was forbidden the words that might convey her feeling.

'We are one', he went on, 'we are engaged together in this enterprise. You regard it as trifling perhaps, a piece of gardening, the obscure speculative exercise of a natural philosopher. I remind you of our high purpose to unlock a deeper power, over nature, over the creation of kinds. It is alchemy, the skill for which the quest has been the drive of history. The calling and the reward could not be higher. It depends on us both, as sole partners, the male energy, the virgin purity —'

She began to laugh. 'You are out of your mind, Father. I have no part in this.'

'You are my daughter.'

'To take care of you, as your companion. But —'

'What?'

'Your gaze is always on me, dark and prying. You imprison me.'

'Few are as free as you. You roam the island like a bird. Only I hold you within the vessel of purity, turning my own burning energy into a casing to protect you. That way I distil both our vital essences.'

'Ignore me, Father, forget about me. To bend me to your purposes, even in your mind, will prevent creation.'

'You are necessary. You, the other partner, are the secret.'

'You have others already – the Chinese.'

'They only further my plan.'

'As do I. Father, be generous. Trust. You are like a jealous monster the way you watch me.'

Popple roared. 'Do not speak in this manner. Purify and discipline yourself, as I have refined the fires that burn in me, and we shall hold in our hands the power of all the world.'

His brow was scarred with thundering lines, long gashes of determination, and his lips drew tight and bloodless, his eyes flaring as he grabbed Ros's shoulders.

'You shall serve the purpose!'

She dropped her head with a sob, her mass of hair falling like a mop, her flesh slumped, fingers kneading chafed fingers in her lap.

'Dear Father, we may not quarrel. We are two alone here. Come, drink your soup.'

She put her arms around him, pressed her spreading breasts against his hard chest and smothered his fierce face with her dirty hair. He was gasping, half-suffocated, until she let him go. And he was pacified.

The wind rattled the leaves and tweaked the sea, turning the regular lullaby to a discontented roar. Always at night Ros felt how far they were adrift, how final their state, the island a shell floating in air and water, the immense undifferentiated constituents of reality. In that mood she craved shelter and a solid place, something more than the bare borrowed huts she shared with her father, and something different from her father's possessive presence. In sleep she would recoil from him. He, contrariwise, was calm as she slept, knowing that arrangements were as he wanted. He was unaware of the submarine currents struggling in her. He was unaware how his strict possession of her risked thwarting his own aim. The secret of alchemy, if he had forgotten, was release.

The wind climbed into a gale, beating the sea in rage. The waves crashed on the grassy knoll, trees and shrubs bent for mercy. The basin where the roses grew was tossed and drenched, but the delicate flowers were resilient.

Popple sheltered under a tree as he waited for the Chinese to keep their appointment. But no one came.

By afternoon the storm had passed, leaving wreckage over the beach. The greasy mercury pillows of the sea rolled and the spumy sky turned orange-pink in the distance where the horizon thinned to its usual steady line. Ros felt brightened, light as a feather after the tunnel of darkness through which she had passed. At the end of the beach she noticed a boat knocking among the rocks. She ran over to see what the storm had thrown up. It was the longboat, half submerged. Water lapped over the gunwales, sinking the hull, and the timbers were soaked and napped, like worn velvet. There was a man lying across the ribs, a carcase propped between the two benches, torso and head, with strips of decomposing flesh torn from it. Flaps of skin peeled back to expose striations of pink-grey tissue, and bones that shone in white knobs. The eye sockets were empty, eyes pecked out. The work of sea, sharks, vultures – or fellow men? Or the storm itself? The hair still sat on the head, parted, the moustache still sat above a lip shrivelled to reveal fine teeth.

Ros shuddered. Her knees went weak and she retched

on to the sand, clasping her stomach as she spewed, fallen into a posture of prayer.

The carcase was Solomon Truro, or his remains.

She dragged the craft ashore until the keel wedged against shingle. The torso had no arms or legs. The bones of the limbs, wrapped in strips of torn flesh, lay in the other half of the boat.

She sat on the beach, not knowing what rite or duty she should perform. Rather than running away, to seek her own survival, she kept watch, with aching head, in a vigil of mourning and commemoration, until Popple found her sitting there when he returned. He examined the death boat washed up on their shore, the shore of the dead man's realm. The limbs, arms and legs, had been hacked off with a cleaver, and flesh stripped from the bones. The technique was quite different from the mess of pitting and decay on the rest of the corpse. Human beings had butchered him and eaten him. Birds, weather, nature had done the rest, returning him at last to the island of which he proclaimed himself king. And if the little boat returned thus, the larger ship, the *Cedar*, would never come back. Leary, Vost and Cramphorn had starved, had mutinied, had disposed of their mad mate-captain and master, not without taking advantage of the only good he offered, as meat. If they could sail their ship, the three of them, they would make for settled land. If not, they would become, in the end, another hollow ghost ship to drift towards the Great South Land until she became a dream, or was swallowed down Neptune's throat. The *Cedar* would never return for Popple and Ros.

But why waste the longboat on a corpse? Replete on Solomon Truro's flesh, had the sailors been impelled by remorse to a ritual of atonement and given the mate burial in a floating hearse that might carry his hacked pieces together for the Day of Resurrection? Why not fling his bits overboard to the sharks? Truro was bound for hell anyway. When there was no fresh meat out at sea, the sailors hung offal bags from their ship to attract hammerheads, which circled so close in their frenzy they could be clubbed to death. But Leary had never liked the business. He never liked sharks. Perhaps the longboat wafting with the remains was intended as a decoy. The sharks would follow Truro as far as he went, drawing evil away from the *Cedar* so that she would sail free of shame with auspicious winds. It was Solomon Truro's sacrifice for his ship. Perhaps that was the explanation.

Popple and Ros dug a shallow grave in the sand. Repelled and nauseated, they tried to confer some dignity, remembering all the while the old villainous Truro, as they took the bits to the pit, dripping, dropping, stinking of fish. The king was covered. Farewell! Long live the king!

The bier his craft they upended, drained and lugged up the sand for repair. Their paltry hope of getaway might eventually rest on the unseaworthy longboat. Yet only a fool would set out to sea in it.

Old Lou was not displeased when the storm delayed things. He was puzzled by the foreigner's fervour. The man had no sense of grace or playful refinement. Old Lou knew that nothing was intrinsically of value except as men placed esteem, and the masters in the foreigner's home country clearly placed the highest value on the results of Popple's work. Yet he wondered how far Popple's commitment aligned with Chinese aims.

Taizao rocked ever so slowly in his hammock as the wind buffeted outside. The disturbed sea caused the raft of boats to groan and strain. A line of hair broke along his upper lip, spots and blotches darkened his nose and chin.

His face was grey and lustreless. His gaze seemed blurred. Apart from his morning exercises on the rock overlooking the sea, Taizao seldom left the cabin. Today, with the storm, there had been no exercise.

Lou Lu had grown despondent about Taizao's lack of interest in activity. Was the boy ill? The cultivation of fine specimens had been a passion with him in the past, in Zayton. If he were not to be aroused by the enterprise in which Old Lou engaged with the foreigners, then nothing would excite his interest. He languished, less from physical affliction, the commissioner worried, than a more terrifying debilitation of spirit.

Lou Lu reported in a matter-of-fact way that they had carried the first eglantine rose to a garden in the centre of the island where the foreigner brushed its pollen on to his plants.

'It may be that a new rose is created,' said the old man. 'If that is the case, the ground will have showed its special properties, perhaps gold, perhaps a sign of imperial status. We do not waste our time. Our activities, which you seem to disregard, contribute to our purposes, our victory.'

'Does the foreign man understand roses?' asked Taizao with a sneer.

'He approaches them like a fanatic.'

Taizao grinned coldly.

'He would benefit from your assistance,' continued the eunuch.

'Leave him be. I should only upset his system. Let him stumble along, and maybe he will achieve something. Why should I interfere? I am no expert.'

'You have knowledge. A gift. Why not give it? It's too important to be left to him. If we can breed the rare plant, it betokens the nugget of gold, which betokens your imperial right. Funds your empire. Your Highness, I feel your absence.'

Taizao looked forlornly at the old commissioner who alone understood.

'As I serve you, so the world of the four seas serves you,' added Lord Lou, to flatter.

To bring the adored prince to the throne was to instil harmony through the length and breadth of the empire. The old man's deprivations, his unending exertions, had no other reason. Without Taizao's claim, Lou Lu was truly a teapot without a spout. Every breath, every mouthful, every step, every pause, every squatting-down of a long life, had been given for the Ming, the Brightness. Losing his control, he shouted at the boy that he must perform his role or the journey was meaningless. If the young man, the Prince of Yong, failed the test, Lou Lu would be incensed by ingratitude and appalled by unrightness.

Taizao gave a supercilious grin. 'You make too much of this gardening. It is an excursion, decked in all finery, little more.'

'You have it in your power to lend solemnity and purpose.'

'Need I go in person?'

'To set an example,' Lou Lu snapped.

'Don't be angry, old man, if I lack the pulse of life.'

About the cabin, about Taizao's body, Lou Lu scented the odour of staleness. He noticed the little puppet theatre in a corner of the cabin and idly drew open the curtain. The painted heads stared at him lifelessly from their rack.

'Their colours have faded,' explained Taizao.

'You will be carried by chair,' offered Lou.

'Through the storm?'

'Not today! Are you completely lost in your dream? Turn your gaze outwards.'

'Outwards? What is there?'

'You are emperor. Out there is your command.'

Taizao sighed, with a high laugh.

'When the weather clears, sir, I advise you to go. Your Highness will grace our next expedition.'

'The old man takes his business more seriously than the foreigner. You miss the functions of court, poor old man. When nothing stimulates me, how can a rose garden stimulate me? I am unresponsive to impressions. I am inert. So leave me, dear Lou, to doze.'

Lou Lu, as if to confirm the prince's teasing, dropped to the floor in the lowest obeisance.

As the eunuch shuffled out, Taizao flexed his toes, watching them with bored astonishment. Down there his toes moved, up here his brain dictated and his eyes recorded. A closed conversation, meaningless except to him, and since he found it meaningless, it must be truly meaningless then. He bent a knee, cracked his knuckles, contracted his belly, and frowned. He lay back limply, vaguely swaying, indifferently breathing, meaningless.

On the fourth day after the weather cleared Old Lou arrived at the rose garden in the number two litter. The finer litter came after and brought Taizao. He stepped out, refusing help from the panting bearers, to begin his tour of the site. Having promised no formalities, Old Lou made no introduction, but Popple could see the different style of the supercilious young man, who looked less rugged than the other Chinese. Lou Lu's eye was kept sharply on him. The young man's attention was soon quickened by the characteristics and construction of particular roses, loose and monstrous on their huge pert bushes. Other Chinese bushes were deposited, for budding and grafting, including one that was the deep brown of soured red wine.

Like a general inspecting his troops, his eyes moving up and down with no intrusion from his hands, no untoward movement, Taizao registered the foreign rose-plants, and the Chinese, and could fancy in appreciative detail the products of their cross. He ignored courtesies to Popple, who stood like an artisan, and complimented Lou Lu.

'Conditions are favourable. The conjunction of elements, earth, air and water, is as perfect as can be. The roses shine like fire. Speed your work.'

'And what is beneath the ground?'

'Dig. Find out,' ordered the young man.

'Not yet,' cautioned Lou Lu. 'Not until our first experiments are completed.'

Taizao turned away. 'Anyway, I've seen enough.'

Ros sat on the grass in the sunshine nestling the tamed solitaire bird in her lap. She was oblivious of Taizao's presence. Her hair shone like floss in the sun and the tilt of her head hooked Taizao's vision from the side of his eyes. He dared not turn directly to her. Ros looked up at the young man. A chestnut brown silk robe was wrapped loosely around his slim form, the large black boots square on black soil, his black hair tied back from his face. The connection between them was wordless, the presence of each penetrating the other as if passing through the window of the eyes to snare heart and soul. She shuddered, pleased, as she stroked the quivering solitaire bird against her belly. Taizao walked straight, his nerves as taut as if he were walking a tightrope. The robe shimmered as he crossed in front of Popple, ignoring him, and the other Chinese, to fold himself up again inside the litter.

The litter was carried back over the hills – when he could easily have walked, thought the girl. Taizao had closed the door of his little cabin with satisfaction, however, wanting to be away from the place. He was incapable.

Unthinking, Ros released the solitaire bird from her

grip. It stirred and stepped away from her, then squawked across the ground and flapped over the fence into some bushes.

'Hey!' yelled the girl, and squeezed through the fence to chase the creature.

As she approached, the bird flapped its wings wildly, flopping from tree to tree.

Again as she pursued, the bird scurried to a tree higher up the slope, Ros panting as she scrambled after it.

The growth was thick as she crashed after the ridiculous bird, up to the crest, finally, where the blue sea on the far side of the island appeared; and down, unsure of her footing, all the way, calling sternly after the stupid wilful creature.

By the time she reached the bottom of the hill, the bird was altogether lost. She was in a grove, where the terrain flattened and the trees thinned; a tremor of anxiety passed through her; she was alone, without bearings. She squatted to the ground, pulling down her clothes to release the pressure on her bladder, warm liquid hissing to the ground. She looked up vacantly at the high sky, the scudding clouds, and heard muffled laughter between the trees. She looked sharply in the direction of the sound, and could distinguish nothing.

Having escaped his duty in the confining litter, Taizao was disgruntled when he got back to the camp. He had wanted to smash his way out of the box of formality and could not bear to go back to his cabin to rock tediously in his hammock. He huffed and sighed at the futility of his situation, the enervating nameless lack in him which he could do nothing about. He strolled, and strayed away from the camp, along the rocks, aimlessly, through the trees.

An aperture through thick tall trunks of palms afforded a vista of the foreign creature, the girl or her twin, transported to the other side of the mountain, with her freakish colourless hair, her weather-bleached skin, her rotundity. Fascinated he watched as she pulled her clothing down to her knees to reveal turnip-pink thighs, and the tawny shadow between them. He arched his back to see precisely. She bent her knees and sank her buttocks towards the ground, with more downward mass than Old Lou the eunuch would perform the same action, and Taizao grinned with spontaneous delight. His breath hastened and his blood began to run in faster rhythmic pulses. The orange stream ran in a steaming dart to the ground, and Taizao laughed, tickled with excitement, pressure, surging, swelling movement in himself, in the same place. Only not the same. He wanted to relieve himself, losing control over what was happening to him, seized by sensations as he watched, captivated by the golden trickle and the faint sizzling whisper. Grabbing himself with puzzlement, he choked with laughter, and she looked straight in his direction. He froze at once, prepared to deny his presence. But as she stared at him, alarmed, curious, inviting, he found himself slowly walking towards her through the dappled shadows of the trees, exposing himself to light and the fire of her gaze.

Her eyes flashed with humour, then sudden embarrassment as she adjusted herself and stood up, with motions of respect yet without any idea of what to say that he might understand. He stretched out his arms, his hands, his fingers, in her direction and continued his steady smiling advance. She stood her ground nervously and they faced each other off across the space, until she twitched her head back over her shoulder, a twist of the neck at once awkward and eloquent, to indicate that she had been *there* and was now *here*, and he likewise, and those who accompanied them and watched over them were still *there*, while he and she were alone, separated, *here*, and was it not peculiar?

He took her meaning and gave a sudden obscene grin, his eyes falling with delight to the puddle she had made. With a word from his language, he gestured that she should come with him to the settlement.

It was the only way she might find her bearings.

Rather than follow him, however, she strode in front, her head high in the air and bobbing from side to side. He guided her from behind with murmurs and signs, and soon they reached the rock ledge where she had secretly watched him exercise the first time she saw him.

The sailor on guard cried out as if the sea had thrown up a monster. Taizao called back that she was a friend, and the man relaxed before the youth's authority. Like a spy, Ros knew the way. With small, careful steps she led him across the pontoon of vessels and planks. She did not know him as the prince. She knew nothing about him, not even his name.

He ran breathlessly after her, less with purpose than a sense of imminence such as he had not experienced before. Another guard was slumbering on the deck by the door to Taizao's cabin and grumbled, dragging himself to his feet too late to salute his master. Taizao opened the bamboo curtain to admit the creature. She went in first, he followed, and threw himself into his hammock, pulling at his great black boots to free himself.

He indicated that she likewise should remove her worn leather shoes. Surprising herself, she did his bidding. It was a game. He began nervously to swing the hammock, watching her and making her feel embarrassed as he waited for her to do something to entertain him. She placed a finger against her chest and said:

'My name's Rosamund.'

She repeated the name, tapping herself, stabbing herself with the finger. 'Ros. Ros.'

He imitated the gesture and the sound. 'Luo-si.'

She laughed.

'Ros!'

Then turning tables she prodded her finger at *his* heart, like a spear. He flinched, his eyes enlarging, and tipped the hammock away. She had no idea how he took her sign. She was determined to have the question answered. She took her own face like a melon in her hands and repeated: 'Ros.'

Then she made a moon with her fingers and moved even closer to the young man's face as if to encircle his nose. His eyes slotted from side to side, his lips protruded. He called out, as if in last-minute defence.

'Taizao! Luo-si, Taizao!'

It was her turn to stumble over the sounds. 'Tuzza,' she tried. 'Tuzza!'

They laughed together, and he shouted something to be heard outside.

He indicated that she could sit on the tiny stool and, after shifting from side to side, considering the position, she clumsily deposited her weight. She was lower than he. He circled her three times, and at last touched the matted curls of her strawberry-blonde hair. She touched it herself where he had touched it, as if to free it from him and resettle it. She wanted to apologize for the dirty mess her hair had grown into. He hissed in amusement, then came closer to touch her eyebrow.

She ducked.

'Get away!'

His slender finger reached out to touch her high pink mushroom nose – and quickly she caught his finger between her teeth, not drawing blood, but holding firm, so he could not free himself without grazing or rupturing his skin. She played with the finger like a puppy with a bone. He gave a high childish moan of astonishment. When her bite released, he held his finger up to check for wounds. He was covered in her sparkling spittle.

Then the guard came in and set the tea things down on a folding table. Cups, chipped in the long voyage, with cracked lids, a clay pot with pumpkin sheen and the tantalizing fragrance of boiling water from the blackened kettle's spout sousing the pinch of cured leaves in the vessel.

Ros's throaty laugh had the quality of a snarl, with tones in her voice that were new to her. If he came near again, she would snap.

The guard left them and Taizao courteously poured the tea. She took a sip, then a draft, quenching the thirst her walk had aroused. The clear liquid concealed strange flavours and its vapour moistened her face. She drank some more and he refilled the cup.

He talked as if she understood him. Undeterred, he seemed to explain, to coax and commend the girl. He drew close and made to pull back the collar of her smock, brushing and pressing her bosom. Sweat broke on her brow from the hot tea. He stared at her dreamily, withdrawing slowly before she could push him away.

His slow arc of movement continued around the cabin as the unknown feelings and sensations spread through his body. He opened a locker and took out a bound cloth, which, carefully unwrapped, revealed a bamboo flute, a tube with holes. He kept his gaze to the ground, to the object in his hands, his head bowed, as somnolently, delicately, he stepped across the cabin to the hammock, and, thinking, dreaming, placed his fingers on the flute, and with dream-like deliberation put the instrument to his lips and blew.

A sharp shrill note chirped out, cloying, unintended, shaming him and calling for greater care and concentration. He blew a long low note, plangent, hollow, disturbing. When his breath ran out he repeated the note, letting it grow into a flat languid melody of unlikely diatonic gulfs.

Ros swayed her head in circles on her neck and rocked her hips from side to side. He improvised, lightening the tune, until the phrases leapt brightly. His eyes were on her now, glinting with merriment. Her body bobbed with the sound, her feet drummed. She moved faster and faster with the music, as if about to boil. Taizao opened his palm in her direction and gestured her to rise and dance. She took a position, pointed a foot, arms curving like fronds, and began to move about the cabin in a springing step, piped by the music. The shrill clipped notes, the lovely tunnelling trills, ran with the dance, calling it on, compelling it forward. Taizao played fast, and Ros jigged into a spiral that became a wild pirouette. Then the flute slipped from his mouth. It was dripping with saliva, and he was gasping for breath. She threw her head back, her bare throat rippling as the blood pumped. She wiped her brow with her sleeve and drained the cup of tea. He laid the flute across his lap and fingered slyly the thickening organ between his legs. He rose from the hammock, the old silk gown chafing his skin, the friction furthering his excitement, as he walked forward once more to fill her cup.

She giggled at him. He reached out a finger and poked her breast. She giggled again. Too much tea. She looked around. There was nowhere to go. She turned to the doorway and found it closed, fastened. A flicker of panic, of recognition – the guard had locked her in with him – increased the pressure on her bladder.

She looked at him beseechingly, hand between her thighs, knees locked together, and, stirring from his stupor of lust, he pointed to a chamberpot in the corner. She could use that.

Although not coy, she wished not to offend. Rudely he made no effort to move away, to avert his gaze, to usher her to a less exposed corner. He stood passively staring, bolted to the spot, and the more he failed to move, the more desperate she became. She could control herself no longer.

He wondered why she waited. After a moment, he mimed the action he had seen her perform in the clearing, squatting down, knees apart, smiling, closing his eyes in an act of relief and comfort. He gestured for her to do the same.

Eyeing him steadily, she lowered her pants to her ankles and settled herself over the chamberpot. Taizao followed her in a squat. He could see between her thighs, his eyes glued to the pink lips, the fan of orange hair, the opening, and the gush of steaming yellow liquid. His breath caught. His heart pounded. She went on and on. He wanted it to last for ever. Intent on her task, Ros failed to notice at first his pleasure, his stimulation, his arousal. She ceased and quivered, patted herself with the sleeve, and stood.

Taizao wheezed backwards to collapse in the hammock. He pulled open the sash of his gown, threw back the flaps and exposed the baggy cotton bloomers from which a little cloth mountain rose stiffly. He rolled the bloomers down to his knees and looked at the thing that had happened to him, crimson-black stalk with a rose-petal head growing from the nest of black hair. He felt happy and dizzy. His abdominal muscles contracted and it twitched a little. He dared not touch, or else.

Ros stared at him as she unbuttoned her smock. Her

breasts drooped, like rare pigeons, warm, solid curves, their rose buds brushed with golden down. She turned a little way from him, legs astride the chamberpot, and released a well-aimed shaft of golden urine into the vessel. The light trickle was like a whisper in his ear. His breath sped as he watched the last drops emerge one by one from the tender scallops of her flesh. His neck stretched against the headrest of the hammock. An itching, throbbing sensation was building in him to bursting point. Something was happening that should not happen yet carried him with long racing pulses that could not be stopped.

Then a grunt broke from his throat, he burst, and pearly white stuff, to his amazement, sprang across his navel. He looked at her with zest, wanting her to appreciate the display; he clenched his teeth to stop himself from laughing. Her presence had caused the mysterious thing that had never happened to him before. She had made it happen, the foreign creature of extraordinary pink openings and rotundities, flesh masses and orange fur. The female animal. She filled his gaze, and his head lolled towards her in adoration, as idly, with a finger, he touched the hot sticky spots congealing on his skin.

'Do it again,' she said. The lips were moist and shining rosy.

'Ssss,' he went, 'ssss . . .', imitating the sound of her pissing.

He took the flute and blew a series of disconnected notes. As she stepped towards him, he lifted the instrument from his mouth and placed its tip against her mound of golden hairs.

'Yowch,' she yelped, 'you get away.'

Then he began once more to play, and she slowly to dance.

X

The convoy returned towards dusk, their work completed. Lou Lu's mind was void as the litter, borne by weary men, bounced over the steep path. The prince's appearance had been sufficient. The day closed quickly, each day cooler than the one before, as summer passed quickly too. The roses would blow and fall, while the hips swelled and ripened for another season. There was nothing to do but wait, and in waiting negotiate steadily with Popple until he agreed to be their guide to Rome.

Lou Lu was glad to settle low on his haunches in his cabin, and bathe face, hands and feet in passive contemplation of the great cause for which he worked, which carried him implacably forward, like an invisible river moving through the sea, inseparable from the ocean's random ebb and flow.

Lou Lu sighed. His toughened soles failed to signal in time that the water was too hot. The attendant came to the doorway, chatting and solicitous for the old man's health and the success of the outing. He came round to his point at last, to mention that the gentleman had a visitor.

'A visitor? Taizao? Who?'

'It's the pig girl.'

The lines of Old Lou's brow spread like bat wings.

'How?'

Taizao had not met her, formally at any rate; no

203

communication had passed between them. He had been indifferent to her presence; she, in her distraction, had ignored him.

'His door is closed.'

Lou Lu suspected a deceit.

'Come, then.'

He dried his feet, slipped on his sandals and tottered ahead of his attendant, his legs rubbing together, his feet splayed in his peculiar walk. The prince's guard was outside, expressionless and resentful as he came to his feet for the commissioner. Over Lord Lou's shoulder the attendant signalled silence.

'Open the door.'

The guard unslipped the latch. The timbers of the boat creaked and cawed, and the floor moved against the rocking motion of the evening tide, and the rubbing, squelching sounds of flesh meeting and sighing.

Lou Lu stepped quietly inside the door, unnoticed.

The girl had a pale glow in the darkness, a blob astride the hammock, like a great peeled pear. Over her back and shoulders crawled hands that left bruising fingerprints, fading immediately, like crabs tracking the sand between waves. She sat on top of him and he lay groaning, sliding in and out beneath. His face hidden, his back and neck bent upward to hold her breast in his mouth, his hair against her white skin in a sweep of black. Her neck was arched, her throat exposed, her head to the ceiling as her hands pressed his shoulders and her thighs squeezed, urging him, as she rose and sank in the saddle.

'Whoah!' She emitted a muffled growl. 'Yes! Oh yes!'

The boy whimpered, yelped. The hammock swooped heavily from side to side and his hands searched for something to steady him. He was flapping upwards, out of the position in which she pinned him, flapping out of himself.

'Bubby, darling,' she cried.

He was expiring. He returned a suffocating groan. 'Aagh!'

It was over once again and he felt his blood had gone into her, as his eyes poured into her at the climax of union. She felt herself receiving him, as if she were swimming in a deep place. Tenderly she held him where he entered her, his last spasms running through her fingers, wave after wave of warmth engulfing her.

Good, thought Lord Lou, declaring his presence. '*Hao! Hao! Hao!*'

Nerveless, they were unalarmed by him. Ros turned to the old Chinese and laughed, and Taizao stared exultantly.

'I've done it, old man.'

They were attracted fiercely to what they had discovered as a new and thrilling potentiality of themselves. They tickled with pleasure, or lapsed into vacant wakeful dreaming, until desire was aroused again, compelling them, giving them direction. They wanted to keep on playing, all afternoon, all twilight, finding new power, learning new tricks, and when energy flagged, Taizao poured Ros more tea and she would drink so much that soon the itch to relieve her bladder returned and she squatted naked over the chamberpot, parting her thighs, gushing steamy liquid, and Taizao grew excited again, his cock like a fishing rod.

Had she worked some potion on the young man, the old man wondered. Or was it that his time had come at last, a delayed maturing, and she took his first seed?

The huts were gloomy when Popple returned. He was content with how the work had gone and disappointed to discover that the fire and the lamps had not been lit. Ros must be seeking creatures in the rockpools with the last of the day. He had not noticed her going. He lit the small lamp himself and sat waiting, and gradually, when she did not come, he grew anxious. He went to the doorway, and to the verge of the grassy mound, and called.

'Ros! Ros!'

And on the shore, 'Ros! Ros!'

The wavelets rolled his cry into something slight and inaudible which they broke against the sand. There came no reply.

He returned to the hut, pacing purposelessly, not inclined to cook. The lamp burnt low, guttered and died, and he was left with the dark moonless night, and the stars muffled by a film of cloud. Her absence was too dread a thing ever to have been contemplated or countenanced. She had always been there; never absent before. He roared at intervals from the grassy verge: 'Ros! Ros!' In vain. If she were injured – if she were lost. She was a tough brave girl, he knew that. She would not panic. If lost, she would wait until first light and climb the mountain. If injured, she would shelter and rest until he found her. Should he not light all the lamps? Should he not light a bonfire as a signal? Dumbly he dragged logs together outside. Fear and anger, running amok in his veins, made him shake and paralysed his thinking. She would not stay away without good reason. That was the trouble.

He roared to the dark empty night in a torture of deprivation, in this hell-tossed place of obscurity, of damp-wood fumes, of sudden entire loneliness. He howled like a wounded hero at the joke played on him. He begged for help from any and every nonexistent power. For the first time he regretted, picturing his wife Delia, ruddy and fine, with a lace collar, eating beef and horseradish from an oak board with Sir Astley Neville at her side. And he saw his son Henry, scarred and medallioned, robust on whoring and high living, thriving on political mistakes, admired by all. He saw the chaste and holy image of Brougham House, and Lady Brougham, who was cloaked by her belief in the comforts of heaven. He recalled his laboratory where, unsung perhaps but his worthy duty, the modest work awaited his return. All left abandoned by his hubris and folly.

The fire went out and Popple had no heart to relight it. He collapsed on his knees, his face flat to the ground, dirt on his lips, grovelling his puny being before the Uncomprehending, the pitiless insentient extent of the world.

No line could be distinguished between shore and sea. Not enough light was cast from the filmy sky even for water to reflect. The rocks jutting from the sea at the end of the little cove had only the merest outline of light against dark. Was it imaginary? From behind the rocks a moving glow lightened and came into sight. Voices, gurgling low with water eddying around the rocks, carried across the bay. Popple lifted his head to behold the form of a little boat, and figures shadowed forth by the light of a paper lantern with the shape of a globe, a moon slowly waxing across the water, the seaman poling – slap, slurp; slap, slurp – Captain Huang, and the girl, hunched under a quilt, her moon face and aureole of yellow hair reflecting the lantern light.

Gusting breeze tugged Popple's hair as he walked solemnly into the black water, waves playing round his knees, his chest expanding, to pilot them in. He saw at once from the warmth of greeting that she concealed secrets. His daughter. He took her elbow, drawing her ashore where he bearhugged her.

'I lost my way,' she explained. 'Chasing the solitaire bird. The Chinese found me. The old man said I should be taken back, though it was dark. He said you would worry. They fear going to sea at night. On such a dark night. You must thank them.'

Popple's Latin was wasted on Captain Huang. But he relit the bonfire and shared thimbles of the remaining liquor. Popple was prevented, in front of the strangers, from venting his rage, the furnace that turned his possessiveness of his daughter to gold. And she – she was able to sit on the grass with her hands clasped about her knees in a self-sufficient reverie. Flames of orange, blood and golden-red danced over her ginger-white skin, which was mottled where Tuzza had touched her.

'We cannot survive without each other,' Popple intoned heavily. 'Never again, my darling.'

★   ★   ★

Instead of dreaming Ros lay in a distraction of half-formed fantasies. Mind and body were uncomfortable, the air hot and heavy with vapour. Night sleep was replaced with clammy restlessness; skin stuck to skin, limbs slid apart. Her flesh attracted unsatisfying thoughts as viscous syrup catches gnats and fleas. If she could not sleep, nor could she dream, and so not imagine him with her. She could only touch herself where he had touched her, and that made her hotter. Summer heat brewed noises and fragrances under cover of night. And the morning, bringing coolness and light, gave only a short respite, a few hours' slow work, before the heat of the day and exhaustion overhanging from a sleepless night hit like a drug, compelling animal sleep through the afternoon and no dreams then either, although she would wake wet with perspiration to prepare her father an evening meal for which she had no appetite herself.

She had not seen Tuzza again. As her father ordered, she stayed in the area around the hut, performing her tasks. Popple shamed her over her absence. It was enough that he chastised her straying. He did not know what had happened with her compliance, and she had no way of telling him, even as there was no way to disguise a changed quality of moodiness that had opened in her. The intensity of his reaction, the strength of his assumptions, based on what he did know, frightened her and made the prospect of his anger terrible indeed if he should know what he did not. His conviction of their inseparableness scared her most. Their conjunction, for him, was chemical. His power came from their compounding. That was what he believed, that only by keeping her to himself, with himself, could he derive the energy to achieve the great goals of his quest.

The main work of the rose crossing was done. The young man had indifferently commended their labours and the Chinese let their interest slacken. What came after was to tend and observe the plants with diligence, to protect them against any enemies the island might throw up, and to wait. At intervals the eunuch commissioner visited the site to watch for signs and omens that the place might produce, following a regime of haruspication he alone understood. Popple came every day. But after the break-through of cooperation with the Chinese, the promise of grand outcomes had faded to a tedious routine. The rose crossing was Popple's undertaking still and he no longer allowed his daughter to come to the garden from which she had gone wandering. He told her he did not need her help; it was engraved on his heart that he forbade her.

He did not say what he might have been told and she dared not ask. The only one with the language to pass on information was the old man, who continued his communication with her father, but she guessed that the young man had not been mentioned. Not yet. For the time a secret triangulation remained between herself, the youth and the old counsellor, undermining her father's wisdom by excluding him.

At first the sensation of having been with Tuzza, of what had happened and what they had done, was enough. She revolved the experience in her mind, reliving it in her body, over and over, as if she were dazedly circling the most beautiful object of art, a treasure created from their impulses and exertions together, the performance of a perfect game. It was enough to savour their deep exchange, to live in the dream space, to inhabit the joy of awakened flesh. She did not need to see him again.

One morning, feeling weak, she rose from the mat and walked out into the glaring light. She screwed up her eyes, the blue splendour of sea splintering in her vision, the reflected light burning her raw, ruddy skin. Her fleece of thick curls fell in front of her face as some sort of protection. Her sweaty, sleeveless singlet chafed against breasts that she supported with her forearm.

'Ya,' squawked the solitaire bird, flapping over to her.

Otherwise the scene was slumbering, quiet.

Her dirty cotton bloomers, threadbare behind, swathed her middle parts, an annoyance.

She crossed the beach and walked into the seawater, sluicing her hot thighs and flopping forward to immerse herself. The water stunned and refreshed her, cool and salty, and she gave her weight like a heavy wet mat to the support of the brine. Salt water filled her eyes. The cleansing sea tingled her body's openings. She snorted water. She dunked her head, shook her locks wildly, stood at last with no strength and waded for the sand.

Exactly at that moment she noticed the cuttlefish wafting on the water with a blue kingfisher's quill stuck upright for a sail.

It was a toy he had sent her. A boat of his making.

Obliquely, unmistakably, the cuttlefish found its way

towards her, slow in its course, inching into her arms. The white prow bobbed with pluck until at last it collided with her belly. With two hands she cupped it and lifted it into the air, light as a thought. The shield-shaped cuttlefish was bone-white and clean. The pert blue feather pierced its heart like an arrow. It was dripping in her hands and she smiled. He had sent it. In an immensity of sea his gift had come to her.

Another day Taizao went out wandering with his flute. He strolled a little way from the pontoon, over the rocks, and found a place to sit in the sun and lazily pipe his music. He strolled further, along the stony ledge, until he reached a shady spot in which to rest. Then, playing a melody of long, close-together notes, he strayed from the shoreline up a path into the jungle, ambling with the aim of reaching the other side of the island. As if pulled by a thread, Taizao was intent only on direction. He reached the first height, and found nothing but a declivity of tangled undergrowth. Determined, he put his flute in his belt and flung himself forward, ascending the final height that rose above the beach on the far side. Perspiration ran when he removed his hat to allow his head to cool. He paid no attention to the crackling sounds that followed his footsteps.

The huts lay below in the grove of shiny trees, on the green breast of the slope above the sea. The sand shone as waves curled idly over the shore. But he saw no one. She was asleep inside the hut, and he sat to play his flute and pipe her out. He played and played. But she didn't appear.

He put the instrument aside in disappointment and sat with his head hunched over his knees watching the scene that lay exposed in the afternoon light, inaccessible to him, inhuman. He hummed, his head tipping to one side.

The noise of feet crashing close over leaves at his back made him jump. Captain Huang laughed derisively.

'Are you following me?' asked Taizao in confusion.

Huang grinned flatly. 'It's my duty to keep watch.'

'It's your duty to stay on the boat.'

'I could have shown you the way, sir.'

'I knew it for myself.'

Huang pushed a flask of water over. The prince splashed some over his head, then drank.

Huang pointed in silence through the trees where the girl had come out carrying a pot to be emptied on the garden bed. She squatted down and picked at the leaves of vegetable plants growing there. Taizao immediately took up the bamboo flute and began to blow a simple melancholy tune that disappeared into the air. She made no reaction. He blew louder, and still she did not turn, until the sound became a screeching little better than a seabird's. As if in response, as if feeling the tug of a string that led to Taizao, she stood up and walked a few paces over the grass, then, as if uncertain of where she was going, clutched her arms round her belly, turned and retreated to the hut. She heard nothing except the drowning shushing of the lagoon, and was gone inside the walls, unreachable.

Merely the sight of her made Taizao flush. She was an ingenious device, a magical creature, to affect him so, through the air, across distance, her image, her power, entering him and working on him in the most thrilling way.

There was needed no other explanation of why they had come to this extraordinary place.

'You can't go down,' continued Huang.

'Not this time. She must come to me again. Can you arrange it?'

'Tell the old man.'

'It's my game. Not his.'

'He's the only one with the means to negotiate. You

were best to enjoy her here.' Huang's teeth were bared. His gums were pink and wet. 'Like a wild doe,' he added. 'I can help you.'

'No, she is to be mine entirely in private. Let's go back. She won't appear again.'

Huang grumpily complied. No sooner had they left their vantage point when Ros came out again and, strangely moved, stepped a circle on the sand, tilting her head to the sky. She knew that someone was aware of her.

Pecking seeds in the grass beside her, the solitaire bird, with the whole world, was undisturbed by the fair-haired, fair-skinned girl's slow dance of invocation on the beach. She must wait patiently until she could answer Tuzza's call. Under no circumstances would she disobey her father.

At the end of the third circle, she fell to her knees, faint with sunstroke, and vomited on to the sand.

Lou Lu was glad. She was the needed tonic to stir animal desire, even if the solving of one problem might create another, were Taizao to become attached to the foreign monster girl. But it was right that the boy should long for her again, to stimulate his blood. The encounter would have to be repeated many times, as ideal regular exercise, until the pulse of energy was restored throughout his body.

The bamboo curtain raised over the window of his cabin, Taizao was staring at a shag diving repeatedly into the undulating surface, taking fish, when the old man came.

'Old man, I want to play. The creature has not come to me again. I fear her modesty prevents her.'

A healthier colour had come into the young man's face, as if he were breathing more deeply. He had energy, now, to play the flute. Where the courtesans and girls of noble families, singers and quacks, and all the women of the mountains behind Zayton had failed, the foreign female had succeeded in igniting the prince's carnal appetite.

Lou Lu chuckled at the prince's readiness with the language of courts. 'She does not presume,' he responded in formula.

'I must present her with gifts, make public tribute.'

'Gifts in anticipation?'

'Gifts of honour.'

He laid on the table a square of silk embroidery showing a phoenix of cinnabar red against opalescent wavelets and cloudlets.

Lou Lu chuckled more deeply. 'She will be offended.'

'She will understand.'

'She will not understand. She will not know the meaning of the cinnabar phoenix.'

'She knows already what passes between us.'

'Her father is a scholar. He will take the meaning with offence.'

Lou Lu understood that Popple was as physically endangered by the absence of his daughter as he would have been by the removal of an organ of his own body. It was imperative not to bring about discord until a pact was made for Rome. The long aim must always be kept in sight.

'Old man, your task is to present this inconsequential gift. Carry it to her father.'

The phoenix's shining wings arched above her back into the sky, her stout legs, like saplings, clutched the earth, her breast swelled in red shadings, her neck extended, her head lifted, her beak opened, her black eye pierced. She was aflame with ecstasy.

'Bring her back here,' ordered the young man.

'Only in accordance with right action. Only as a permitted guest.'

★

In the corner Lou Lu gritted his teeth, as if a wire were twisting through his body, for the painful expulsion of water. He had stones. Troublesome perhaps, Taizao's infatuation could become a strong element in the achievement of the goal. The dart of anguish as he squatted was a regular foreshadowing of the risk of failure. The girl must become Taizao's companion, a plaything to educate him in his capacities as a man. The girl's father must appreciate the esteem the prince conferred.

The sea being calm, the old man chose to go by boat, with Captain Huang and the boatman. His body weakened by constriction, Old Lou had no lust for the ferrying back and forth, the go-between work that had so long been the essence of his life. He was weary, as he lifted frayed sandals and scuffed feet into the boat once more, aided on both sides by his colleagues. The deep ripples on his brow stretched and he spoke not a word, narrowing clouded eyes to gaze across emptiness to the horizon. His jaw protruded below fleshless cheeks, his teeth were clenched, and the breeze brought a runnel of mucus from one nostril. It was Captain Huang, not Lou Lu, who carried the gift of a woven silk square.

Huang hollered as the boat approached the beach. He hollered again, and after long silence, suddenly, the girl burst out. She ran straight to the shore waving wildly. Her hair was a bush, her clothes hung dirtily. Her haggard yellow-grey skin made her look like an old banana. She was peering, Lou Lu knew, for the prince, and not finding him in the dazzle her face turned fearful, her eyes blanked, and she stood emptily. She gave no greeting. Instead she backed slowly away as the boat came forward over the little breakers to be carried up the sand, until she turned and hurried away to the security of the hut.

Wearily Lou Lu allowed himself to be helped ashore.

Carrying his sandals, he waded through the foam to the land, while Huang supported him and boatman Jia dragged the boat. The girl's behaviour showed confusion and denial as much as forlorn longing. Why did the father not emerge? If she was alone, she would be frightened, Lou Lu considered, or perhaps forbidden to deal with the visitors, as if they had come to seize her. Or did she want that? He must seek clarity, stiffening his arm to make his companions pause.

He sank on to the sand, pulled his knees up under his chin, and waited for the girl's curiosity to draw her out. Eventually she took a few measured steps from the door and peered at the visitors – the old man in front and the tawny colleagues behind. She wanted to run to them and gossip, to plead for explanation, or she wanted to conceal from them everything, distressed by what she had already exposed. She moved sidewards like a crab, keeping her eyes on the old man, Tuzza's friend, and came up against a lime tree whose branches provided a fork on which to sit. She cringed against its strength, until gradually, playfully, her legs began to swing.

Popple found them facing each other in the hot sun, the old man crouching by the beach, Huang and the boatman on guard, and the girl perched in a tree. He was alarmed at what they might have done to Ros. When he found out that she was insisting on seclusion in obedience with his command, his harshness embarrassed him. He kissed her, stroked her cheek, and with the firm swagger of one who had been working at his tasks all day went boldly to greet Lou Lu, whose bones groaned as he rose to his feet.

'Old friend.'

'Old friend.'

They gripped each other as estranged partners. Popple remarked on Lou Lu's failing health, and Lou Lu found

Popple wilder than he remembered, with piercing eyes and overloud speech.

'The days grow long as we await our journey to Rome.'

'The garden must grow, before we can account for the fruit of our enterprise.'

'Can we not plan for departure?'

'We must continue to chart the winds and tides.'

'Our young gentleman requires preparation in the ways of Rome. He would be grateful for the honour of your conversation.'

Popple frowned. 'I should profit the more from some preliminary instruction in *your* language, if you consider it possible.'

'We must meet more often.'

Popple invited the old man to take refreshment, signing Ros to make preparations. The girl sullenly lifted herself down from the fork of her tree. Lou Lu called Captain Huang near. They entered the hut and drank tea, as if they were neighbours, relations, villagers on a holiday visit. Tea made with the leaves that had been an earlier presentation from the Chinese. There was warmth despite themselves and formality without friction.

Face down to the steaming vessel from which he drank, Captain Huang in an expressionless way observed the girl. She was silent and dutiful before her father, revealing no longing, nor the excitement they had glimpsed in her when their boat came towards the shore and their cry went out. With tender regard she refilled their cups and was still.

'I have recorded seven hundred and fifty types of plant and zoological life on our island,' boasted Popple. He had ledgers to prove it.

Lou Lu was amused. 'What are their uses? Which do you plan to take with you? Which are good for trade?'

The Chinese carried all they needed and had little impulse to experiment with native products. Where familiar categories applied, they might assimilate unfamiliar substance to what they knew. One kind of grass they called bamboo shoots and ate in the accustomed fashion. Gull's eggs were chicken's eggs. Seaweed was sea ribbon. For Ros and Popple it was different. They applied scientific principles, acted as pioneers. They were prepared to stay on the island, whereas the Chinese bided their time.

'The types of things on the island are inexhaustible,' said Lou Lu, 'more than ten thousand, as are the myriad things in the world. Between our island and the universe there is no boundary. Things cannot be numbered. As our presence here proves, another is always likely to arrive.' Then he asked the worrying question. 'How many types will you number before you have enough?'

'Precise counting is required if the mathematical riddles and other signs are to be revealed. The number is important. I must count to completion. Our island is small, circumscribed.'

'Can we help you count?'

'If you count, who will know if we are not counting the same specimens over and over? Who will tell sameness from difference?'

'I fear you grow tired from the labour. Can we not help you?'

'I must be at the centre of the counting. I must do the work myself. My daughter looks after me.'

Lou Lu looked over his shoulder at blank-faced Captain Huang, who carefully slid the gift out from his jacket and passed it to Popple with a bow of his head. Popple felt the warmth of Huang's body still on the parcel as he unfolded the bundle of grass-woven cloth in front of them and unrolled the shining silk, a square of brilliance such as he had never seen. Ros gasped and her fingers jumped to stroke its deep glossy surface, jewelled colours on blood sheen. At once she read the image of the mythical uplifting bird as Tuzza's secret beckoning. She said nothing. Captain Huang cast his eyes down. Lou Lu gave a faint dignified smile to Popple, as if to solemnize the gift. And Popple, peering at the fine workmanship, thread by silken thread shaping a picture of such animated detail that light seemed to dance through it in an illusion of brightness, shuddered, the quality of stuff having such a texture against his finger pads.

'I have never known such a piece,' he complimented.

'Yours – if you will join us at a feast to celebrate our hundred days on the island. I invite you.'

Popple folded the phoenix embroidery in half, as if its lustre made an indecent intrusion into the rough hut. He covered it with his hand. 'I accept,' he said.

'And your partner?'

Without consulting his daughter, Popple said yes. Lou Lu stood, Huang behind him, and they returned to the boat for the journey homeward before dark.

Popple frowned at the purpose of their visit.

'We'll be at their mercy.'

'Trust them, Father. We have no one else.'

Popple clamped his teeth, the jaws of a trap closing. 'Our strength is all in ourselves. They must not wedge between us. Never!'

Popple's desire for Rosamund had been sublimed, as in a chemist's burner. The impurities of flesh combusted in dark fumes of nocturnal torment and denial until, in a pure blue flame, a perfect hard crystal was formed, the clear quintessence of purity, an impression of God. Girl bud and rose, her virgin purity was the core, immaculate offspring of his tainted coupling with hot ambitious Delia, mud that bred from his seed pure beast and pure spirit, his belligerent son Henry and his daughter Rosamund. Ros had coupled with him on a journey to the farthest extremities, to a life of strenuous labour, rags, filth, sustenance ever more meagre, struggle ever more thankless, discomfort tending always to the brink of distress, existence of unending satisfaction. For what? For the single pure idea, for possession of the knowledge and the power, of which her purity was an essence. The immutable energies of their souls cemented them to each other unbreakably.

As the wet summer came on, and the island became wilder and more sultry, their challenge was to achieve a final abstraction from the flesh of the world, from shell-gathering, bird-shafting, grain-grinding, weed-tending, flower-copulation, in order to enter into a timeless higher realm of Being. Popple's work of mind, his compilation of records and his physical toil in the garden, were stages towards finding the keys of mental control without which growth itself had no meaning, a random lushness from which no one profited, not even four-legged beasts. So Popple, reviewing the shabby pilgrimage of his life, tormented himself with translating the body's frustrated energies.

He had delved deep into the arts of plants, tilling and sifting that rich black soil. He had lifted himself into more theoretical knowledge, Natural Philosophy and Radical Theology, Cosmology, Astronomy, and the Science of Change. He supported the king's cause but not the man, neither Charles the First nor Charles the Second. He acknowledged the need for blood sacrifice to purify the realm, and felt soiled when the butchers, removing their aprons, turned out to be not holy priests but a coarser brand of politician. Unwisely he tried to graft himself on to trunks of patronage, first with Lord Brougham, melancholy prayer-master, then the opportunistic beef-fed Puritans of the new regime, the Society of Fellows, who were inventing a new kind of superiority to suit their wide-girthed acquisitiveness. At last, through mismanagement, through desperation, he had escaped to his own unfettered fate. He grudgingly recognized his wife's role. In seeking her self-interest, Delia helped him aboard the ship that no doubt she saw as his water hearse. Instead the vessel had tossed him ashore to the path of his high vocation. Did Delia grieve for her daughter's loss? She had never felt for the girl, preferring the bully son. It had been Popple's recognition of Rosamund as his spirit bride that saved them all, and rather than touch his daughter's virgin part, he had burned himself, his seminal fluid calcined into a sprinkle of bitter stains, like carbon specks. And now he possessed her as his essential partner in their final ascent to Truth.

A mage, a scientist, Edward Popple felt himself approaching that state, only through Ros's help. Fire scored his veins, twisting his lust to restraint, to a crystalline will to protect her. She must not be touched, she whose purity led her to walk with spirits, the virgin essence which combined with his male energy in a burning transformation to give the last and most exalted grasp of the world, the universe of the four elements, the solid land, the infinite sea, the clear air, the moving heat, and the fifth element encompassing the zone of time, ultimate power over creation and destruction; that was the point on which Popple set his sights.

While he waited for the crossed rose to generate the symbol of his undertaking, his daughter became more than ever his love, his life, his world, sole breath and presence of his universe.

XI

Great events oft from little causes spring, and it is a
remarkable fact that the most important improve-
ment of our garden Roses in the last century was due
to the introduction from China of a minute Mende-
lian gene, so small that it is quite invisible to the
naked eye ... A pair of these genes, one from the
father and one from the mother, is present in every
growing cell of our best modern Roses ...

Dr C. C. Hurst,
'Notes on the Origin and Evolution of our Garden
Roses'

(1941)

On the appointed day clouds gathered over the western sea
in creamy scoops of pearl and fluffy purple, piled atop
shifting castellations of brilliant white and foreboding slate.
They set off early in clothes that were salt-stiff from
seawater. They used the last piece of soap on their skin and
hair and felt clean. Popple took his oak pipe with silver
mouthpiece, and a gathering of mouldy tobacco leaves, as
a presentation. On the way Ros picked flowers to weave a
garland for her neck.

They passed through the rose garden. The blooms had
turned salmon flesh and brown as they dried, opening
wide and dropping petals, shrivelling into relics. The dead
petals turned slimy insects' wings that disappeared into the
earth, leaving behind strong glossy foliage to flap abun-
dantly from robust stems. Popple was proud of his garden,
and, as they passed, paid homage with Ros to one particular
bush.

'This plant is unlike all the rest,' he said. 'This rose contains the meaning of our journey, the evidence of our purpose, the proof that we have been here. In this rose we move forward to a world made new, and what comes after.'

'You rave, Father.'

'Do you understand, daughter, how the world means nothing unless we can follow the spiral of its creation, find a thread that leads through time to the reality that lies beyond time? This rose, which I am making, is part of that thread.'

'It must be a pretty rose then.'

He flashed his teeth in joy.

'Like you, the prettiest.'

At last they came down the steep path to the Chinese camp. The sentry ran ahead with the news. Captain Huang stepped across from the raft of boats in his usual attire and indicated the plank where they should cross. Ros, who knew her own way, nevertheless accepted his guidance. Through the awning, held open by attendant hands, Lou Lu appeared splendid and imposing in a stiff wide court robe. An almost imperceptible nod was his greeting, his hands clasped ceremonially in his sleeves. Happy to see them, he ushered his guests aboard the craft which was decked out in all finery.

Ros had brought her solitaire bird on the outing, a chain round its neck. She tied it to a sprit on the deck.

Feeling the yield and rock of ship-shape timber beneath his feet, Popple was all of a sudden lighthearted. He tingled as if weightless with the sensation of flight. For the first time since Solomon Truro had left the island there was the prospect of a departure.

The eunuch commissioner's jade-green sleeves rustled as he led below deck where chairs were arranged in a square around the brocade-covered low table, and teacups set out.

Lou Lu showed Popple to the western seat, eastern facing, while he took the adjacent southern seat, leaving the girl to sit east, and Captain Huang standing. The southward-facing northern seat was left empty.

The guard, who had foul garlic breath, poured amber tea. There were little dishes of dried crab in front of each place. Ros's eyes roved impatiently.

'Destiny has joined us in a hundred days on this uncharted island belonging to no emperor. But ourselves,' began Old Lou in his prepared pig Latin.

Popple understood.

'Joined us as friends,' said the old man, raising his teacup. 'Drink tea. Welcome aboard our floating home, the envoy of our civilization.'

'A high and gracious civilization,' complimented Popple.

'One day you will know our language and read our records.'

'You are familiar with courts. I am not. I am a humble scholar only, called by fate to study the book of nature. The records and secrets of your civilization I am keen to learn.'

The old man nodded graciously. 'You seek information that our people have gathered long ago.' A shudder of ecstasy passed over Lou Lu's smile. 'We can hasten your work. We journey together.'

It was the question of motive that perplexed Popple. Though they might share common purpose, what other visions underlay their activities? To bond or remain separate was the challenge, and they enacted a ritual of exchange while concealing deeper untradeable aims.

Food was brought, remarkably gathered, reconstituted

and prepared, steaming and fragrant. Still the fourth chair remained empty, although a saucer and the twin ivory sticks used for eating were set there.

Popple asked: 'Is it your custom to reverence an absence? Who is the fourth at our feast?'

'The young man,' said Lou Lu. 'It is his privilege to come when he will.'

Ros drank her tea nervously, knowing that if she drank too much her bladder would burn. She could barely contain herself in the uncomfortable cabin, with the incomprehensible conversation.

The food sat, like an offering to the empty place, and Popple said to Ros in English: 'Be careful what you eat. Strange condiments can cloud the brain.'

Lou Lu whispered to Huang that Taizao should be informed the visitors awaited his pleasure.

'The boy is shy,' added Lou Lu. He showed Popple how to use the chopsticks, deftly clicking the air. Popple laughed as he fumbled. The girl slipped them over the ivory mound of her flesh, pivoted on the forefinger, between thumb and index finger, and lifted a flake of dried crab meat into the air. Then dropped it carelessly.

Taizao came in with an air of reluctant obedience. He wore the chestnut robe, his hands concealed in the sleeves. His straw sandals he slipped off at the edge of the grass matting. Popple made to stand and extend a hand in greeting, but the young man failed to respond, except to stare bashfully at the bristling visitor. Lou Lu stood, despite his age, the ingrained motions of obeisance, and only the awkwardness of the moment, the limited space, the concealment, or rather, calculated ambiguity of the prince's standing before the eyes of the foreigners, prevented him from plunging to the floor in deep prostration.

Taizao took his seat, avoiding Ros's gaze entirely.

225

Enough of a prince not to wait to be invited, Taizao picked up a tiny cup of the wine that had been poured, raised the half-walnut vessel into the air in an expression of welcome, and threw back the contents on to his throat.

'One hundred days,' Lou Lu translated his toast.

'Aagh!' gulped Popple. The spirits descended in a convulsive swallow, stung the belly and made his head swim.

Ros's knees began to knock together, her thighs rippled.

Lou Lu plunged his chopsticks at a dish and transferred food to Popple's bowl. Popple struggled to get the morsels to his mouth, where they slipped down without giving satisfaction. At last Lou Lu called on the foul-breathed guard to sit beside Popple and feed him.

They had emptied several more cups of spirit when Popple took the turn to propose a toast.

'To the sharing of wisdom, and the sharing of power.'

Lou Lu happily obliged, and seized the moment to bind Popple to him.

'Our power can only be consolidated when we reach Rome. Let us delay no longer. Promise you will guide us there. Brother in the enterprise.'

Flushed, Popple could only smile and nod. 'Yes! YES!' he said. 'When the winds are favourable they shall blow us straight to Rome. That I can promise you.'

'The Christian pope shall receive us.'

'There are friends in Rome of whose help we can avail ourselves. English fathers. Architects. To frame an alliance.'

'The Christian pope shall cooperate with us.'

Popple had an enthusiastic vision of a great universal ecumenism in which his highest truth would be crowned, subliming and absorbing knowledge and beliefs from the four winds into a pinnacle of single immutable beauty. Atop he would stand, eternal omnipotent wizard. He was aflame, drunk and a little queasy.

Taizao slipped from his seat to a cushion on the floor, slumping in a loose-limbed curling heap. The guard brought his bamboo flute. His eyes closed dreamily as he blew, or opened a little to envision the girl in an unfocused question, for a glancing instant, before closing again, as the thin yearning melody crept through the hollows of the cabin and the timbers of the boat. His taut lips against the reed were swollen and purpled.

'Excuse me, Father,' said Ros, 'I must relieve myself.'

Huang jumped to attention, understanding the situation, and ushered the girl ahead of him. Taizao played on with lower breath.

Lou Lu leaned forward to Popple. His bleary eyes were red. He took Popple's hand.

'We must not miss the meaning of our meeting,' he said. 'It is a unique conjunction that will lead us to be – the greatest men of our time! So posterity must judge us. We have no choice. We must act to rectify the order of ages and put the governance of the greater world to rights. We must act not for personal ambition but as the agents of the magnificent enterprise of universal empire.' He clutched Popple's hand ever more tightly. 'You must tell us when the favourable winds blow. You must tell us what bearing to take by the stars. You must know how many days to sail in a certain direction before it is necessary to change our course. You must commit yourself to our negotiations.'

'Is your ship seaworthy? The worst seas are ahead.'

'Our ship follows the design of a segmented bamboo, the most slender, supple and enduring of plants, its qualities manifest when set against its opposite, the great flood, whose wish for dominance the bamboo triumphantly resists. That I guarantee.'

'I don't know how you sail.'

'You guide our course. I assure you of our means to follow.'

The two voyagers were face to face in intense conversation, eyes searching the other's eyes as if the mysteries of the cosmos were held there, mixed with hot enthusiastic alcoholic breath.

Edward Popple would agree to a compact with the eunuch commissioner; he would join their voyage. But not until he was growing the new rose of the world to take with him to Europe. He must continue extemporizing for several months, until the time was ripe. That motive he enforced to himself, like cold rock hidden in the swirling fumes of his brain, as Lou Lu, ally, manacled his wrist with his bony fingers in friendship.

Taking his flute meanwhile, Taizao slipped away from the cushions, crawling low and silent across the bamboo-covered floor in a rustle of bronze silk, like a water dragon.

Popple jumped up with shock at the realization that he and the old man remained alone in the cabin. Lou Lu's hand round his wrist held him and steadied him.

Tuzza nibbled her lips as if they were squirming fish, biting to bruise them and crush any bones. Their tongues played like two eels, teeth knocked together, eyes squirmed. Joining hands, they giggled happily, appraising each other then casting again. Tuzza latched the door of the cabin, climbed into his hammock and dragged Luo-si on top of him, fumbled to open his sash, exposing his flat belly, and pulled at her bloomers to see the golden fur disappearing into shadow between her thighs excite him, and where his finger squeezed, the rose-pink mouth. Laughing, slapping his hand, she pulled away the swathes of cloth in which he was wrapped to bare his chest. She sat astride him twiddling the tiny knobbles of his nipples, the only protuberances on his board-flat chest. She dragged his robe away and had him stark naked. He was breathless with embarrassment, the thing flopping about in her hand like a sea-slug. She pulled off her smock so she could boast to him her own solid breasts.

'Ss-ss-ss!' he hissed, tickling her. She bounced up and down on him. 'Ss-ss-ss!'

She had drunk so much wine and even more tea. His tickling fingers were like fluttering moths and crawling silkworms all over her body. He was supine, like a baby or a frog in the slow-rocking hammock, his legs wide apart and his toes squirming, reaching to clasp her. He was beyond himself in delight. Only one thing remained.

'Ss-ss-ss!' he went, tickling her without mercy.

'No!' she cried. 'No!'

He continued until the point came where she could no longer control herself and the warm fluid gushed from her in a steaming fountain, a golden bow. Moaning, he pushed her above him with strong locked arms, and she rose on her knees, squeezing his narrow hips with her thighs, spraying him from neck to groin with the stinging liquid. His desire raced as she bathed him. The thing flipped upright, purple and twitching. He clawed at her in laughing, gasping ecstasy. She slid her body down over him as piss dripped from the hammock like jungle rain.

Popple opened an eye and found the world sideways, his face pressed into a silk cushion, his head thick and weighty. The world tipped a little on its axis as he roused himself from drunken sleep. He was alone in the cabin where the banquet had taken place. Clambering to an upright position, he peered through the tight mesh of woven bamboo blind and saw the heavy slate-green sea and writhing

229

edifices of charcoal cloud. He felt the imposing energy and breath of an aroused cosmos, as if, initiate of its secrets, he were being drawn across heaving dark waters into an explosive mystery. Before his eyes the lightning veined through the cloud and he put his hand out, reaching for the staff of power. Then he snapped to the awareness that his hosts had abandoned him. Had he thrown up? And his daughter, left to her devices, where was she?

The timbers creaked and groaned. The doorway opened from the banqueting cabin to an antechamber. The other side of a sealed-off partition he heard knocking. He pressed the timber wall, its grain leading his fingers along a split to the point where the crack opened and he could peer through at the hammock rope bumping against wood. A ringing, resonant sound. He saw in the hammock the white flesh of the woman showering the slumped black-eyed man in golden tea. His golden-locked Ros.

With a scream he raised his fist to smash the partition, when the force of Captain Huang and the guard closed on him, the one gripping his wrist, the other his trunk, and he was pulled, shouting in vain, down a corridor to another chamber for an audience with the eunuch commissioner.

As if willing a violent disgorgement, Popple's body reacted to his daughter's pollution. He wanted to slaughter those who had turned her into an animal, and his shaking state went beyond rage to the spasms of convulsion. His eyes were like furnaces. Although he moaned from his gut, his tongue, flaying in his mouth, prevented coherent speech and blood-flecked froth oozed where he had bitten himself. He shuddered as Captain Huang and the guard settled him on a chair. She was gone. He hung his head, expelled breath from deep in his belly, and fell silent and motionless. They had seized his daughter, ripped away his best part and, with the loss of her, his power was gone. No doubt she had been bewitched, and the wounding shame would kill her when she came to her senses, or else the change would hold and she would become a woman of brass, separate from him.

Lou Lu sat motionless, his habitual polite smile quietly subduing his pleasure – at the satisfaction of achieved outcomes, not the suffering of his friend, whose fit he hoped would pass. He looked pitilessly at Popple, pardoning his excessive reaction, which was based on misapprehension. When he understood, the foreigner would be calm and content. The rage must burn, the frenzy race, his entrails must be ripped, and afterwards he would see what was being offered in friendship's name.

'Be still.'

Lou Lu emitted his command with almost no movement of the lips. He sat, legs wide, gown gathered around his knees, spine straight to bear the shreds of his flesh, balancing the skull, the shiny wrinkled skin, the wisps of hair. Hands rested on his thighs. Clouded eyes gazing impassively as he waited without impatience in the realization of the unquestionable rightness of the moment that had been reached, the execution of the work of centuries.

'Monster! False friend! Devil!' growled Popple.

Lou Lu made no reaction. Let them curse in their language. It had no force.

'Are we your prisoners?' asked Popple.

'You are our esteemed guests. Accordingly, I explain the cause of our hundred-day celebration. The Son of Heaven pays your daughter the highest honour. He takes the female as consort. The Emperor of the World, the Lord of Brightness, the Omnipotent of Four Seas, Taizao, Prince of Yong, marries with the foreign princess as his wife. Do you understand my information, sir? The young man is ruler. Your Rosamund has attracted him, inspired him, and they join as clouds and rain.'

A manic glittering excitement showed on Lou Lu's face, cooling Popple as he became aware of it.

'I reveal to you the identity of the young man. He is the Throne of China.'

'That is your excuse for the rape of my daughter? Give her back. Let us leave in shame.'

'We owe you the greatest gratitude, my friend.'

'Where is she?'

In part Lou Lu's placid self-containment was a sense of timing. Taizao and the girl must not be interrupted. Yet what had been commenced was already too far underway to be cancelled. He was not anxious and need exert himself only to quell anxiety in others, to instil patience and understanding, while processes continued to grow to perfection.

On cue, as their discussion reached this point, the boy and girl entered the chamber, decently clad, their hair disciplined and colour high, their faces glowing with satiety and joy.

Popple gulped, crouching on his chair. They stood side by side, and Ros looked at her wretched father, whose eyes flooded with tears to see her.

'What have they done to you?'

'What have *I* done, Father? It is with my compliance. I have followed my desire.' She knelt beside him, her arm around him, her head unbowed, as she whispered tenderly, 'I beg your pardon.'

He looked at her with swimming, uncomprehending eyes. 'You are no longer chaste.'

'I am carrying a child.'

Popple's eyes screwed up in a last wrench of resistance.

Lou Lu spoke without a waver in his voice. 'You

understand the honour that has been offered, the reasons for our gratitude. Together we ensure the continuation of the imperial line of Ming, dynasty unending, in which your destiny is implicated. You will come with us to Rome, to seek military support from the Christian pope in defence of the rights of your own heir, my friend. A marriage ceremony is proposed, here on our island.'

Taizao's eyelids drooped. A mole on his chin was bruised where she had bitten too hard. He was pleased with the release of his capacities. He could do it again and again, and listened to Lou Lu's speech as if drugged, caring only for the pretexts by which he could keep the girl-creature available to him. He laughed in response. And laughed again, as if he were an idiot.

Popple was unversed in the ways of courts. At last he made his simple reply.

'For today I ask one thing only. Please allow myself and my daughter to return to our side of the island. That is all.'

Lou Lu's equanimity was unperturbed by the paltry supplication, a test of good faith perhaps.

'Take her away, friend.'

Taizao moved a hand in protest. The eunuch commissioner ignored him.

'She is your responsibility, and no greater responsibility could there be.'

'Thank you, friend,' acknowledged Edward Popple with difficulty.

Ros had a look Edward disliked when she came to him, when they were alone. She touched his hand lightly, a gesture balanced between cautious sympathy and exquisite flirtatiousness that she had never used before. He was disgusted. Her face had changed, features that had been girl-like, delicate, preciously innocent, were revealed in their animal nature, lips curled up from kissing, teeth that could bite, eyes that could roll, fluff on the lip like the wires of desire below, candid brow that provided a wide space of knowingness for the new power she had discovered. She was guilty and not sorry, conscious of having wounded her father, but with no remorse. She was in an ecstasy of love with Tuzza, and could only find pity for her father – which angered him the more.

He looked blankly at her changed shape as she touched him.

'Father, might we not stay here awhile, until we are rested? The return to the other side of the island is so strenuous, for you especially, after the shock you have had.'

'For you,' he blurted, 'in your condition. You think we should stay with them now to be their slaves, their toys?'

She feared the intensity with which he distorted the Chinese motives, that were not anyway the motives of the lovers. Popple gripped her hand, harshly, as if to parody her lighter touch.

'Obey me! You are my daughter. We go today, even if we drag ourselves to exhaustion through the jungle. We must maintain the world we have built here.'

'I have not said I will not accompany you, Father.'

Her note of conciliation prompted Popple.

'We at least need to think carefully.'

They were too tired to make their own way. Lou Lu ordered Captain Huang to ferry them. Taizao pleaded to join his beloved for the ride and Lou Lu dismissed the idea. No risks were to be taken.

Popple gave nothing to Captain Huang's efforts to be respectful and comradely, as he poled. Ros tried out her Chinese. The sounds made bile churn in her father's gut. He turned his head sideways and spat into the lagoon. His mind kept working on how, or rather why, he had been deceived. To what end? For the Chinese youth to have seduced his virgin daughter, what purpose did it serve? All their talk of offering the empire, the peacock throne, was a laughable gesture here on this barren shore. A few dirty, ragged men running short of provisions, with nowhere to go and no means of getting there. If the young man were so special that he warranted having his lusts satisfied on the one pure creature on the island, the one human female of any description, then arrogance and contempt in the highest degree let them think they could do so, as if she were simply theirs to possess, or might as well be, to trick and sweet-talk into compliance, a low unpardonable betrayal of all the talk of partnership the unscrupulous old man had pursued. A girl deprived of a mother or other female company with whom she might have canvassed the questions of acquiescence, the discipline of urges and desires. A mother who in any case had been lax. Delia, a bad example, a lesser type of woman than Rosamund should have been. And he, a father who had never sought to counsel her, tormented himself to the ends of the earth so as to preserve her sovereign symbolic purity from the threat of himself. Why had he never suspected? Why had he, her father, never imagined? Was he to blame? Popple boiled, as the craft moved slowly, silently, over the cool calm water.

It was dark when they returned. Popple helped Ros on shore, taking her hand, and gruffly sent Huang back with no lantern. The violation was irreversible. There could be no forgiveness, no civility. The question was one of revenge, and the agonizing struggle to understand the meaning of what had occurred. She should never have been there, the sole blessing of his ruined life, impregnated now by a yellow-skinned stranger who claimed her as his queen, her egg poisonously fertilized by his seed, her purity polluted, Popple's own – English – blood and seed mingled with, infected with, the foreign element. What monster would come out, or would nature herself abort the miscegenation?

Weeping now, on her knees, dragging her hair and tears over the earth before him, she swore she loved the man. It was her own doing, as a woman, her own decision. Why could her father not believe that?

'Am I never to find a partner? Am I a nun then, never to breed?'

'Not here on this place. Your breeding stock is reserved for a higher destiny.'

'This place is my destiny.'

'You are a child.'

'I *was* your child. Your logic is that you would breed on me yourself, on one child breed another rarer still.' Her eyes pierced him unresistingly as she drove the accusation in. It was too horrible. 'Why are we arguing, Father? It is already too late.'

'Unless you kill *your* child.'

'You wouldn't make me.'

'I will have my revenge.'

'Then we become enemies. My child is me. My bud. My fruit. My own rose.'

'My dear, you are not to blame in this. You have fallen victim of a stratagem by which the Chinese seek to take possession of us totally.'

'And we are the beneficiaries of this – this happening.'

'How so?'

'In knowledge, in power, in survival.'

'Is that all?'

'And, for me, in love.'

He stared at her with profound and forlorn thoughtfulness and added: 'The force that moves the stars.'

'The bond includes you, Father.'

'You talk of carnal desire. The eunuch knows well how to manipulate what he cannot experience himself.'

'I believe he understands but cannot execute.'

'Except through others,' roared Popple sourly. 'I would have his balls!'

He did not tell Ros of his plans to poison the Chinese. There was a fungus that grew among the elevated roots of the great banyan tree in the shadowy part of the jungle. It glowed phosphorescent purple between the stained black contours of the tree roots and the slimy jungle floor. It had captivated him when he discovered it and he collected some specimens to dry. After picking he had been afflicted with spasms that rose from his groin across his chest and rippled round his heart. He attributed the attack to the mushroom's penetration of his system, through the pores of his skin and the suction of his lungs. If a little contact could inflict such pain, the consumption of larger amounts would be lethal.

He hatched a plan, and dissimulated.

It would continue to grow inside her, unfurling, revolving, expanding, until it pushed out, discarding its husk for a longer journey, kicking, reaching, turning as it cajoled the encasing world to bear it forward into destiny. The island was only its temporary home. Her child must be nurtured by the larger world, by civilization. Ros saw, as she contemplated the growth within her, that they must leave the island. She was turning too, and the conclusion she arrived at was to go with the Chinese. They had boats. They had means of transport. And judging from what they professed of their purposes, they intended to continue their mission.

In the decisions her thoughts quietly deposited, Ros was already an agent of the larger processes of procreation: the survival and prosperity of her offspring. If the Chinese promised that her child would be ruler of China, so be it.

'You say the child must be abandoned, Father. But I shall have it first. That will bear me no pain.'

'More pain than you can imagine enduring, and danger to your survival in this wilderness. It is a monstrous birth, remember. It may not come smoothly.'

'If it were to end before I reach term.'

'Poor creature. I don't believe we can make end of it so lightly, though the witches of home, of the moors behind Hull, would have fine uses for its foetus.'

'Father!'

'The first human being born on this island belongs to this island. To be reared by wilderness itself with the tortoises and wingless birds. Give it to the island.'

'Abandon it?'

'A gift, a sacrifice.'

'Like a lamb dropped in the field by a mother with no milk. A dropping – No!'

'Do you prefer sacrificing it to the Chinese?'

'You will love it, Father.'

'It will be outside my power.'

'Is that what fills you with hatred? That I have escaped your control?'

'You have not escaped my love, daughter. That is never possible. Hear me, I have been considering. We have until now been reasonably content with our island. We have not been driven by mortal danger to attempt to flee. We have assumed, making virtue of necessity, that we were to stay here. Yet we can leave. We are not prisoners. We can make a boat and sail. We have tools. We have axe, rope, cloth, knowledge. Seeing the Chinese sails of woven

238

bamboo, I understand how it is possible to make sail and rigging of palm fibre.' He talked rapidly, convinced. 'Let me try. When the wind is favourable, when the sea is calm, we shall sail.'

She hoped he did not believe himself.

'Where?' she asked. 'Sail where, Father? We don't know where we are. We don't know where we have come from, except from mischance. The last of our colleagues sailed away with high hopes and was washed up on our shore hacked to pieces, his longboat smashed. How? By whom? There is terror out there. You risk our lives, our baby's life, on an untested craft, on a directionless ocean, with what provisions, where we will turn and turn as breezes play, our own imperceptible whirlpool, until we are sucked under, or taken prey, or dried out, or at last perish in the vortex of our own helplessness.'

His dim eyes looked in bewilderment from the dark mane of his hair.

'We shall sail to another island. Another island, like this one.'

'Father, you are mad.'

'You have trusted me before.'

'You have not been endangered before. Do you not see?' she insisted. 'You risk, Father, a singular act of apostacy. We have come, by what forces, to this place. A chapter of miracle and misery, a most unlikely outcome, pushing the limits of credibility and luck. This island proving itself to be a fortunate place, at the furthest margins of possibility. Our survival here, our frail bodies, through furnace heat, wet, disease, growing accustomed, blessed and preserved, far beyond our capacity or our desert. And you presume to talk of another island! You dare! There is no other island for us, Father. To this island, small, hidden, as remote from them as from us, came a party of seafarers, by some design, they claim – a design that blithely encompasses error and accident, from which it is indistinguishable. The Chinese. The emperor of China. Parked, encamped, on the other side of a hill, a valley, a cliff, from our settlement. Eventually the one youth and one maid on the island meet and conceive for each other a passion surpassing the ordinary. Desire that replenishes as soon as it is satisfied. Love, and in that love a further conception. Nature intervening for her due. Worlds meet, Father.'

'You are unnaturally articulate, my dear.'

A smile widened on her straining face. 'You see, Father, the illogicality, the improbability, the pattern, the wonderment. Whose devising? More than one god and goddess have been at the work of harmonizing, Father.' Popple thought of his rose, and stayed silent. 'Can you deny that, Father? To deny the evident intention of the powers in whose net we find ourselves would be a stubborn wilfulness of petty man indeed. A suicidal presumption –'

Popple was nodding in concurrence. 'Such as marks our nature.'

'I will not have it mark *my child*,' she concluded.

'Your message is that we should unite with the Chinese to discover common purpose.'

'It is given us,' she whispered, taking her father's roughened hands.

He thought of his rose. He had opened the swollen ripened hips to extract the comma-shaped seed, encased in pulp, for planting in the ground. And as the seed waited in the moist island soil, the change was occurring, even now. Slowly the new kind was entering into being. It would grow to become the summation of the species, fragrant, multiple, repeating, combining all the colours of creation. It would be his progeny. The rarest flower of the world.

'I do not deny,' he vowed.

'Father, we will go to them, and you will grant permission for me to marry the young man, and the child will be born with a name.'

His daughter, after all that had happened, desired to be respectable. What name could the child have?

'An exchange of gifts and signs,' he agreed simply.

Clouds flashed blue and black as the prince broke through their surfaces into columns of moist air that lifted and plummeted him. He soared through a strange architecture of air and water and obscured light, pipes and chutes, crags and gulfs, lightning crackling to and from his body as he twisted and arched, as if he were its heart. Electric fire ran down his spine, along the crests of his back. Born from the turbulence of atmosphere, Taizao the dragon spiralled down, rose playfully, spinning like a kite frenzied by air, his immense corporeal substance, smooth scaly belly, spiny back, pearl eyes and whipping tentacles, glowing branched horns, heaving against, buffeted by, thrown back on surging fountains of air and plunging waterfalls of spume. Taizao dreamed he was the dragon, the divine force stretching his length in an undulating rainbow across the bright accumulations of cloud of a night sky, elongating at will, humping and cresting in surf mountains, stars in the sky echoing the coals that burned in the sides of the dragon, the moon a nacreous ball he could toss. Earth below received his rain and his mists, the once-more returning pageantry of cloud, giving life, drowning the creation in fecundity, so much sperm. And spread below as in a diagram, as he coiled overhead, the walled spaces of the palace that was his lair.

Taizao dreamed he was the dragon emperor, ruler of myriad things, of ten thousand years. Conscious of his dream, not lost in it, he invested the dragon with his mind, his own eyes seeing through those pearl globes, the power his power. By mental effort he was able to keep himself immersed in the dream, until he discovered the source of his transformation, his potency, the lightning rod breaking into depthless cloud. She, appearing –

The phoenix bird flapped and fluttered in the cloud, her wings outstretched, her back arching, rising upright on taut legs, her claws extended, a shuddering gold emblem in an ecstasy of fiery light as the dragon circled.

A modality that Taizao barely knew, he who had known neither mother nor father, who scarcely remembered the succession of maids and nurses who tended him. Who had been unmoved by woman therapeutically applied. Yet he identified as memory, or recovery, the sensation of infinite sustenance, heat, pleasure, exchange, bliss that the dragon experienced in the phoenix, lover with lover, element with element. In dream the dragon arched his back and somersaulted, an endless quivering spring.

When Taizao reported his dream to Lou Lu, the old man nodded in more than his usual acquiescent patience with the prince. An exhalation of breath followed the slow nod, the chin tucking deep into the throat as when a head bows in prayer, the eyelids drawing down in obeisance to an invisible world that was correctly revealing its purposes. Lou Lu's energy was ebbing. He was pacing himself, eking out reserves that were already measured in months not years. He was waiting for this moment. That it had come brought immeasurable relief, which he restrained, not risking false hope for the last arduous steps of the ascent. He knew the meaning of the dream. More than mandate, it reported the vacancy prepared. How, why, could not be understood. But time was drawing near for Taizao to reclaim his throne. The usurper in the dragon's court would be driven out. The omen was most clear and most powerful; a matter now, in practical terms, of bringing in those on the other side of the island.

The Chinese divers found pearls in the oysters they gathered. The eunuch ordered a tiny chest to be fashioned from the native casuarina pine, polished and inset with slices of coloured stone, an object of exquisite craft to hold the pearls.

Huang was sent to deliver it, set on a bed of pink frangipani flowers in a basket of raffia.

Huang had come to resent his role as ferryman. He was a loyalist through and through, and loyal to the eunuch as behoved his commitment to the cause. But understanding the need for unquestioning service, as in the discipline of a ship, he wondered at what point the old man's judgement could be called in doubt. For Lou Lu, journeying for the Yellow Springs of mortality, was dealing with a spirit world of memory, posterity, and rites of vindication beyond what any of them might actually know if they stayed on this island. Huang had no time for the island except as a temporary mooring. Finite, exhaustible, however pleasant, the island was a temptation to delusion, to complacency, offering recompense for nothing. Their object was the capital, the palace, dominion. Huang was a politician of sorts, an erstwhile administrator of certain rank, a practical man with a career that was assured if the restitution of the true regime took place. That is what he served. It was a waste of time to parlay with the foreigners in the intricate moves of courtship for little more than to satisfy the prince's lust. Admittedly, thankfully, a perverse object had belatedly been found for the prince, to whom they all pandered, more because Lou Lu was besotted with the boy than to further their strategic ends. Yet what were empire and majesty at their peak, if not the unquestioned necessity of providing for some mortal fellow's appetites? Huang would not rebel. He would merely grumble as with surly tanned mien he laid the exquisite offering in the hands of the foreign wizard whose uncut hair and whiskers tumbled to his breast.

To accept the gift, Popple placed his palms together in front of his heart, as he had seen the Chinese do. He inclined his hands three times, the lines around his eyes wrinkling, his pupils glittering, as he noted to his private amusement what a pagan and actor he had become. What unexpected forces he was invoking. Ros bounded over and hugged him. They agreed to a return crossing with Captain Huang.

PART FOUR
Rodrigues, 1653

XII

On the reef the waves broke in garlands of bridal spray, dissolving and renewing in endless tribute. Their line bound the depthless indigo of the great ocean to the benign jade of their lagoon. For the wedding a tortoise feast was prepared. The protuberant neck of the oldest of the tribe was slashed, the blood drained and preserved for a warm tonic toast. The beast was lifted by the shell into a roasting pit of hot stones and embers. Palm fans aired the fire. In deft anatomy the Chinese cook had removed the large liver, and the gall bladder for Taizao to consume, crushed in coconut wine, to assure that his seed would be as abundant as the fishes of the sea. The creature's brain and the sweet white flesh of its shoulders, stewed with glutinous matter from its bones, were reserved for the honoured guest, Edward Popple, doctor, former supplicant to the Society of Fellows, anti-church believer, supposed servant of a nameless king.

The stubby limbs – part leg, part fin – bigger than a dunce's cap, were brewed with plates from the underbelly of the carapace to make a rich soup that Lou Lu drank with relish, its surface floating with the leaves, like miniature waterlilies, and orange trumpet flowers of nasturtium. The snout and white swimming eyesockets poked back at the old commissioner with an affinity that was lost on no one. They guessed that the tortoise was more than a hundred and fifty years old and might have been the eunuch's sire.

The Society of Fellows would have appreciated an anatomization of the rare giant earth tortoise, which might be traded lucratively to extinction.

Flesh, oil and wine intoxicated the members of the party into making speeches as best they could, one speech meeting with another, cementing the fated, the unavoidable, the sensible alliance. Lou Lu, the senior, presided over the rudimentary ceremony, an exchange of silver rings made from beaten coin.

The feast was testimony to the salubrity of the island and ingenuity of its new population. The tortoise was their symbol, marvel of the place, and a sovereign creature that both English and Chinese could claim. Popple knew he had worn the comedian's tortoise shell on board the *Cedar*, an object of ridicule after Captain Macqueen let the crew know he was a cuckold, his place on board secured by his wife through Sir Astley Neville. And the Chinese worshipped the sacred beast of longevity and strength. The tortoise bore on its back the universe as a great slab of stone inscribed with the final meanings of existence. Length, endurance, survival. Final sums. The last laughing word. The tortoise symbolized their cause, their union, as Lou Lu managed in his speech. The Latin *testudo*.

The other dishes were cabbage palm hearts fried with the shallots that grew like willing grass in the sandy decline where the Chinese had established their garden; and the marrows that sprawled, legacy of the Dutch, in a web of trip-ropes for the long-legged birds that came pecking; baby squid and a pig-faced fish; a bundle of crisp beans, picked with the spinach leaves and the basket of limes from Ros's garden; and pancakes of flour ground from the second generation of wheat, once she had picked out the sugar ants. In a single inflection of less-than-complete magnanimity, Popple had urged her not to bring the new flour, since the Chinese did not savour it. But they had long since run out of rice and resorted to eating flour from ground roots. The wheat flour tasted better.

A solitaire bird, plucked, glazed and roasted, lay in another pan in front of Popple who gazed mournfully at its ungainly defenceless swanlike shape; its goose cooked, he smiled sourly. Impelled to share the joke of his own language, he called to his daughter loudly.

'The goose is cooked! The goose is cooked!'

But the Chinese laughed more than she did. She only gestured at the ring of perfect peeled hardboiled solitaire eggs in sauce on another plate. Her new in-laws knew how to provide.

Taizao recited his poem, which the old man translated into Latin as:

Across vast oceans
solitary islands meet.
Sun joins moon.
Day and night
come together
without end.

Popple sat with the poison fungus powder hanging by his groin in the pouch inside his trousers. He felt the piece of green stone from a flaw in which was carved the black rose, his cause. Warm beside it he could feel the thickness of the phosphorescent powder, concealed in darkness. It pleased him to finger his power. He could sprinkle the purple grains in the old man's soup. He could poison all of them. But he yielded, allowing his will to fail. He heeded what his daughter had said. He could not oppose what had been brought about.

Ros wore the embroidered phoenix around her neck as a bib. On her head was a veil of muslin over roses entwined in her curling hair. When Taizao lifted the veil, he sniffed the sweet fragrance of those roses, a delicate wafting tenderness never before known in the flagrant vegetation of the island.

Popple felt jealousy drive through his nervous system like a fine wire entering through a decayed tooth and drawn out through his bowels, jealousy with the chill of death.

They reclined on dry grass, in a clearing among the palms and pines, as dark came on. The bridal garlands around the reef glowed like bone, sending freshets of breeze with friendly murmurs of the ocean as they shattered into blackness. Through a warm dry night of stars, cloud mounted over the crags above, promising rain to the island, straining to rain in a teasing intimation of cool relief, then vanishing at last without trace, leaving the land not quite suffering, but disappointed.

The night of the wedding was a prolonged flirtation between heaven and earth, clouds and mountain, in which all participated who celebrated at the feast, the humans too coming to share the land's state of patience.

Towards first light they smelled the rain coming. The pearl-pink sky was thick with spongy clouds, as the prince led Ros to their bed. She was drunk and dishevelled, tired and overstuffed. She pulled away from him, and stood for a moment alone, unsupported. Her hand lingered over her breeding belly, and her brain was fired with the sensation that all herbs and beasts, all liquids and stones, all water creatures, the hanging canopy of watching stars and passing clouds, the cosmos in totality, witnessed the moment of which she was the very centre.

She stepped across to her father and dragged him to his

feet in front of the assembled group. As she had quickened and swelled, so he had grown gaunter and older. She knew the feast was against his grain. She knew that, despite appearances, her desire was not approved and her course deprived of his assent. He who had formerly been her only one.

Her hands rested on his shoulders, his on hers. Tears rounded like pearls and trickled from his staring eyes.

'Let me go, Father,' she pleaded. She already put her request like a queen.

He had no idea what words to say. His tongue snaked and bloated in his mouth, choking him. A gusting breeze heaved the palms overhead and the native pines hissed and sighed. He was shaking. On the reef the bridal garlands were shivers of silver in the oncoming light.

A splutter of words came to Edward's lips, smeared against her ear as they embraced.

'Go. Live.'

And she was gone.

The sun rose in fire over the crags, herding the last straggling clouds to a distant fold, dispelling a last hope of rain, and the sky turned once again to its usual unblinking blue.

Late next afternoon he set off on foot with a long staff. He was not ready to be encompassed by them. Against their entreaties he returned to his solitude, endeavouring to give the impression of a man who refused to abandon his purposes. All night he had been vividly tormented by dreams of home – sweating with nostalgia for the paradise of his civilized world, for Brougham House, good place of a green commonwealth, of dedication to the arts of justice and science. So far away that world of people who elaborated what language might allow!

Looking at him the Chinese knew his pilgrim meaning, his lonely purposeless ascent into a mountain hermitage. It was all a language of signs and they were not deceived.

He had slept and restored his frame, and the food he had eaten renewed his steps. At the first rise he paused to look back at the motionless camp, the ship like a nut shell on the surface of the sea, the awnings limp in the windless approach of sunfall, the mirror sea running into light, islets scattered like a girl's shuffled-off slippers. He turned in retreat from the sight and passed over into the cooler descent where wild arbours opened to his sinuous path, comfort and relief brushing his shoulders as if birds had lifted their claws from his neck. Spiders swung their trapezes away from him. The black earth-crabs ran down his legs into their burrows. He breathed regularly, deep into his chest, and the noose stayed tight around the pouch of poison at his groin.

He reached the rose garden towards dusk. The first blooms of red damask had already browned, while others, fully open, sucked in colour more intensely as the light faded. White damasks shone like lamps, their fragrance, hovering in the air, conjuring up young green apples. He recalled their taste wistfully, his mouth rinsing with saliva. So much sweeter than the monkey apples of the island, sticky fibrous insipid fruit that Ros had learned to boil down to glassy syrup. Other bushes had early buds coming on, the Chinese graftings producing vigorously, to afford good material for further experiment. Scarlet tapers of hips were abundant in the late-maturing specimens. He looked in vain for chance hybridizations where the promiscuous bees had flown, but all was growing as managed and intended. Within the clearing was order, created or interpolated, fed by dark fertile soil and the radiant blaze of sun, sweet rain and the gushing ichor from the ravine beyond.

He checked the roses of his secret pollination, which only he knew, which he alone cared about, and found that buds had formed on the double yellow. He peeled one open – a buttery colour and a delicious hint of fragrances that the original Chinese dwarf had lacked. But time was needed for the plant to prove itself.

The other special rose was at an earlier stage still, the buds hard green cones that revealed nothing.

'So we shall see,' he nodded, speaking to himself.

The effervescence in the air began to fall as light rain. He felt it on his cheeks and, making no effort to cover himself, he sat down on a boulder to enjoy the sprinkle. The garden offered shelter enough. No one waited for him at his hut and the fire would be out. From what was there need of shelter here? From himself only, his mind, and his poison. The rose leaves fluttered and prinked, fur and thorns responsive. His huge weary wide yawn gulped the clammy air. He bent his arms round his knees and bowed his head, his eyes slipping closed. Imperceptibly the gentle distillation of rain reached through to his knees, drenching him. His staff rolled to the ground from the rock where he had propped it. Water permeated his hat. Unaware in his sleep he tumbled off the seat, snuffling like an animal, and curled up in the manner of a fern frond on the wet grassy ground. Changing location for the night, a flock of golden bats flew overhead, screeching, and failed to stir him.

The rain eased as he slept, and the moon rose above ragged departing clouds, a half chunk of candid silver cocked low over the wooded crest of the hill. Steam seeped gently from the earth becoming cool nocturnal air as, taking her way, the moon disappeared and soft, grey light stole over the incline. A pair of rainbow lizards allowed their colours to appear as the sun's rays reached them. The solitaire bird that had stood nervously among the roses, watching Popple sleep, began to strut with dawn excitement, declining to eat the strange rose fruit. A trio of fodies flitted with insistent variation on their call of a semitone interval. Shyly, obliquely noticing, the gathered life was bewildered by the hot damp pile that lay on the grass, a dugong without water. Yet the creatures approached, protective and curious, drawn by a power in the man's presence. From a blue sky overhead, through swimming fragrance, bees, flies and motes of pollen, light came down amongst the mild clatter of leaves. Edward opened first one eye, screwed against his sleeve, then the other, wide to the mighty sun. He blinked. He stirred, stiff and sore. He pulled himself upright and rubbed his sticky face, separated the shag of hair around his head, and sneezed.

The creatures looked startled.

He sneezed again.

In the clearing of the rose garden in the middle of the jungle of an unknown island, he was transformed. His daughter had found her partner and he a new family. The cause awaited him, he rejoiced. He had found his power. He was at the heart of nature.

He unbelted his pants and squatted behind the boulder to relieve himself of the waste matter of the feast. He passed water. The breeze whistled under his bare buttocks.

He sneezed for a third time.

His pants were like damp hide. He pulled them off and went to wash himself at the stream that gurgled down from the spring in the mountain crevice above the garden. He had forgotten about the leather pouch hanging from a tight cord in his groin. He struggled to undo the ties. The carved stone he removed first, and tossed its hard artistry in his palm. The purple grains of the phosphorescent fungus, carefully folded in a page of Harvey's Latin, exposed to air, had a hue like the purpled metal of a dagger.

He emptied the paper into the bubbling cascade. Purple crumbs scattered the surface of the stream as the water from the spring that fell past his rose garden carried the poison away.

The passion that burnt him in one furnace with his daughter was released, releasing him from possession, as she had pulled herself away. A strange heat was spreading through his palms, his hands were hot, his fingertips alive with the advent of wizardry. He walked through the garden brushing the leaves of his roses, caressing most carefully the last and most important bush whose buds were still the hard green tips that revealed nothing.

He resurrected his staff and walked on.

He was losing himself.

He would construct his own seaworthy craft, he thought.

But he had no need to escape now. He was his daughter's guardian and would do all he could to help her to her dynasty. He would not ignore his duty to join his cause with theirs.

Popple sorted the notes he had made on the characteristics of the island, those words, those categorizations, a struggle for precision that was in the end little more than mimicry. Without the described object there could be no identification of what he described, no recognition of his description, only erroneous longings, wistful approximations that had their value, he reassured himself, as he bound the bundles in twine and packed them in his ship's surgeon's chest.

He moved his dwelling-place to the Chinese settlement. In sign of esteem quarters of his own were provided. They were cramped and unprivate. Ros kept him company for meals. She had another chamber of her own where she spent the nights more often alone now, without Tuzza, as her term neared. The rest of the time Popple sat with the old man trying to talk.

Plans were incessant for the departure to Rome. On Popple's advice Lou Lu ordered creatures penned or caged: the solitaire bird, the fody, and the long-legged pink bird of India. Lime, coconut, pandanus and other plant specimens were potted for transport. Baskets were woven and stocked with fruit and vegetables; fish salted and dried; aloes prepared in bulk for trade. A frenzy of oyster gathering occurred, day after day, until the reef was stripped and they could stomach no more, all for a handful of pearls. A travelling diet was worked out. It was on the backs of the giant tortoises that their vitality would ride, and since the tortoise in its turn was found to favour palm hearts and monkey apples, many baskets of these were set aside as fodder.

Cartography and navigation were also important. Solomon Truro had come back mutilated. Those early Dutch had vanished. No other vessel had crossed the horizon as long as they had been on the island. Was it possible to leave? Popple believed they could negotiate the reef through which only luck had piloted them on their arrival, their two vessels sharing the same luck, approaching different sides of the island through two rare passages in the enringing reef. Beyond the reef lay the featureless sea. Where were they? Looking at the stars by night, they interceded for knowledge. The stars moved tantalizingly closer. They could chart any number of journeys from topsy-turvy star to star, stars different from those at home, journeys to unknown ends. How these stars told them where they were on land or water Lou Lu and Popple could not agree. Their estimates of where they were deviated starkly. Somewhere, they agreed, in the great green sea formed by the triangulation of Europe, Africa and

Asia. Or was it a square? Was there a fourth, unknown side towards which they had travelled? There were no answers. Popple's practical conviction was that the trade winds blew them hither and would blow them hence, in season, back along the route to Europe. To take the winds on trust, argued Lou Lu, without any marks, could have them blown through the gap over the fourth side into the realm of frozen eternal darkness. Anywhere! Who said the winds were benign? So they contended, divided even as to north, south, east and west, here where the sun and the moon moved differently. Despite the insistence of the magnetic needles, there was no accepting the guarantee that east was east and west was west, nor that north and south had not been exchanged. They had only their chart of the island. The island itself they could not place anywhere. Yet on an auspicious day they would sail.

The yellow rose flowered into splendid double-tissue cups of rich butter yellow, and smelled as sweet as apples and cloves. It was a prize. As overseer of the transfer of rose stock to the ship, the damask, the China, the grafted roses, Popple personally saw to the potting of its cuttings. The transfer of the double yellow plant itself he would leave to a later moment. The grafted roses, meanwhile, took their place in the ship's rich nursery behind the bamboo shutters that could sensitively adjust heat and light.

Only the last rose was not yet ready to be touched at all. The still-green buds were ripening and he must wait.

Lou Lu feared the foreigner's solitude and obsession, and had come to distrust his horticulture. It was destiny that mattered to the old man as he pared the strength and energy remaining him to achieve his ultimate goal. At nine years old he had been taken to court. At ten he had the operation. He had screamed like a piglet before the knifer clapped a gagging hand across his windpipe and blood ran down his sleek legs like hot soup before they stoppered the wound. He was already thinking love thoughts, aged ten, that were warm and slow, like silkworms with no consciousness what their sticky ooze could become. Thereafter court-craft became his love, as on ladders and ropes, with gripping fingers and agile toes, he climbed the sheer cliff to achieve the highest ascent, his circumstances glued to those of the dynasty. When the earthquake opened the mountain that stood beneath the foundations, causing overturn and collapse, the craft of survival, of which he was master, had taken a more practical form. He carried in his arms Taizao, Prince of Yong, his child, his son, his spoilt pampered adored one. No obstacle was insuperable, Lou Lu knew as he recited what had happened: their establishment at Zayton, the extinction of the rival claimants, the elimination of the other line princes, the ship, the voyage, cast ashore, the wizard and his daughter, the female who could charm the prince, his emission, her conception . . .

Chinese men feared to witness birth. After her waters broke, Ros was confined in a separate cabin, her hair tied back in a scarf, ropes to hold and boiling water prepared. She laboured with no help from midwife. Outside, the Chinese grinned and chuckled at her cries. Huang restrained Popple in a grip to which he at last submitted. Lou Lu, the nearest thing to a woman, came to Ros's aid when after many hours the moment of delivery was reached, and took the baby into his bony carapace of hands. He cut the cord to make it squall, a hungry thing, a girl with black hair and green eyes.

Stooping, Lou Lu washed the infant and washed the mother's thighs. Then he presented the baby to her, his contribution complete. Ros felt the tightening pull as she took the creature to her breast.

The men trooped in to behold. Taizao took the child carelessly into his grip, a wrinkle of astonished and disdainful humour on his lips at what had been produced. Popple blessed his daughter and her baby, a granddaughter, in the name of life. In an instant he loved the little thing to distraction.

She was theirs. Popple and Lou Lu liked to sit at night under velvety dark with the mother and babe, and Taizao at a distance piping on his flute. The sense of pause was uncanny.

Then Rome. Popple had committed himself to guiding them if they agreed to accept his directions. Gradually the cargo was all transferred from land to vessel.

Late at night they sat, the wind blowing from the east.

And on one such night the camp was especially quiet. Time came for Taizao to lead his wife and their child to bed.

'Goodnight,' wished Ros. 'Goodnight, Father.'

She offered the baby's scalp for him to kiss.

A little later Lou Lu stood and bowed, in silence, indicating that he was tired and would retire too, leaving Popple to sleep.

Popple stood on the rocky ledge, stretching his legs in the moonlight, restless He had the impulse to wander, to postpone sleep.

A compelling unease led his steps away from the camp and the shore back up into the hills, over the crest to the ravine and the familiar track to his rose garden.

He approached in darkness. He heard sounds – voices, grunting, scraping. In the dark he could dimly see the group of men digging.

He yelled out, and it was Captain Huang who came running from the darkness to block his path. No word of explanation was given.

The Chinese had dug a deep pit in the rose garden, excavating the basin almost entirely. Some of the men were down so deep that their heads had disappeared under the earth. With a wild and desperate howl Popple flung himself about in Huang's iron grip, commanding them to stop.

Tossed-up rose bushes stuck at sharp angles in the mound of loamy rubble, half-buried, uprooted with brutal indifference.

Breaking free, Popple was thrown to the ground and sprawled lengthwise. He had no weapon; Huang blocked his every charge.

Then Huang barked a series of orders. The men climbed out of their pit. They abandoned whatever they were doing and scurried past Huang, in hastening single file, back along the path that led in the direction of their camp. Huang's eyes stared ferociously. His brows rose in fury and his teeth were clenched and bared. On his face was an expression of extreme shame and disappointment that looked like self-contempt beneath his evident rage. When the last of his men had been counted, Huang gave Popple what passed for a nod and strode after his party.

The rose garden was destroyed.

Popple was paralysed. He had no conception of their motive. The vengeful rampage of some incomprehensible whim, or distortion, some savage madness. He ran about righting any roses he stumbled across. One or two were standing, isolated, in outrage. Others had been rooted out. In his search he found the double yellow upside down with black loam smearing its flame-yellow cups. He fell to his knees in the dirt and sobbed over the rose in abjection. His wife Delia came into his mind, her strength against his possessed weakness. She stirred him. Summoning his will, he righted himself and began his dogged return to the camp, determined to have the explanation and justice.

The shadow of the new day was already reaching from beyond the extremity of the sea when he mounted the ridge above the bay. He looked down, his eyes arrows to the spot.

Ship, boats, awnings, planks, the baskets and cages and pens, the Chinese, all gone without a trace. Gone! Ros and the infant gone!

Across the water, past the rocky protuberances that could scarcely be called islands, beyond the breakers on the reef, the chain of white turbulence that had imprisoned them, some way out from the one passage through the reef, an indistinct moving shape, another kind of island, was visible, sails raised, dark against the incoming light as she was borne into the deep-blue main.

He let out a roar of shock. They were gone. *She, gone.* Everything gone. Vacant! Void! He raised a hand. To wave? To stop them. To call them back, fatuously? To curse them. To beckon their return to fetch him, the forgotten passenger?

Not forgotten. The casualty of a trick merely, a consequence of destiny. In a groan of utmost grief, Edward Popple collapsed.

Lou Lu had ordered his men to dig for the gold under the wizard's rose garden. They had until dawn to find it. At first light they sailed, with or without the gold, and without the contrary wizard, onwards to the empire of which Taizao was dragon ruler. Lou Lu had absorbed what he could of the foreigner's navigational knowledge, his knowledge of the stars. They had one giant tortoise to eat for each day of the twenty-day crossing to Malacca, their staging post on the way back to China. The beauty of their ship, her multiple sheeting attached to the battens of the sails like puppet's strings, was that she could sail against the wind.

Ros woke from an impassive sleep sensing a change in the tang of the air and a different light seeping through the weave of the cabin's bamboo blinds. The motion did not concern her, since she was used to the nightly lulling of her shipboard bed, but when she looked out, to see in every direction the moving swell and its curlicues of foam, her first instinct was to check that she and her baby girl were not alone, had not been put adrift.

'Tuzza,' she called. She hurried to where he was sleeping. 'Where are we?'

He half-opened one eye, closed it again.

'Wake up!'

Two eyes opened, unfocused, remote. She was frightened.

'Tuzza, tell me where we are.'

He lay with a blank, detached expression on his face, as if he were in a dream.

Clutching the baby to her, Ros pulled aside the hanging that sealed the cabin and crept out to the deck. On every side was sea, vast and featureless in the fine weather. The many-panelled sails made plucking sounds as they stiffened in the breeze, propelling the craft. A tumult of emptiness and exhilaration filled her. They were travelling again, they were moving on, pursuing the larger world. Yet there was no bearing, and not a sign of the dear island, left behind as if it had never existed. Why had her father not roused her to bid the island farewell?

The twenty giant tortoises in a pen on the upper deck were composed in formation, grazing on the greens they had been given. Those at the corners erected their necks above the backs of the others to gaze for danger across the void of blue. Behind the tortoises she saw Lou Lu, watching near the prow. He flicked a glance over his shoulder when she approached, babe clasped close.

'Where's Father?' she asked. 'Where is he? *Pater meus!*' She knew he understood.

With an arm outstretched behind him and the flat blade of a hand, he indicated the distance they had left behind. Her father was with the island. He was there.

Lou Lu did not face her. There was no propriety in discussion.

'You've left him and taken me? You mean my father's back there? My father did not tell me. There was no hint that our going was nigh. You've said not a word. You didn't tell him either, did you? You didn't give him the choice. You tricked him. Left him. Abandoned him to die. Murderer!'

Lou Lu understood the torrents of her passion and called for Taizao to take her and calm her.

'We are not out far. We can go back. There's time. He cannot be abandoned like this. Father! I beg you.' With her babe in her arms, she was on her knees to implore the old man. Her eyes were dry. Outrage convulsed her, until the baby started to cry and she needed to be steady to feed her. As the baby suckled, Ros looked out distractedly. The little one was intent on satisfaction at her breast.

Ros pierced the eunuch's bleary eye with her realization. 'You want my baby, and me for the time my breasts can give milk, to provide feed like a tortoise.'

Tenderly she dislodged the babe's mouth from her nipple, making her yowl and squirm in vehement protest. She held her in her arms as she moved to the side of the ship and, before Lou Lu's gaze, extended her arms over the rail. She hung the mewling, writhing little thing out over the great sea.

'I demand you return for my father. *He* must decide.'

Old Lou chuckled, knowing what a mother would never do.

Ros was frozen, the child flailing her limbs as if acting a capacity to fly and swim.

Taizao stepped towards his bride across the deck, his expression steady and blank. When she saw his face, her hardness broke into a jet of tears. She pulled the baby back into her breast and curled her head around her child in horror at what she had been tempted to. Then Taizao led the girl back to the cabin and had a guard put on the door.

Huang remonstrated with the eunuch. Huang who had never been drawn into intricate discussions with the foreigner but had observed him, as he ferried him back and forth, absorbed in his solitary obsession, a clear and single commitment that posed no threat. The Chinese had only to engulf him. The suspicions of his treachery, the decision to be rid of him, came from the eunuch, for whom the concealment of gold was the sign – or rather, raised a doubt about the successful outcome of their mission if they were forced to rely on someone who was capable of hiding his deepest store.

Lou Lu calculated that under the rose garden on which Popple so doted was gold enough to prove beyond argument Taizao's claim to the throne. East or west, the gold would buy necessary force to ensure the prince's accession. On the eve of the day that had been secretly determined as auspicious for departure, Lou Lu ordered Huang to find it. At first light they would sail, come what may.

They tore away the nurtured surface of the rose garden, mowing down the thriving plants in blind indifference to the gardener's care, going deeper into stone and against basalt boulders that each time promised in vain to be the core of gold. They excavated a crater – and found nothing.

The wizard's arrival under deep of night confirmed to Lou Lu that his guess was correct. However crazy the man, however much he failed to understand the worth of what he knew, he had a hidden purpose. That Huang was caught in the act and no gold found doubly angered Lou Lu. At the last minute, without consultation, in the petty malice of a eunuch's revenge, he saw and seized the opportunity to sail without the unhelpful foreigner, snatching child and grandchild in a single retributive move. Deft and neat, he showed the callousness of one without generation, so Huang remonstrated. There was no gold. The foreigner concealed nothing except his connoisseurship of the rose. The protest that had possessed Popple to the bowels when he encountered Huang like a thief in the night at his work, as Huang was witness, was a lament for his rose work undone, the frenzy of a man falling on upturned bushes, his slain ones. Huang was ashamed of the Chinese distrust and betrayal. He gave a rasping laugh to expel his disgust. Although they were foreigners to one another, enemies if you like, servants of opposing and ultimately perhaps incommensurable interests, they were also human beings who gained nothing from mutual destruction for the sake of falsehoods of imagination.

Popple had not tricked them. There was no gold. And now they had their unworthy treatment of him to launch their voyage and sail with them till landfall.

Lou Lu shrugged, showing no remorse. 'There was gold. *Is*,' he insisted. 'The wizard managed to hide it. Then let him live on it.'

'Let him at least live,' sighed Captain Huang.

★

265

Old Lou had grown confident in his absorption of the foreigner's navigational knowledge. He could read the stars as he read Taizao's dreams. No longer was there need of Rome. The empire was ready to receive the dragon prince, returning from exile. No need to wait for the wind's turn from east to west. The beauty of the Chinese ship prevailed, able to sail against the wind.

More than twenty days passed, more than twenty-five, more than thirty. On the fifteenth day they had begun to ration the remaining five tortoises. After the first of the roses on board died, Captain Huang did his best to sustain the others with the limited water, the men's urine, and to move the plants on to the deck when it looked like rain. Lou Lu was unconcerned, staring into the emptiness ahead, sea and sky, as the ship sailed aimlessly now, all his proud fading effort set on conjuring a landfall.

After the twenty-fifth day the weather turned fierce, to unrelieved parching heat. The sailors complained and doubted. Ros stayed in her cabin, fanning the babe as she fed on her milk. Taizao reverted to sulky silence, stroking melancholy words on the back of papers he had used already, or blowing relentless, repetitive tunes on his bamboo flute that warped in the salt air.

In an idle hour, when the baby was asleep, he came to Ros with a pot of tea, made her drink, obliged her to open her ginger lips and cover his bare skin as before with her hot amber stream that was concentrated from the lack of drinking water and the expression of milk, for him to stir and rise and have the sensation, the gushing oblivion, of pleasure. Her power over him was undiminished.

Huang could not help his smile, stroking his whiskers as he heard them laugh. Their pleasure alleviated his anxiety as he waited for the empty prospect of sea and sky to show something. Anything.

On the twenty-third day Lord Lou Lu succumbed to fever. The eunuch commissioner of the Ming lay in his hot cabin shuddering as he might have done if he had fallen on ice while skating on the frozen ponds of the northern palace. He burned as if his brain were a crucible. Whatever he ate or drank was regurgitated, even pale tea. His skin turned egg-yolk yellow. The impression of his bones showed through. His eyes were rare stones veined in cock's blood and yellow topaz.

He spoke in his delirium of their broken-backed voyage, the imperial progress that bore Taizao, Prince of Yong, Son of Heaven, to the central throne. He called for the youth to sit by his side for hours and squeezed his hand as if it were the ship's tiller.

At a certain point the fever subsided and the old man was able to creep unaided to the prow of the vessel.

What is it to have tied yourself to a political destiny, an aim as fixed as the evening star, invisible for one part of the cycle, a beacon in the other? To near completion? For the way is unswerving, rigorous, narrow, and every step, every stage, demands compromise and deviation, to travel the widest conceivable arc, the most roundabout of itineraries. Is the end always in sight, unchanged, or does the always shifting state of affairs change the end itself, eventually beyond recognition? How to recognize then the arrived-at point as the original purpose? The last animation of his supple brain worried Lou Lu. Dying, as he knew, he had completed his destiny. Or had he completed it, or not? A political purpose may be beyond the destiny of a single man. A motion of power, a process of states, a line through the raw stuff of history that describes at last, wondrously, the desired pattern. If not, then still to come. One holds to the fragment of the pattern from which the whole can be remade, as a principle, as Lou Lu had held tenaciously to his tether on the person of Taizao who now, with heirs (only a girl so far), was making his way. Sleep at last. Lou Lu could withdraw into the tortoise shell and sleep. But he ruminated . . . If there were an error . . . a misdirection in the course . . . the mistaking of an illusion, then . . . only then . . . only come what may his journey was complete and in that fact he must trust insistently, loudly. Were things not as they should be, the journey would continue in a patient tacking to port, spiralling to the goal. The end in sight, the ship on course.

'Taizao,' he murmured, his hand in the youth's hand a structure of bones made fire as his fever viciously devoured him. His vision blurred. 'My boy! Lord of all things!'

With Lou Lu's body stretched on the cabin floor, a new command had to be established to decide what to do with the deceased. The eunuch commissioner had been master of such ministrations. Without him to advise they were becalmed in inconsequential and irresolute consultation, until through inaction it was agreed that the corpse should not be cast overboard. Lou Lu must be brought on shore. Efforts were made to clean and perfume the remains, laid with rough rites in a shroud of his robe of rank at the aft of the ship. The Chinese howled their grief, the noise poured out, disappearing, eerily over the sea. Ros and her baby declined to attend. A watch was set against seabirds, which might prey on the carcase, and so they sailed, with their decomposing cargo, until at last on the thirty-seventh day, famished and drawn, they reached land. A promise broken as much as kept. On receipt of payment, underwritten by display of arms, a native guide was persuaded to pilot them to port – Malacca after all, another stinking twenty-four hours away.

In Malacca Captain Huang was able to make contact

with the Arab shipping community, the cronies of their original captain, Jin, and for the price of a few pearls had their ship refurbished and crewed for the onward journey. Captain Huang thereby established himself in full command. Naturally taciturn, he made no attempt to explain to the Malaccans where they had been, why, or what the outcomes were of so evidently ill-fated a voyage, save that they were returning whence they had come. From the chapter of Ming loyalists in the mixed Chinese community of Malacca, exiles, halfcastes, cut-throat traders, lunatics, fanatics, hopeless cases, and those grown fat-bellied on a foreign shore, Huang was able to unearth the gossip of China. The Ming remnant prepared a requisite funeral rite for the corpse on board, without having to be told who the curly-wigged gold princess was and who the winsome young man at the head of the mourners. After cremation the bones were shaken free of orange ash, broken and stored in an urn for the last stage of transport.

EPILOGUE

Wei Chi: Before Completion

Things cannot exhaust themselves.

I Ching (Book of Changes)

They entered Zayton harbour in a choppy squall. Rain fell like sand scattered on the sea. When the ship bumped against the dock the crew taken on at Malacca hurried across a plank to shore, leaving Huang on board to make good the vessel for disembarkation. What was this world, thought Ros as she looked at the mass of interlocking white houses and black roofs blocked down to the water-front that to the others was home?

The sailors who had run ahead came back with officers of the new Ch'ing overlords. Zayton had gone round in their absence, as Huang had heard rumoured in Malacca. Changed sides. The governor wanted no trouble. They arrested Taizao, seizing him as he waited listlessly in his cabin, unwilling to go ashore to his realm. They tied a rope around his wrists and led the foreign woman with her baby in procession after him. The urn of Lou Lu's ashes was borne to the governor, for whom the matter would win distinction. A portion of the pearls, the remaining roses and other specimens from the island were delivered to the authorities – excluding the one solitaire bird, which had died en route.

Captain Huang got his reward: Admiral Huang of a notional imperial fleet. The double yellow rose he kept for himself, having ensured its survival. It flourishes in his courtyard garden in the hills above Zayton, filling the four walls with a fragrance that visitors envy, who comment that it smells sweeter than any they have ever known.

More than a century later it will migrate to a mandarin's garden at Ningpo to be inherited by Sir Robert Fortune, trader and amateur rosarian, who will take the rose to London, giving it his own name. Fortune's Double Yellow.

Taizao, Prince of Yong, was separated from his wife and child for the journey to Peking. An unknown assassin, presumably acting on orders, strangled him in his cell in the middle of the night, somewhere on the way across the dusty Yellow River plain. Who knows what happened to his remains? Quiet obliteration was the best way to deal with any element that might rally the people against the new power. Ashes blown with dust, strewn in flood, sedimented as silt over the plain.

The foreign woman was presented to the Manchu emperor to appease his taste for novelties. She failed to stir his desire, however, although she was pink and plump and the shine was restored to her golden fur. Her greatest use, once she was installed in a back apartment of the palace, was to rear the child. The black-haired green-eyed child, miscegenated offspring of the last of the Ming line, with a breeder from the western seas, might revive the emperor's palling energies as a concubine for his middle age, if she grew up to match her strangeness with grace and beauty. The emperor smiled and despatched them, and thereafter neither mother nor child would leave the Forbidden City for the rest of their lives. Nor did the emperor foresee that he himself would die before the baby reached proper girlhood. It was the eye of his son that she eventually caught.

His son, the Kang-Hsi emperor, sired fifty-six children

altogether and it was his joking boast that at least one carried the seed of the extinguished dynasty.

Under supervision of the imperial gardeners the child's mother grew her father's rose in a secluded part of the palace. Huang had given her that much at least. An envoy had come from Zayton with a cutting and, after concerned scrutiny of the object, permission was granted for the lady to receive the admiral's gift. Otherwise she had no contact with the world she came from. She was not shown to foreign visitors. It is barely possible to speculate on the slow process of forgetting, or uncontrollably flaring hope, to which she submitted. In the end she lost even her own language, all but a few words that continued as snatches of baby talk to be exchanged in adult life between mother and singular child. Lost to speech, while elaborate structures hung in Ros's dim brain, torn spiderwebs that no house-keeping could quite clean away – the crazy story she told her daughter in Mandarin, who loved to hear, and laughed at where she came from.

Delia Popple sat with Sir Astley Neville among the oak panels of the Society of Fellows' chamber where the servant had shortly replenished the coal in the grate. Tiny specks of falling ice left a pale rime on the stony ground outside and around the windows, through which a grey-white sky imposed.

From silver the knight poured a thick brew of chocolate into two cups waiting in their saucers.

'Bitter? No,' he cooed. 'Not if you stir in several spoons of this –'

The white crystals sparkled, like ice, in a silver bowl of their own.

'Sugar from the island plantations,' he smirked.

As her lover instructed, Delia relished between her lips

the contrasting mixture of black bitterness and white sweet, of grainy mud and warm syrup, and her heart began to beat faster.

Although her husband had been absent for a matter of years, Delia had not yet felt free to remarry. She could not help imagining that, were she to make a second match, Edward would cheat her by turning up. News of him had been scant. The original captain of the *Cedar*, Macqueen, had been sent back to England by the Dutch asylum at Cape Town, for a handsome price met by the Society of Fellows – fine sort of trade for an asylum, to ransom its inmates – and he had recounted the mutiny for the Society's records. Nothing had been heard of the *Cedar* since. Either she continued as a rechristened pirate ship or she was lost. The Society wrote her off.

A further vexation to Delia Popple was the unexplained disappearance of her daughter Rosamund; a heavy burden indeed to lose husband and girl, leaving only the son Henry to care for her, and many tears she had let fall, her tresses tangled as she languished and pined on the barrelling bosom of Sir Astley.

To whom else should she turn, putative widow of the sea? The knight steered well through the troublous times, as commonwealth gave way to protectorate and looked more and more like turning right round to newfangled monarchy. A grouping had formed to run the nation, slyly resetting the ship of state for whatever form of government should be adopted. Those changing tides, those shuffling hands, those scuttling crabs of allegiances had suited Sir Astley Neville, who became a key advisor, a figure to be consulted in any calculation. Fitting therefore for Delia Popple, unable to remarry, to find solace and due appreciation of her capacities with Sir Astley, whose London mistress she became.

'A rare treat, dear,' smirked Delia before going on to the subject of her son Henry, who had been overzealous for the king and had required, on Neville's counselling, a period in the service of a Puritan grandee to dye himself truly in the new colours. But Henry was tired of that now and wanted to come to London.

'Astley, get him a place in Parliament.'

Neville rubbed his myopic eyes. The boy was dim. And young. No matter. It would be done.

'He shall comply with you in everything,' she undertook.

It was a numbers game, he reminded himself. Only a numbers game.

The chocolate had mottled the woman's cheeks. They burned scarlet. She felt the need of powder.

'Does it move you,' he asked her in a spirit of scientific enquiry, 'the chocolate? See if your tit is blotched too.'

She dug it out. The blushing grape, redder than when he last chewed on it, made the mass of man guffaw and shake. The thing he called his unholy rose thickened in his breeches. He wanted as much as could be managed, as much as would fit. As far as he could reach.

'Henry thanks you, sweet,' she said, recomposing herself and draining the sticky black sludge.

So Henry Popple, gent, came to sit in the House of Commons. Civilization steps forward. Whether the view is through a magnifying glass, as close as possible, or through a telescope from the greatest distance, the worlds revolve.

*   *   *

Edward Popple stood like a pole, watching as the ship sailed away. He stayed motionless until her shape began to blur, hidden in the movement of the sea, and his determination that he could see her was little more than fancy. As the dread thing occurred, he was incapable of lifting a finger to stop it, incapable even of believing it to be happening or seeing it for what it was. He watched incredulously as the more powerless he became. Completely powerless as he cast about for explanations. Even as she sailed to vanishing point, it might have proved to be a mirage or a conjuring trick. Leaving him with only the inevitable, indigestible truth.

He could always make his own craft, he reminded himself. He could sail after them – to Rome? Alone for ever, with no chance of reprieve? Never to see her again. Never perhaps to see human face or share language, thought, ideas, with fellow creature. Never to read human gestures, or touch skin, or chart the span of life. Inconceivable, impossible, a prospect too terrible, too final, for mind and heart to hold. He, who found no companionship from God. Was this his reward? Sovereign of the domain, king of the island, fertile, life-sustaining, peaceable, friendly island, known as an intimate, not in words and names, yet in contours and moods, venturings, withdrawals, daily life and death.

So he would content himself. Knowing and loving this place, and the knowledge and love it provided, without need or love of what lay beyond. Until the lost world faded from dreams and nightmares too. He would remain the first and last man, traversing the peaks and streams of the island, tending his sustenance, his garden, gazing placidly at the lagoon and the breakers everlasting beyond and the sky not empty but peopled with weathers, unless the creation threw forth a mate, unlikely, better not, and when he died at last the island would be left alone, like him, unmolested, his memorial. Could his human heart bear it? Or would he be human no longer, what is human without society, without the species? He was a freak of nature in this place, a failed trial, a creature that brought its own extinction closer with each day it lived.

The island's varied topography made the weather conditions as changeable within the space of the day as in England, only more spectacular since the range of heat and cool permitted the air to play out wide and vibrant dynamics. As the Chinese ship sailed, the weather was cruelly fair and serene, azure sky, whipped-cream cloudlets, indigo-dyed sea, and all the trees on shore dancing and dazzling an approving festival of goodbye.

Then clouds gathered and piled darkly up as the sun rose overhead. Popple at a loss, like an abandoned dog, came down to the shoreline, the rock ledge, the encampment, to sniff about hopelessly for signs or remains, and further towards the shore, waded up to his knees, as if to go after them. In his heart he waited for their return, hope the most uncontrollable of the dispositions. When hope at last took leave, despair came rushing in a dumping wave.

The sky grew overcast and blackened, and Popple shook himself free from purposelessness to a conviction of tasks to be done. The whole world was gone, and his rose garden lay despoiled, in need of repair. A gaunt shaggy pilgrim, he took his staff and made weary steps back up the slope. He was a picture of the hermit of mountains and waters. He arrived without hurry at the top of the crest, and meandered into the valley. He was whistling Ros's song of her horse Nelly. The palm leaves waved at him, and large crimson tropical blooms nodded, glowing the more intensely as light dimmed. The little birds looked and laughed, knowing they had him for themselves. One after another the solitaire birds stepped out through the trees to watch. Flightless, defenceless, helpless should they ever be introduced to a world other than the one they knew, their stumpy wings ballasting their elegant waddle and their

high necks undulating with a told-you-so enthusiasm, they stepped with dignity towards the man as he passed. In absurdity, of which they were unaware, in fatuous grace and quaint noble gliding through a landscape of their own, they outdid by only a little distance the man himself, who was the true solitary. In the dappled shade he mused at the paradox of a multitude of solitaires, and longed to speak with them.

Was he mad? If not now, he would be at last, he sighed, mopping sweat from his brow. A little further would bring him to the rose garden, and the birds were following.

He roughly reinstated the roses that had been plucked from the soil and ditched sideways. The earth around their roots needed tamping down, they could do with water. He busied himself as the air thickened and cooled. In the cracks of his labours gulfs opened to reveal his isolation, his loss of his daughter, and his granddaughter, and the old man and Huang, the Chinese for whom he had hatched a querulous affectionate respect. All plucked out. The cracks, opening on abysses, revealed the test of himself that lay ahead. Of what was he made? What was he? And the fear. If he could wash away his mind and become as bird or tree. But he was the sovereign of the island who must journey to fabled riches of knowledge there. Such was the high aim for which he begged strength.

Speckles of rain frosted the leaves, followed by droplets and a steady shower. He had no care to take shelter, no care whatsoever to protect himself. To save his clothes from drenching and going mouldy he stripped off and stowed his garments in a bundle under a rock. Of his shoes, his belt and knife, and the pouch containing the jade, he divested himself too. His hair and beard were a black and knotted dripping fleece. Water filled his eyes a

he stood naked in the falling rain, the clouds above charged with glittering shafts of light.

In their digging rampage the Chinese had not touched the special rose. One of those standing apart, the bush had been missed in the darkness. Its unharmed buds were swelling to open. Bare in the showering rain, Popple approached with awe and reverence before his tumult settled to the simplicity of a mind detached from singular griefs and able to join in equitable compassion for all things; a pitiful creature approaching the rose, breathless and eager, eyes running. Specks of purple phosphorescence glowed in the darkness, in the soil about the stem of the rose bush, and as quickly disappeared in brightness as clouds made way for light. The spring's stream carried the poison crumbs in its course and fertilized the rose, Popple realized, the rose cross-pollinated, with his own hands the only bee to touch it, manipulating pollen from the double Chinese yellow to his blood-deep damask in an experiment of colours. Approaching, he saw the buds open. As the rain bounced off the leaves, the sun's rays played variously with giving and taking shades and hues. He drew closer, to make sure it could be no illusion of light. The flower was black. He bared his throat to the delivering sky and emitted a cry that mixed gasp of doom with peal of glee. A partaker in the event would have shuddered for the wretched being, who seemed to cast off his own spirit in triumph. There was no one to bear the news. He slipped. He stumbled, and clutched at the rose bush to steady himself. The wood snapped in his grip and gouged his palm with thorns. He kicked the wet earth at the root of the rose. His bare toe stubbed a sharp hard period. There was a dull metallic ring. Exposed to air, the obstruction in the dirt glittered as gold.

Popple shouted. He was mad. He would make his own

craft and sail. He swore it. The place was making a fool of him. How could he risk putting to sea with the rarity of his discovery, the one and only black rose of all the rose fanciers of the world? He began to laugh, until he was breathless with open-throated laughter.

'Bloom, flower,' he demanded as he fell over on the ground and rolled up into a naked muddy ball. 'Bloom' he spat in bitter defiance. The greatest discoverer of them all.

ACKNOWLEDGEMENTS

I gratefully acknowledge, among the many sources consulted in the writing of this book, *The Southern Ming, 1644–1662* by Lynn A. Struve (New Haven and London, 1984; kindly lent to me by Professor Carney Fisher), *Hidden Power: The Palace Eunuchs of Imperial China* by Mary M. Anderson (Buffalo, New York, 1990; reference provided by Dr Geremie Barmé), *Roses: Their History, Development and Cultivation* by Rev. Joseph H. Pemberton (London, 1920), *The Old Shrub Roses* by Graham Stuart Thomas (London, rev. ed., 1983) and *The Vindication of François Leguat* by Alfred North-Coombes (Mauritius, 1991). I also wish to thank Walter and Jo Duncan of Hughes Park, Watervale, South Australia for telling me about the rose, Helmut Bakaitis of Leura in the Blue Mountains for growing it, and Claire Roberts for help of every kind. Work on the novel was assisted by a writer's fellowship from the Australia Council, the Australian Government's arts funding and advisory body.